Virgin Flight

By E.V. Bancroft

2023

Butterworth Books is a different breed of publishing house. It's a home for Indies, for independent authors who take great pride in their work and produce top quality books for readers who deserve the best. Professional editing, professional cover design, professional proof reading, professional book production—you get the idea. As Individual as the Indie authors we're proud to work with, we're Butterworths and we're *different*.

Authors currently publishing with us:

E.V. Bancroft
Valden Bush
Addison M Conley
Jo Fletcher
Helena Harte
Lee Haven
Karen Klyne
AJ Mason
Ally McGuire
James Merrick
Robyn Nyx
Simon Smalley
Brey Willows

For more information visit www.butterworthbooks.co.uk

CATALOGING INFORMATION
ISBN: 978-1-915009-27-2
CREDITS
Editor: Nicci Robinson
Cover Design: Nicci Robinson
Production Design: Global Wordsmiths

Acknowledgements

I am so grateful to everyone who has given their time and expertise to bring *Virgin Flight* to fruition.

Firstly, thank you to Nicci Robinson from Global Wordsmiths/ Butterworth Books for putting up with my quibbles during editing and leading me through the whole process through to publication.

Special thanks go to the wonderful staff at the Maidenhead Heritage Centre which houses the ATA museum and also a spitfire simulator, which certainly got the adrenaline flowing.

Every author seems to need a person who will read and critique the roughest of drafts, and I'm very grateful to Annmarie for ploughing through my ponderous ramblings, challenging and making suggestions. I'm lucky I have some awesome beta readers in the Swallows critique group: Joey Bass, Valden Bush, Jane Fletcher, Lee Haven, AJ Mason, Maggie McIntyre, and Sue Still. I know the book is so much stronger because of all your input. Thanks also to Sue, Dave, and Kev for their encouragement throughout.

Thanks to Em, who has been supportive in her unique way, and Jerry the cat, who has been a total distraction as I've tried to work.

Finally, I'd like to thank you, the reader, for taking a chance on me and giving me such wonderful feedback. It's such an honour. Thanks.

Dedication

To Em, thanks for distracting me with lots of cat memes.

And to all the forgotten pilots of the Air Transport Auxiliary
who flew unstintingly for many years and who are
an inspiration to everyone who has been
told they can't do something.

Author's Note

Inevitably with an historical fiction, you have to decide whether to be absolutely faithful to the timeline and sensitivities of the time or alter things slightly for a modern audience. Throughout, I have attempted to be as authentic as possible, while tweaking the timeline a little for the sake of the narrative. If anything offends, that's at my door.

Prologue

1934, England

BERYL JENKINSON WIPED HER hands on a rag and stared up at the darkening sky as a de Havilland Tiger Moth came into view. She followed the path of the aeroplane as it made its steady progression across the sky, just above the tree line.

The engine of the plane coughed and stuttered, then died. Beryl watched in horror as the plane descended and waited for the dreaded plume of smoke that seemed to be the companion of many air shows. She called out to her mother, "A plane's down, I'm going to help." Without waiting for a reply, she snatched the first aid kit from the workshop and jumped onto her bike.

Her legs pushed as hard as she could, standing up on the pedals, and the sweat from her forehead dampened strands of hair on her face.

"Please let him be okay," she said. It wasn't until she reached the gate that she realised she should have asked her mother to call an ambulance. Beryl threw down her bike and clambered over the locked gate. She steeled herself to peer over and inhaled sharply, dreading what she would discover.

Instead of a furrow-gouged trench deep enough to bury a man and a flaming tangled mess of metal, Beryl saw an overalled figure standing by the nose of the plane at the end of the field before it dipped down towards a stream. As she approached, she noted the engine cowl was flapped back, exposing the engine, like a chest ripped open to see the organs inside. It was fascinating, recognising the same parts she was used to seeing in the cars she helped to service in this frail but beautiful biplane. "Hello," she said. "May I help?"

The figure turned, and Beryl almost dropped the first aid kit she was still clutching. The woman had perfectly arched eyebrows, deep red lipstick, and short hair cropped close to her head in the style of Jean Batten after her record-breaking flight to Australia that had been splashed all over the papers earlier in the year. And she was just as glamorous.

"Perhaps."

Oh, that voice! Low and sultry with a strong French accent. Beryl had to squeeze her legs together. She was burning up and dipped her head so the woman wouldn't notice. "I'm Beryl. How may I help?"

"Enchantée. I'm Odette. I'm with the flying circus, but there's a problem with my fuel line, can you direct me to a garage where I can get a replacement and telephone the rest of the team?"

Beryl smiled and wiped her clammy hand on her overalls before she shook Odette's elegantly manicured hand, noting the nail polish matched her lipstick. "You're in luck. My family runs the local garage."

"Perfect. I didn't notice the cut fuel line on my pre-flight checks, because it was covered in oil."

Beryl looked at the fractured pipe in horror. "Sabotage, you mean?"

"Avec regret. I'm sure I know who did it."

"You could have been killed if you hadn't made such a skilful landing." Her cheeks warmed again; she hadn't intended to say that aloud.

"Thank you. Not all the men in the flying team want a woman aviateur. Or maybe they hate the French. I was offered lots of flying and thought it would be fun."

She shrugged as if sabotage was just another risk she encountered on a daily basis.

Beryl swallowed. "I can get back here in half an hour with a replacement. Will you be all right till then? Or would you like to come with me? Are you hurt?"

"No, I can't leave the aeroplane. It will be dark soon, so I'll sleep under the wing." She shrugged her elegant shoulders again; shoulders which belonged more in a ballgown than flying overalls.

"You can't sleep here. It's uncomfortable and cold at night."

"I've done it before. My boss is very strict about protecting the aeroplanes. People steal mementoes."

"But they're not strict about someone trying to kill their pilots?" Beryl wasn't sure where the sudden anger had come from, but her mother said it would land her in trouble one day. She grimaced, hoping she hadn't offended this elegant woman who had dropped from the sky, but Odette didn't seem perturbed.

"My boss would be cross, because he wouldn't want to lose one of his aeroplanes, or one of his trained aviateurs. At least he welcomes women. There are two of us now, as well as the wing walkers. He says it adds a touch of glamour." Odette raised her eyebrow with a slightly mocking look before blooming into a full smile.

Beryl's insides burned, and she took a couple of deep breaths. "Can I bring you some food and blankets?"

"Ah, that would be very nice—along with the fuel pipe."

"Of course. I'll be back soon." Beryl ran back to her bike and cycled till sweat trickled down her back and the dynamo light buzzed brighter than she had ever seen it. *Wow*. A beautiful female pilot had landed in a field next to her. All her dreams were coming true.

She barged into the kitchen and her family, who were eating, turned to stare at the whirlwind that had entered the room.

"There's a woman pilot who needs a new fuel pipe because someone sabotaged it, and she's in Mathersons' fields, but she can't stay because she's not allowed to leave the aircraft. I said I'd take her some supper and blankets," she said in such a rush she had to catch her breath.

Her mother shook her head. "A young lady can't stay out all night, and it's too dark to fly out safely now. I won't hear of it. She'll come and stay here. She can sleep in your room, Beryl."

"She won't leave the plane."

"Nonsense. Your father and brother will go and guard it tonight. It seems fitting since they didn't let you go to the air show today and left you looking after the garage instead. Don't look at me like that, Fred. It's only fair. Go and collect her. I'll pull together a meal for you both and change the sheets."

Despite the grumbling from her dad and John, they knew better than to disagree with her mother when she was in full matriarch mode. So, armed with a tarpaulin, new fuel line, and the tent pegs from John's tent to hold down the tarpaulin, they squeezed together in the front of their new Bedford pick-up truck.

When they arrived, Beryl proudly introduced Odette to her father and John. John nodded repeatedly when he shook her hand. Beryl hoped she hadn't made a similar fool of herself.

"I am quite all right staying with the plane."

"I won't hear of it, and my wife would make my life hell if we let you sleep out all night. John and I will take it in turns. I promise we'll keep it safe. I've also brought a new fuel pipe and tools, so we can fix it first thing in the morning. I've done some work on the Gipsy Moth before, so it'll be good to get my hands on a Tiger Moth."

"I can't ask you to do any repairs on my aircraft. I'll be here early in the morning to do them myself."

Her father grinned. "No hurry. Any excuse not to go to the eight o' clock service."

Beryl had never seen him so in awe, or so gallant.

"Thank you very much. I'm sure my boss will give you all free passes to our next show around here."

"Wow, that'd be wonderful." John's eyes shone.

Were her eyes twinkling with the same amount of hero worship as his were?

"Now, John, if you take first watch, I'll run the ladies back home."

He would never have called Beryl a lady, so that was clearly for Odette's benefit. John nodded and pulled his jacket up tighter. Beryl was grateful she was not having to sleep outside in a cold and lumpy field.

The pick-up truck jostled Beryl closer to Odette on the bench seat, and she had to suppress a sigh. She was sitting next to a real live aviatrix—a very glamourous, exotic aviatrix—and she basked in happiness. She didn't care how long and bouncy this journey was. They bumped again and shared a smile. This moment would be etched on her mind forever.

When they arrived home, Beryl reluctantly climbed out, introduced her mother, then showed Odette her room. "I hope you'll be comfortable," Beryl said. To Odette's eyes, the room probably looked small and shabby, its walls adorned with curling newspaper clippings of various flights by Amy Johnson, Amelia Earhart, and the recent addition of Jean Batten's flight. To have a real live woman pilot in her room was thrilling and the most exciting thing ever, bar none.

"I'm sorry you have been ousted from your bed." Odette smiled as she studied the yellowing articles. "You like female pilots, I see. Is it the women or the planes you like?"

Beryl turned her face to hide the blush. Did she know about her? No, of course she wasn't asking if she liked and dreamed of women, their smell, their softness, touching them. But always in the abstract, though Alice Goodenough, with her gap tooth and long pigtails, interjected herself occasionally. But Alice Goodenough was just a girl compared to this real-life heroine sitting on Beryl's lumpy mattress. Odette gave her a quizzical look, possibly because Beryl had taken so long to reply. "Oh, yes. I'd love to fly, but we can't afford it. I'd hoped to study engineering at Manchester University, but I have to help in the garage, so I'll never go."

Odette nodded. "We fly from Stag Lane, where de Havilland have an aeronautical technical school. Maybe you could go there. I know the engineers work on and develop their aeroplanes. They allow women too. Your Amy Johnson was there." Odette tapped at the articles of Amy's historical flights, not just to Australia, but also to Japan and Cape Town.

Beryl closed her mouth tight. Could she? Her mind freewheeled like a bicycle hurtling downhill. She huffed. "My dad would never let me go." That Odette had even thought that she could was too much. "Shall we go for supper?"

"Thank you." Odette followed her downstairs and dipped her head as she entered the kitchen.

Beryl's mum was fussing about. She'd laid out the best silver and crockery and the tablecloth with the extra embroidery to cover a stain Beryl had made as a child when she'd knocked over her blackcurrant juice.

"Please sit down."

Beryl wondered if her mum would break into a curtsy, her bob of the head was so low.

"Is bacon, broad beans, and parsley sauce okay?"

"Everything is delicious, I'm sure."

Odette's smile was warm, and Beryl was fascinated by her brightly painted lips, how they moved and pouted when Odette spoke.

Odette raised an eyebrow. "Do I have oil on my face?"

"Sorry," she mumbled and rushed to help her mother bring in the dishes. She needed to get a grip of herself; she was behaving all lovey-dovey.

Odette began to eat her food, almost shovelling it in. "Thank you. I'm hungry. I didn't have time for lunch; there was such a long queue for trial flights."

"You tuck in, dear. It's lovely to see someone appreciate my cooking."

Her whole family was being barmy around Odette. "Do you have another show tomorrow?" Beryl asked, trying to steer the conversation back to a more interesting topic.

"No. We have a free day."

"You do?" Beryl tried not to let her excitement show. "When we've repaired the fuel pipe, I could show you around the area."

"No."

Beryl's hopes sank in a wash of disappointment.

"Have you flown before?" Odette asked.

"Never. I wanted to go to the air show today, but I looked after the garage when my dad and my brother, John went."

"I'm sorry you didn't get to fly. I'll take you up tomorrow."

Beryl couldn't have tethered down her smile even if she wanted to. "Really?"

"Yes."

Beryl clapped her hands, then held them pressed under her legs so she wouldn't make a fool of herself. "How did you get into flying? Where did you learn? Why did you come over to England?" Beryl knew peppering Odette with questions was probably the last thing she needed, but she didn't seem to mind her runaway enthusiasm.

"My *friend* taught me in France. She was a very good aviateur."

There seemed to be something significant in the word friend, or maybe that was Beryl's wishful thinking. She picked up the past tense. "What happened to her?"

A sadness passed over Odette's face and raw pain was exposed for a second. Odette took another bite. "This is delicious."

It really wasn't that special, but it was obvious she didn't want to elaborate. Why had Beryl been so impolite to overstep the mark? It was none of her business.

Odette continued to eat, then she put down her implements across the plate with a satisfied grunt.

"Would you like some more?" Beryl's mum asked, hovering like a hummingbird.

"No, thank you."

"Just some cake then. Or we have Bakewell tarts."

Without a second's delay the sponge cake was sliced and placed on the rose-decorated, best china plate, along with a jam and almond tart with a cherry on top. She gave one smaller piece of cake to Beryl to remind her she was the host and therefore was expected to share, but Beryl didn't care. She would have given all of her cake to Odette and more just to spend more time with her.

"Anything else?" her mum asked, as Odette picked up the crumbs from the plate with her finger.

"Could I have a bath?"

Her mum turned scarlet. "Of course. We only have a tin bath that we use in the front room, I'm afraid. I'll go and stoke the fire in there. Beryl, can you fill the kettle, please?"

Maybe sensing she had asked for something too complicated, Odette put up a hand. "But if it's too much trouble—"

"No trouble. It'll just take a few minutes. Finish your tea or it'll go cold." Beryl's mum hurried away to set up the arrangement.

Beryl rose to fill the large cast-iron kettle again on the range.

Odette blushed. "Sorry, I didn't think. In my digs in London, we have an indoor bathroom."

Beryl shovelled a scuttle full of coal on the range and opened it to increase the heat, then placed both the kettle and a large saucepan on the top. She turned to face Odette, desperate to put her at ease. "It's okay, we're used to it. I'm sorry it's not glamorous."

Odette snorted. "It's not glamorous where I live, but it's home until I can bear to go back to France." She took a sip of tea and shuddered. "I'm used to sleeping under the wings in the hangar when we travel sometimes."

"I'll get you a towel." Beryl ran upstairs to the linen cupboard and scoured the pile for the fluffiest one. She pulled out the newest, navy coloured towel and skipped down the stairs.

Odette was reading the newspaper placed flat on the table, tracing each word with a finger. She raised her head and smiled. "I'm trying to improve my English."

"It's perfect."

Odette bit her lip in a way that made her seem young and vulnerable, not a confident pilot. "That's not true but thank you."

Beryl trembled, starlings fluttering in her stomach. Their gaze met and held, Odette's chocolate-brown eyes darkened, and the twinkle was replaced by something deeper, something Beryl didn't know how to explain, but her body tingled. She handed over the towel in a trance, her breathing fast and shallow.

The moment was broken when her mum bustled into the room and indicated Odette should follow her to the front room. Her mum returned, switched on the wireless radio, and picked up her sewing, settling into their ordinary evening routine.

Except there was nothing ordinary about it. Beryl stared at the crossword, unseeing, aware that in the next room, Odette was naked in their tin bath. She fidgeted as she waited, and it was a full seventeen minutes later before the kettle boiled again.

"I'll see if Odette would like some more hot water," Beryl said, affecting nonchalance.

"Thank you. I don't want to miss my programme."

Unleashed, Beryl snatched up the kettle with the cloth, careful not to spill the boiling liquid and hurried to the front room. She cleared her throat and tapped on the wooden door. "I'll leave more hot water outside."

"Come in, Beryl."

There was something about the way Odette said her name that liquefied her insides. She carried in the hot kettle, focusing on it to ensure she didn't spill anything nor saw anything of Odette. She made to put it down beside the tin bath.

"Will you pour it in?" Odette whispered.

Beryl raised her eyes and was relieved, though disappointed, to see Odette was sitting up in the bath, her arms wrapped around her knees. Even so, Beryl deliberately avoided looking below Odette's chin, despite her imagination doing cartwheels with excitement.

Odette laughed. "Oh, Beryl, have you never seen another woman naked before?"

She shook her head, feeling like a child castigated for not knowing something she should have learned as an infant.

"You English are such prudes! Pour the water behind me. Thank you. I can't tell you how much pleasure this is."

What did she mean? Was she just referring to the bath? Yes, she must be. Beryl crouched beside the bath, so close she could feel its heat and smell the lavender soap. If she just reached out, she could touch Odette. "Please stay forward. I don't want to scald you."

She poured a glistening stream at the edge of the bath and stirred the water with her other hand to mix it, her fingers so close to Odette's tantalising body.

"That's so nice. The water was cooling."

Beryl stole a glance at the pale smooth skin of Odette's back, as elegant as a swan's. The starlings in her belly fluttered lower.

"Wash my back?" Odette held out the soap bar.

"I..." She wanted to explore every inch of her body. Of course she did. But what would her mum think if she came in?

"Please."

Beryl placed the kettle on the mat covering the Axminster carpet. She took the slippery soap and rolled it around in her hands to lather it up. "Are you ready?" she asked, her voice at a higher register.

"Yes, please."

Odette's skin was as soft as down and goosebumps raised to her fingertips.

"Are you cold?" Beryl asked, not quite believing she was actually skating her fingers over another woman's body, so much smoother than her own.

"No, that's wonderful. Don't stop." Odette glanced over her shoulder. "That's nice, yes?"

Beryl swallowed and nodded, unable to speak in case her voice betrayed that her body was reacting in strange yet delightful ways. Her heart thumped as if she'd run from the fields, and she was overheating all over.

"How old are you?" Odette asked.

Beryl whipped her head up. "Sixteen. How old are you?"

Odette sighed. "I'm twenty-two. Maybe in a year or two..."

She seemed to mutter the last to herself as if unaware she had spoken. Odette leaned back in the bath, causing Beryl to stumble backwards as the water sloshed perilously close to overflowing, but she didn't care. She couldn't help but stare at Odette's lean body shimmering under the water, her small breasts with dark nipples, and the triangle of hair at the meeting of her thighs. Beryl's heart pounded in her chest. She'd never seen anything, or anyone, so beautiful.

"When you're older," Odette said, not unkindly. "Now you need to go back to your mother." She smiled and trailed a hand over her breasts drawing attention to them in a way that made Beryl sag at the knees. "Thank you for the water."

Beryl nodded at the dismissal, ashamed of being too young, too inexperienced. She grabbed the kettle and shot out of the room, trying to regain her equilibrium before re-joining her mother.

All night Beryl wrestled with the sheets on the camping bed, reliving the vision that was seared onto her brain, and a new awareness hummed in her body. She had just been initiated into the wiles of women, and it was thrilling and frustrating to be sent away. Not that she blamed Odette; she was being respectful. And tomorrow, no, today, she was taking her up in an aircraft. All her Christmases had come at once.

"Throttle set. Contact," Odette said before she swung the propeller.

There was a splutter and cough before the propeller caught in the whirling invisibility of a hurricane that smacked Beryl in the face. She shrunk behind the glass half-moon windshield for protection.

A few seconds later Odette was leaning over to double-check Beryl's harness. She caught a faint whiff of lavender amongst the oil.

"Okay?" Odette mouthed.

Beryl grinned and gave a thumbs up. Odette returned the smile and patted her shoulder before sliding into the seat behind. Beryl adjusted her goggles for the umpteenth time and wrapped her scarf tighter against the nip in the air.

"Ready?" Odette asked down the pipe that connected the cockpits.

It was difficult to make out her voice above the clattering. The plane vibrated like a dog on a leash straining to go, and she felt equally eager and shaken up. Her father stood by the wingtips smiling at her, and she waved at him.

"Chocks away," Odette shouted to him.

He raised his thumb before withdrawing the rope with triangles of wood that held the wheels in place. The aircraft serpentined to the edge of the field across the rough grass, catching the ping of a stone against the underside and the swish of the grass, pulling them back as they taxied. Beryl was surprised she could see nothing in front but blue sky, but by jinking from side to side, she could see glimpses of the way ahead.

"I will do my checks at the edge of the field," Odette said.

Engine noise reverberated in Beryl's brain, but it seemed to shake her alive as though she had been slumbering, as if she hadn't lived or experienced the extremes of life. Finally, they came to the far end of the field and the brakes were applied.

"Flaps, ailerons, empennage," Odette said, trying to give a full commentary on what she was doing, but half the words were snatched by the wind and scattered to the air. "Ready for take-off?"

"Yes." Beryl hoped her voice didn't tremble and was relieved Odette couldn't see the cramping in her stomach. She didn't feel so brave now, in this vibrating, rolling monster of a machine.

"Enjoy."

With a surge of power, the aircraft bounced across the grass. The side hedge blurred as they hurtled forward like a galloping horse heading for the jumps. The tail rose, giving forward vision, and the wheels felt lighter until the metal, string, and canvas contraption eased into the air. They rushed over the hedge, fronds of leaves slapping the underside, trying to drag them down, but they floated over the next field and climbed higher. It was noisy and smelled of oil, and her cheeks stung with the bitter wind, but still she grinned. Beryl tugged the hat close over her ears, grateful for the borrowed goggles, and squealed with delight. This was freedom.

Hills became pimples, and they reached a height just above the steeple and the treetops before banking towards the town. The place she'd lived in all her life sprung into a chaotic map: the church, the school, and the cars like Meccano toys, chugging down the roads. She felt she could put a finger out to stop the traffic or meddle in their lives, like God.

"There's your house," Odette said down the tube.

Beryl turned to their house with the workshop and the two pumps outside, though they were just distorted dots from this angle. "I see it!"

Too soon, they left the town and followed the river downstream.

"Would you like to fly?"

"Yes, please." Beryl thought her heart would burst, it was hammering so hard inside her chest.

"You have control. Keep it level with the horizon and follow the river. I'll do the rudder."

The stick moved like a spoon in soup, and it was harder than she anticipated to keep the river in sight, constricted as she was by the blind spots of struts and bits of engine and wings. "I'm flying," Beryl said as if anyone else could hear, but she didn't care. If she died now, she would die happy.

The time passed as rapidly as the ground below them and soon they returned above the field.

"I have control," Odette said, taking the stick. "Follow my movements on the control stick." She flew over the field to check it, then around for her approach. "I'll sideslip to lose height, and it will seem strange."

The wing tipped, and Beryl stared out of the side of the cockpit at an odd angle. They skimmed the top of the hedge as they came in, and all forward vision disappeared as the Tiger bounced as if it was caught by the tail and was trying to fight for freedom. But Odette tamed it, and they taxied to where her father waited. Odette cut the engine, but the vibrations continued in Beryl's head, a reminder of the taste of freedom. Her jaw ached from excessive smiling.

Odette quickly said her thanks and goodbyes and promised to keep in touch and kissed Beryl on both cheeks.

Beryl almost didn't want to watch as the plane taxied to the field edge, and the grass bowed down behind the propeller, as if in worship. The aircraft lifted off and headed towards the morning sun. Beryl shaded her eyes and squinted until there was a tiny speck in the sky, her cheeks still tingling where Odette had placed her lips.

"Let's go back home. Your adventure's over," her dad said and wandered back towards the gate.

Reluctantly, she followed, not wanting to return to her humdrum life.

Two weeks later, when she had given up hope of ever hearing

from Odette again, John handed her a formal letter. Not wanting to open it in public, Beryl ran off to the toilet and locked the door behind her. Her hands shook as she prised open the brown envelope. Inside was a letter from the de Havilland Technical Training School inviting her for interview in a week. She clutched it to her breast. Now she had an opportunity, but more than that, Odette had not forgotten her.

Chapter One

Six and a half years later. January 1941

ODETTE WASN'T SURE WHETHER it would be a student or the English weather that would kill her. Maybe she was still shaken up, as they all were, by Amy Johnson's death a week ago. Amy was such a good pilot, yet she'd been forced to ditch her plane miles from where she should be after hitting bad weather. The rumour was that she'd said she had a dodgy compass. If someone who had flown across the world could get it wrong, couldn't they all?

That was no way to think or talk, and Odette would not fall into that negative attitude. She hoped she would not have made that mistake if she'd been in that position. Not that she was arrogant; she just had no reason to worry about any consequences because no one would miss her. But now she was responsible not just for herself but also for assessing a student who would be let loose to deliver these aircraft for the Air Transport Auxiliary soon. She dared to put her head into the slipstream to peer left. The cloud was thicker there, almost to the ground, but that's where they needed to go. She shivered, no longer able to feel her exposed face. Sometimes she wished she could grow a beard for warmth. She pulled up her lucky scarf, but that left a gap where her Sidcot flying suit ended. An open cockpit was the least appealing thing in January in one of the worst winters she had seen. Yet she wouldn't change it. She tried to see where they were. The student, Joyce, was not taking the pre-determined route and had overshot her turn point.

Joyce was studiously following the railway line into London

and hadn't noticed that the river Thames had peeled off to the South, so she needed to avoid the barrage balloons of London and head north if they were to complete the cross-country exercise safely.

Odette wasn't supposed to assist in an assessment, but it was better to be safe than brave. She wouldn't take risks with a student in the plane.

"What is your heading?" she asked down the Gosport speaking tube that connected her to Joyce.

The reply came back muffled.

"What time do you need to turn, according to your dead reckoning?" she asked.

"I need to turn now?" Joyce's rising intonation betrayed her uncertainty and fear.

"You tell me."

"Yes."

She sounded more certain now and banked to the left. They were engulfed in a dense snow cloud, thick and all-encompassing. *Putain*. Odette could see nothing ahead. They weren't supposed to fly in cloud, but the weather didn't know that, and this hadn't been forecast for another two hours. It seemed as though they were banking hard to the left, and the altimeter dropped dramatically. They were in danger of spinning out.

Years of experience in the flying circus kicked in. Every nerve tingled, and her heart pounded, yet her mind clicked into being cool and logical. The turn and slip indicator showed they were banking right despite feeling they were going left.

"Straighten your wings. Use your turn and slip indicator. Keep it dead centre. When it's straight and level, do a gentle turn one-hundred-and-eighty degrees, and go on the reciprocal course. There's an aircraft factory beyond the railway line that has a runway, and we'll put down there. That's it. The airfield is almost dead ahead."

"It doesn't feel straight."

"Trust your instrument. Your mind is disoriented by the cloud." It was ridiculous the ATA wouldn't even teach basic instruments to pilots, saying that it might "encourage" them to fly in poor weather, but a simple knowledge when they were caught out could make all the difference. She exhaled as the windsock and hangars came into view, distorted by a drift of white.

"You're not worried, are you?"

If only you knew. "In an incident, you need to think, be logical. Yes. See that building? It's a hangar, and the runway is to the left. Can you see the windsock? Which way is the wind?"

"Behind us."

The normally confident socialite sounded scared, or maybe the tremor in her voice was the cold. Joyce took no correcting action on the stick. Whether it was fear or the confusion of being in a whiteout, her brain seemed to have frozen. Odette could take over, but that would crush her confidence. Joyce would be flying cross-country on her own shortly; this needed to be a learning experience.

"So you'll need to land which way?" Odette asked, keeping her own panic at bay. She should have seen that snow cloud sooner. Flying was all about preparation, attention, and expecting the worst. She'd become distracted by her thoughts.

"Into wind," Joyce said.

Without further prompting, Joyce brought the Tiger Moth into the circuit and called out her downwind pre-landing checks. Odette scanned the runway as they flew parallel to it. Fortunately, it appeared clear, and the fine paper of snow was rapidly being obliterated. Someone on the roof fired a Very pistol, and a red mist settled in the falling snow like blood. She just hoped the flare was for them, and they weren't about to collide with another aircraft.

Downwind, the storm wasn't as bad, but as they made their sweeping approach, it was difficult to see through the curtain of white. "Talk me through what you are planning to do."

"Establish the approach. Give myself the maximum landing distance. Slow as possible about one foot off the runway."

"Good." Odette hadn't flown with Joyce before but was relieved she seemed more confident and focused now. "Be aware as you touch down—it could be slippery. Good, the snow hasn't settled on the wings yet."

As they made their final approach, they flew into a blizzard, the ground barely visible through the thick swirl of snow that filled the cockpit then melted against the heat of her legs. She tightened her harness in case they slid off the runway, not that they could really see it now; just a patch of white remained in the grey of the snowstorm and lines of blue-white indicating the field edges. She followed Joyce's every move with her hand on the joystick and her feet resting lightly on the rudder pedals and fought the instinct to take over.

The plane dropped the last foot and skidded wildly from left to right, spraying snow in an arc. Joyce wrestled for control, and they taxied over the thickening snow.

Fortunately, there was a member of the ground staff braving the elements to come and meet them. He indicated a slightly more sheltered place beside a hangar to park. He flagged them to stop by crossing his arms above his head, then slit his throat to indicate cutting the engine.

Odette said, "Well done," but Joyce didn't reply. Odette wriggled out of her seat to brush away the snow slipping down her neck in icy rivulets and saw that Joyce had her head in her hands. She leaned forward and touched her shoulder. "You're fine. Your guardian angel was looking after you today. Well done. Unbuckle yourself. That's it." Odette helped her as much as she could in gloved hands with frozen fingers.

The ground crewman stepped onto the ledge, muffled up in several jackets and scarves. "We were just about to close the airfield. Come inside."

By the pitch of the voice, the ground crew was female. That

was unusual, but in the war, women were performing all sorts of roles that were considered men's work.

"Thanks. Can we phone our home base?"

"Of course. We've heard there are problems on the rail into and out of London this evening, and no trains are running, so if you and your other pilot would like to stay at our lodgings, you're very welcome."

Even more unusual. Normally, ground crew would not be so forward. Such an invitation came from an officer. But this wasn't a military airfield. Maybe it was because Odette was female, she was worried about them getting back. "Thanks. Can we decide when we've checked the weather?"

The crew woman twisted as though looking left and right. "It's snowing."

So a bit of a smart one. "Now, yes, but that wasn't what was forecast, not for two hours. Perhaps it will clear. But I suppose it will be dark by then."

Joyce had stepped off the plane and was heaving up her guts. The fear had clearly got to her. Odette couldn't stop her teeth chattering, a sign she was shocked, or cold, or more likely, both.

"I bet you're glad you didn't do that inside there," the crew woman said, pointing inside the plane. "Why don't you both go into that hut over there and get a cup of tea. I'll pull a tarp over the cockpits which will keep the worst of the snow out."

Odette was grateful for her kindness. "I need to—"

"I'll tie her down, and you don't need to worry about security. We have a twenty-four-hour operation here, and guards."

What she wasn't saying was that they were trying to maximise the number of aeroplanes that came off the line.

"Thanks." Odette led Joyce to the hut, out of the wind and the snow. They stamped their feet as they entered and without a word, huddled by the pot-belly stove and rubbed their hands trying to bring the feeling back. Chilblains be damned, Odette needed to be warm.

The door at the back opened, and a woman came through. She didn't seem surprised to see them.

"Caught out, I guess. Hello, I'm Maisie, and I'm in charge here. Do you need your wee chits signed?"

She had a broad Scottish accent, and Odette had to strain to understand her. They shook hands. "I'm Odette, and this is Joyce, who just flew amazingly to get us in. We don't need chits signed, thank you. We're not delivering. We were on a cross-country training flight. We were caught in the sudden snowstorm."

"Aye, it's filthy out there. Would you like a tea? We've no biscuits, I'm afraid."

Joyce nodded. Her skin was still grey, and her eyes were dull as if she was still in shock. Odette pulled up a chair for Joyce to sit on and one for herself. As Maisie bustled about organising tea, Odette leaned forward. "Do you want to talk about it?"

"Thank you for talking me down. I froze up there. That's never happened before."

Odette removed her flying helmet and shook out her hair as much as she could, but it was so cold, it was like an icy lump. "That's why we start with an accompanied cross-country. Do you know what you did wrong with the navigation?"

Joyce shook her head then paused, cocking her head to one side. "I went too far along the railway line."

"Exactly. Sometimes it's easy to become mesmerised by following the lines. What would have happened if you'd continued?"

"We would have gone into the barrage balloons and within reach of the ack ack guns?"

"Oui. And it would have been very hard for them to tell if we were friend or foe, even if the cables didn't get us. So your dead-reckoning calculations and time keeping is really important when you're navigating."

Maisie handed them both a brew of tea, so dark and thick, it would probably rip their throats out.

"Thank you." Joyce's hand shook as she took the mug, and she almost missed her mouth when she put it to her lips.

Odette smiled. "Don't burn yourself now. I don't want to have to fill out an accident report. The paperwork would kill me. You flew brilliantly; well done."

Joyce sipped her tea, and her posture softened.

Odette sighed with relief and smiled at Maisie. "We have a game back at base to find the strongest tea whenever we land, and I have to say this is a prime contender."

Maisie coloured slightly. "It's probably been on the boil for half an hour. We thought we were done for the day." She grinned.

The door burst open, and a drift of snow blew in, complete with the ground crew woman wrapped in a heavy coat, flying hat, goggles, and scarf that covered her face and was iced with a layer of snow. She shut the door, unpeeled her hat and goggles, and shook out her hair.

Beneath that bundle of clothes was a gorgeous young woman, and she offered her hand to Odette with a broad smile and twinkling eyes, as if she recognised her. Odette was certain she'd never seen such a natural stunner in such ordinary clothes before.

"You probably don't remember me, Odette, but my name is Beryl Jenkinson, and you gave me my first ever flight when you stayed at my house."

Odette frowned. She would have remembered a stunner like this, but she couldn't place her. Then, she must have given hundreds of trial flights over the years, if not thousands. She couldn't seriously expect her to remember her, could she? Beryl's smile faded, and Odette realised she had committed the terrible British sin of being impolite. She shook Beryl's hand. "Oh," she said. "Pleased to meet you."

Maisie poured tea into an enamel mug and added a splash of milk from a chipped jug. The fire crackled in the stove and the fumes mixed with the smell of wet wool, creating a pungent aroma. Beryl turned her gaze back to Odette who dropped her hand.

Beryl's joy disappeared leaving just the mask of a smile. Clearly, Odette didn't recognise her at all. Disappointment chilled Beryl to her core. Why would a flying great remember a nobody like her from six and a half years ago? She couldn't exactly admit that she had a picture cut out of the newspaper with Odette amongst a group of the ATA women, the "glamorous pilots" that the journalists raved about as heroes. Odette was certainly Beryl's hero. As she stared at Odette, willing her to remember, she started to shake, although whether that was nerves or the cold, she couldn't say.

Maisie held out the mug of tea, and Beryl gratefully wrapped her hands around the enamel to warm her fingers. It wasn't often a star arrived at the airfield. She met Odette's eyes and couldn't help humiliating herself even further. "You gave me details of the aeronautical engineering college and provided a reference."

Slowly, recognition seemed to register, and Odette's eyes became as wide as piston bores. "You are the girl whose house I stayed in? Who I pushed out of your bed? But you are not a girl anymore; you're a gorgeous young woman."

Beryl could not have stopped the blush if she tried, and there was no point trying to pretend, but whether it was the compliment or that Odette remembered didn't matter. The glow that rose from her core made every cell tingle, and she didn't feel cold anymore.

How amazing to be seen, to be recalled and to be appreciated, and by this exotic woman. She had always tried to hide her feelings about women when she was around Maisie, but her adoration could not have been clearer. And she didn't care. Odette called her gorgeous. It wasn't what Beryl saw when she looked at herself in the mirror but coming from Odette... Her heart picked up speed, and her wide smile made her jaw ache. Although that could have been her face thawing out. She needed to arrange some words into a coherent sentence, but her tongue refused to move, so she nodded and took a sip of tea to give herself time to recalibrate herself. "You had a fuel pipe that was sabotaged by a fellow pilot—"

"Ah, poor man. He died a few months later when his plane spun into the ground. Nothing to do with me." Odette raised her hands.

How odd that in flying, death was as much a constant passenger as it was in war. But if they were to continue to fly, they had to shrug, box up their upset, and bury it. Shuffling by the stove reminded Beryl there was another pilot in the room, shrunk into her seat and cradling a strong tea. The woman's face was wan and her hands trembled, but she raised her head to meet Beryl's eyes.

Beryl sat beside her in the huddle around the stove. "Hello. I'm Beryl. That was some spectacular flying to come down in this weather."

The woman returned Beryl's smile and seemed to physically expand in her seat at the compliment. "Thank you. I can't tell you how glad I am to be on the ground. Pleased to meet you. My name's Joyce Sidden."

Now it was Maisie's turn to be wide-eyed, possibly at Joyce's very plummy accent. "Joyce Sidden? Of Swan Walk, Chelsea? I'm Maisie, although you probably know me as Mairead Stewart. You came to one of my father's parties once."

"Mairead Stewart! Wasn't it at one of the airfields he owns? Although I guess they've all been requisitioned now."

It wasn't often Maisie called herself by her proper name, and on a day-to-day basis, it was easy to forget she was from the upper classes, because she never acted superior. Beryl always wondered if it was because she was Scottish, and she related stories of a strict upbringing in a cold and draughty hall.

"Yes, but my father got permission for me to be involved in helping to run the airfields for the Ministry of Aircraft Production, so I can take over when the war ends."

Everybody took in a breath, not wanting to consider that maybe the war wouldn't end, or if it did, that it wasn't in Britain's favour. It had already gone on for fifteen months and seemed to be escalating. St Paul's Cathedral had been hit by incendiary bombs in December, and the whole country was holding its breath, gritting its teeth, and concentrating on the here and now, clinging on to hope when there was no rationale for it.

"Do you still go up to London much?" Joyce asked. "We should all meet up there."

As Maisie, Joyce, and Odette conversed about the nightlife in London—which Beryl had no interest in at all, thank you very much—Beryl sat back and sipped her tea, which had become too strong even for her. The conversation rolled over her, and she slowly warmed through, every nerve of her body tingling as it came back to life with pins and needles. She was reluctant to move and disturb her joy that Odette was sitting beside her, laughing and joking as if she'd known Maisie all her life. Odette's flying suit brushed against her overalls, and she imagined what it would be like if—

"Oh, we haven't contacted base," Odette said.

Beryl rose, grateful for the interruption to her inappropriate thoughts. "Let me show you where the telephone is."

As Odette followed her, Beryl was conscious that she was probably trailing a line of melted snow.

"There you are. The operators will put you through." She pointed to the phone in Maisie's office.

"Thank you."

Odette caught Beryl's arm as she walked away. She fixed her with a gaze that seemed to delve deep within Beryl's private thoughts. Beryl couldn't help staring back at Odette's lips. Odette had even applied lipstick since arriving in the hut, drawing attention to her delicate cupid's bow.

"I'm sorry I didn't recognise you," Odette said.

Beryl shrugged, trying to cover up her disappointment. "You've taken hundreds of people up. Why would you remember me?"

"But I *do* remember you. I remember a kind girl who gave up her room for me, who had pictures of women pilots on her wall, and who brought me extra hot water for my bath. A girl who was thrilled when we went flying and had a natural affinity with the air and the plane. I didn't connect that young enthusiastic girl with this beautiful woman." She indicated Beryl's body. "Did you do the course?"

Beryl stretched taller. "Yes. I'm an aero engineer, but there aren't many jobs for women. I wanted to join the ATA, but I didn't have enough hours. I took this role so I could still be by aeroplanes."

"D'accord. Let's talk later. I want to know everything that's happened to you."

Odette's voice was so deep and sultry, with the French accent—Beryl wanted to snuggle into it. She didn't like to say there wasn't much to tell. "Of course. Let me know if you have problems getting through." She nodded towards the telephone and skipped down the hall to where Maisie and Joyce were still comparing notes. Her dream had just blown in on a snowstorm even if it was for just one evening.

Chapter Two

"WOULD YOU CARE FOR a bath?" Beryl asked as she showed Odette into her room. She snatched up a cotton vest that was strewn over a chair and stuffed it in the laundry basket.

Odette pretended not to notice, focusing instead on the bedroom with unashamed curiosity. Frilly, flowery, and pink really wasn't Beryl's style at all.

"We're not allowed to put up anything on the walls," Beryl said, turning almost the same shade as her bedspread.

Odette grinned. "Do you still have a tin bath?"

"No, we have modern conveniences here."

Beryl's face glowed, and her eyes shone as she stared at Odette with the same gleam of desire so many people cast Odette's way. She wasn't arrogant but knew what that look meant. Why didn't they just acknowledge they were attracted to each other? And Beryl was such a beautiful woman, radiant with that clear openness and enthusiasm that Odette envied and wished she could embody. Odette wanted to pull her close, inhale the scent of innocence, and let it cling to her.

"What a glorious bath you had, all the better for soaking in and being pampered with extra hot water." She couldn't resist teasing when Beryl had such an interesting reaction. "Had you ever seen another naked woman before?"

"No." Beryl turned and whispered, "Or seen one since."

She must be, what, twenty-three? She was older than Odette had been then. By the way she looked down and curled her shoulders, shrinking into herself, Beryl seemed to have shifted from excitement to shame. Odette had wished to tease and flirt, not to embarrass her. She touched Beryl's forearm, and heat seeped into her fingertips. "I wasn't mocking you, Beryl. I loved that evening. Can you show me where this bath is?"

Beryl lifted her head, and Odette kept eye contact, trying to understand what was going on with her. "And I promise I'll only have the regulation four inches of water."

"Or maybe two of us could get in together, and we can have eight inches," Beryl said.

Odette's heart picked up pace. Given how wide Beryl's eyes were, that comment had slipped out without filter. The girl had a crush on her. Was she still dreaming about that flight years ago? She really hoped Beryl didn't have a picture of her tacked to the bedroom wall, along with Jean Batten and Amy Johnson. Although she supposed Beryl might be using that fancy Sellotape now. A shudder passed through her body, and it wasn't the cold. Odette couldn't live up to the heroic aviator reputation, to be glamourised for the one thing she could do. It was a sham. She was hollowed out and going through the motions.

Beryl cleared her throat with a nervous laugh, bringing her from her thoughts. "I don't know where that came from. Sorry, just joking. You have a bath first; I'll use the same water. I'll get you a towel. Oh, Maisie might be in there. Wait here."

Beryl shot out of the room like she was in a single-seat fighter, causing Odette to smile. Her fluster was adorable, and the young girl, so anxious and desperate to please, peered out from the eyes of the beautiful young woman.

Beryl was clearly besotted, which was flattering, and it would be so easy to initiate something with her. It had been many years since she'd been tempted by anyone. After Simone's death, she'd been so closed off and angry, she didn't dare open up and let anyone in to witness that.

She unzipped her Sidcot flying suit and wriggled out of it, before hanging it over a wooden chair by the small fire to dry out. She loosened her tie and was removing her uniform when

Beryl burst in, stopping just in front of Odette.

"Oh, sorry. I didn't know you were undressing."

Beryl threw the towel in front of her face and started to withdraw, but Odette caught her hands. "Beryl, come here. You've seen me naked before. I can tell you enjoyed what you saw. Are you saying you don't enjoy what you see any more? Have I become too thin, with shadows around my eyes? Am I... how do you say, haggard?"

Beryl's eyes widened again, and she shook her head vigorously. "No, no. You're beautiful, but I didn't want to intrude on your privacy—"

"Don't be such an English prude."

Beryl half pulled away but stopped. She squeaked but no words came out then she cleared her throat. "No, I won't," she whispered.

It would be so easy now to just lean forward and take those lips onto her own, but she didn't want Beryl to think she would kiss her out of pity or to immerse her in her confusing hidden world. Beryl would need to seek it out. She didn't want to be the one to corrupt her purity. The longer Beryl could hold onto that the better. Much better to hold onto her innocence than to become as sullied and jaded as Odette.

Yet they were so close, their faces drawn together. She was fascinated by Beryl's surprisingly feminine lips and how she chewed them when she was anxious; all Odette needed to do was to stretch a little. She didn't think Beryl would object. Beryl's wide pupils, parted lips, and excessive swallowing were clear signs that she was as invested as Odette was.

Banging on the door made them both jump.

"The bathroom's free," Maisie said.

"Thanks," Beryl said, still staring into Odette's eyes.

"Hurry up, you two. We want to get out to the pub," Maisie said. "This calls for using some of our petrol ration."

Beryl blinked twice as if switching on her brain again. "We'll be quick," she said then turned back to Odette. "We *could* take that bath together."

What had she let herself in for? A kiss would have just been a bit of fun, but the anticipation had unleashed a disturbing stirring in her that she didn't want to examine. Beryl moved close. Odette shook her head and placed her hand on Beryl's chest. "Beryl, we can't do this. It would only be a kiss, it wouldn't mean anything to me, but you would probably want something more and I can't do that." She should just bathe and get out. "Where are the towels?"

Beryl stared at her for a few seconds. "They're in the airing cupboard. Follow me."

She swung around and marched out of the door. At the airing cupboard, Beryl passed over a towel and gave Odette a watery smile.

"If you need to get to the hard-to-reach places, give me a shout."

As she followed Beryl to the bathroom, Odette wondered how she had bungled it so badly. She needed to set Beryl straight that this was light and fun, not intense or significant. In another world and another place, she could be drawn to Beryl, wanting to shield her from the unpredictability of the world, to show her the delights and explore the flights of female intimacy, to protect her. Not now. Not here.

Odette shuddered. She couldn't risk being caught. If she was thrown out of the ATA, would they send her back to France? She would fit in with neither occupied France nor with the Vichy regime's motto of "Work, Family, Fatherland." She could not become a dutiful wife tied to the stove and be nothing more than a baby factory in France. No, she needed to stay in the ATA and quash Beryl's infatuation before it went any further. It was too dangerous. But more dangerous than Beryl's crush was the shifting of the gears of Odette's heart, unlocking after so many years. That was terrifying.

Chapter Three

THE OTHER THREE WOMEN snagged a wooden table while Beryl sorted out the drinks. As she waited to be served, she looked around. The Horse and Hounds could be any country pub with its old oak beams, low ceilings, and dark wood panelling halfway up the walls. Rough plaster above the panelling, now yellowed with smoke, was covered in faded photographs of the local area and paintings of horses and hounds. Not very original. Cigarette smoke clung to the ceiling. In one corner, a piano was covered in columns of sheet music. In another, a darts game was in full flow. The place was filled with old men, a few stout women in scarves, and the rest were mainly RAF officers and WAAFs in loose groups, standing and sitting in every available space. The navy-blue ATA uniforms of Joyce and Odette stood out and were attracting sideways glances. Beryl would love to be wearing that uniform. It was enough for now to be associated with them, to revel in the aura cast around them. The glamour girls. She didn't care about the glamour, all she wanted to do was fly.

Beryl paid, mentally calculating if she would have enough to last until the next payday. She picked up two drinks and went to join her group. It was a seething cave with complete blackout curtains. The whole pub was packed, smoky and dark, punctuated by little pools of light, making it difficult to manoeuvre to their table.

"Darling, can you bring some coasters over here?" Joyce asked.

Beryl's cheeks heated. Why hadn't Joyce said anything after she arrived at the table? She suspected Joyce enjoyed the attention. Certainly a few of the RAF boys had turned when Joyce called out and were watching the new arrivals. It made Beryl cringe. She almost preferred the distraught Joyce who had just had a terrible flight landing in a snowstorm.

"I'll get them when I go back," Beryl said quietly as she placed the drinks on the table.

Maisie rose. "I'll help you carry the rest."

Beryl didn't need a hand carrying the additional drinks, but this was for Maisie's benefit. As they threaded their way through the tables, it was an opportunity for Maisie to smile and flash her eyelashes in some courting rituals in her not-so-subtle goal of bagging a RAF officer.

Maisie stopped at one table where four men sat drinking beer and leaned over. "Do you mind if I take these spare coasters?"

Blushing on Maisie's behalf, Beryl hurried to the bar to pick up the remainder of the drinks and an extra couple of coasters. What was with the mating rituals? They were no more than animals, desperate to rut.

"Thank you, boys," Maisie said.

Beryl followed her back to the others and perched on a worn, leather-covered stool.

"Here's to happy landings," Joyce said, and they all raised their glasses. Joyce turned to Odette and fixed her with a dazzling smile. "And to the most wonderful instructor I know."

She clinked glasses with Odette, who accepted the accolade with a nod. Joyce took a large swig of her gin and tonic as if she thought this might be her last drink ever.

Odette's sip was smaller, more refined. "It was you who landed the aeroplane. You did very well."

There was something about their intense gaze that caused the hairs on the back of Beryl's neck to rise. Were they flirting, or was it just the understanding you had for someone with whom you'd shared a scary or significant event? She wanted to be the one who had that connection with Odette, without having the scary event, of course. Her toes curled in her shoes. She didn't want to be jealous. It wasn't a helpful emotion, and she didn't care for that version of herself.

The three of them laughed at something, and Beryl observed them. Maisie was a revelation, her Scottish accent becoming stronger with drink. So did Odette's French accent, which was doing something to Beryl. Thinking about that almost kiss had her tingling all over. Then Odette had ruined it by saying if she had, it wouldn't mean anything.

How could a kiss not mean anything? It would be an opening and exploration into whole new worlds. It was an intimate promise of more to come. Yet to Odette it was nothing. She probably had people kissing her most days, men and women. Her face still flamed from the memory, and she imagined her lips tingling at the touch. She would just have to accept it was never going to happen, so she may as well make the most of being in Odette's orbit right now.

Someone at another table dropped a glass, the sound of which broke into her musings. Desperate to bring the conversation back to Odette and to satisfy her curiosity, Beryl asked, "What have you been doing since you left the Flying Circus? Did you join the ATA straight away?"

Odette laughed and took another sip of her gin and tonic. "No, I did flying training for the Civil Air Guard, then worked with army liaison, towing drogues for the ack ack guns and target practice on the south coast. It was well paid, and we had closed cockpits."

The women oohed in envy.

Joyce put down her glass, already empty. "Why did you leave?"

Odette shrugged. "They really weren't very good at judging the distances, and I was fed up with being a sitting swan."

"Sitting duck, you mean?" Maisie asked.

"No. Because of my name, they called me Swan from Swan

Lake."

Joyce and Maisie laughed, and Beryl smiled, but she had never seen the ballet. In her house, all conversation revolved around the intricacies of the combustion engine, and none of them had time for anything as frivolous as ballet. The only reason she knew Tchaikovsky wrote the music was because her mother listened to music on the wireless, much to her dad's disgust. She shared her dad's view and could contribute nothing to this conversation, yet Odette seemed as comfortable in that world as she was talking about flying. They all had so much more in common than she did.

Joyce turned to Odette. "You are a fantastic pilot and a wonderful instructor, but surely you must've had some dangerous moments?"

Anguish washed across Odette's face then disappeared quickly, as she smiled. "I prefer to focus on the great times flying. Up in the sunshine, above the clouds, taking people for their first flight and seeing the thrill and enthusiasm on their faces, especially when they are at one with the plane."

Odette looked at Beryl with such intensity, she felt naked. Her heart sped up to double time, and her chest expanded. Odette really did remember their flight.

For the first time all day, a warm tingling feeling spread to Beryl's toes. What she would give to fly again, to be equal to Joyce and Odette, flying daily, even in horrible conditions. They had purpose and meaning in their lives. Sometimes, a brush with death infused a person with life, encouraging them to squeeze it and shake out every last drop, just as Odette was doing.

Odette held Beryl's gaze. "Why don't you apply to join the ATA? We need enthusiastic great pilots."

Beryl didn't want to expose her vulnerability. That had been her dream, but it had been crushed. Even at Civil Air Guard prices, she had struggled to find the cash for lessons. And her dad always seemed to need her to do extra hours when she had a lesson booked. Beryl lowered her eyes. "I don't have enough hours," she whispered and stared at her glass of the watered-down bitter shandy, pretending to be fascinated by it.

Odette placed her hand on Beryl's arm, seemingly oblivious to the fact that the hairs raised at the touch. Odette was so unthinkingly tactile, it was confusing and exciting all at the same time.

"Soon they are changing the requirements, reducing the number of hours needed. I've heard rumours that they will be looking for women who have less than two hundred and fifty hours if they pass the flying test."

Beryl searched Odette's face to see if she was teasing her. "Really?"

Odette smiled and nodded.

"What do I need to do for a flying test?"

"Give me your address, and I'll send it to you when I have the details. They're going to change the test too. At the moment, it's doing circuits, spin recovery, a short cross-country, and a landing. You already know the engine side. You'll be fine."

Beryl felt as if she'd been given a jolt from the spark plugs. Could it really happen? "You think I can do it?"

"Why not? It sounds like the perfect match to me."

The perfect match. Beryl would love to be Odette's perfect match, but she had made it very clear that wouldn't happen. This foolishness needed to stop, and she should make the most of having Odette's company rather than wishing for something that could never be. "What planes have you flown with the ATA?"

Odette's lip curled in disgust. "At the moment, the bureaucratic idiots won't let us fly operational aircraft, so just a few old Oxfords as well as the Tiger Moths."

How humiliating to be a brilliant pilot and be held back because she was a woman. Beryl's anger rose, but Odette shrugged as though it was no more than she expected.

They continued to talk about aeroplanes and for the first time ever, Beryl revelled in the conversation; it was something she could contribute to and be nourished by. They spoke as equals sharing an interest and weren't condescended to by any men. She lapped it up, wanting to relish every last drop.

"Good evening, ladies. We wondered what such beautiful women were doing unchaperoned on such a horribly cold night. Maybe we can snuggle in and warm you up."

Really? Did anyone fall for that line? Beryl looked up to see four men in RAF uniforms, the same ones from which Maisie had borrowed the coasters. So, her courtship dance had worked. Despite the unwelcome interruption, Beryl was impressed at how easy it was, for Maisie, anyway.

Maisie batted her eyelashes. "Ah, gentlemen. Come and join us. We were just talking about the Hurricane. We're desperate to get our hands on one. You must have flown one."

The tallest man blinked twice before replying. "That's classified information."

If he was going to say they weren't allowed to say anything because of the war, Beryl was going to throw up. She and Maisie had heard such tales in the pub that the Jerrys would have had a field day. More than once, they'd had to tell the flyboys to shut up.

"We're just starting flying training on them, so we wouldn't know. Hello, Odette," another man said and turned to his mates. "This is Odette de Lavigne. She taught me how to fly. She's a brilliant teacher with thousands of hours."

Odette smiled and preened at the men's attention. "Charlie, I'm glad to see you haven't splattered yourself on the runway yet, despite your best efforts. Are you going to introduce us to your friends?"

Why was she inviting them to sit down? Now the conversation would all be about them and what they were doing, just when it was getting really interesting. Beryl sipped her drink as one of the men pulled up a stool beside her.

"Hi," he said quietly. "I'm Mike. Pleased to meet you."

She smiled. "Beryl."

"Nice name."

It really wasn't. It was very ordinary, just like her.

"Do you fly as well?" he asked, nodding at Odette and Joyce.

Odette's eyes shone as she chatted, her face powdered and her lips bright red, drawing Beryl in. She'd asked Odette earlier why they brought skirts in their overnight bags and Odette had told her that it was regulation, and they had to look as feminine as possible when they went out. Stupid rule in Beryl's opinion, and she should have said so.

She turned her attention to Mike, who flicked his gaze back to her from watching the rest of the group. He looked uncomfortable so she smiled at him.

"I've got one hundred and fifty-three hours, but that's not enough to join the ATA. I'm hoping they will change their criteria for joining."

"Blimey. I've only got thirty-seven hours. To be honest, I'm a bit scared about going on to the faster planes so soon." He bit his bottom lip.

Beryl nodded. He was probably just as frightened about the war. "You'll get the hang of it quickly."

"I'll need to. The Jerrys are making mincemeat of London."

He sounded as though he was from East London, not what she'd expect in an officers' pub. She was tolerated here because she was Maisie's friend, and Maisie's dad owned the pub as well as the company and the airfield.

"Yeah, I know what you're thinking, what's a cockney like me doing as an officer? They must be desperate. When I volunteered, I said I wanted to fly. I passed the test, and here I am."

He grinned, and she could imagine him charming his way into and out of lots of trouble. Interesting that he didn't seem the same as the other three pilots. He was cheeky rather than arrogant. She liked him. Beryl scanned the other men. Charlie was leaning back with his arm resting behind Odette's chair, while he curled her hair in his fingers. She was so tempted to throw a drink in his smug face, but she had to be polite. She turned to Mike, who must have followed her gaze and seen she'd been staring at Odette and giving Charlie the evil eye. A diversion was needed, pronto.

"Fancy a game of darts?" she asked, nodding towards the dartboard in the corner, away from the crowd.

"Yeah, why not?"

She thought she was a mean darts player, but Mike was a notch above. Playing kept her mind off Odette, although she couldn't help glancing across, noticing how she threw her head back as she laughed. Jealousy did not make for smooth or accurate darts throwing, but it was satisfying imagining Charlie's head at the end of her point when it made a thunk in the cork.

There was nothing to be jealous of. Just because she had harboured a vision and dream of Odette since she saw her in the tin bath all those years ago didn't mean she had any claims. Odette was playing with her, teasing her, and messing around. Her flirting with Charlie proved it. Although if she was really truthful, it was Charlie who was coming on strong, and Odette was being friendly but didn't really seem to be encouraging him. Beryl missed the board altogether with her next dart, and she stepped back to let Mike take his turn.

"Glad I didn't have any money in this, or I'd be skint by now," she said as he finished the game.

Mike laughed. "Misspent childhood. Better than nicking cars anyway."

They returned the darts to the bar and slowly threaded their way back to their table past the raucous drinking games.

"I spent my childhood helping at my dad's garage, playing around with engines and dreaming of flying." She glanced at Odette, who was laughing at something Charlie said. She couldn't believe it hurt so much to see Odette being the centre of attention with all the RAF officers. What she would give to have Odette's attention, to have her dark eyes focused only on her. She fantasised about conversations with Odette with her husky voice and the accent that made her melt inside.

Beryl endured the rest of the evening, becoming increasingly concerned that Odette might go back with Charlie to his digs, even though her bag was at Beryl's.

Beryl was a freak. Why couldn't she just want men like everyone else and be satisfied with making a home and having children as soon as the war was over? But it just didn't interest her at all; she was thrilled by the light sound of a woman's voice and the curve of a woman's body. She cracked her knuckles to reset herself. "We have an early start tomorrow," she said to Maisie.

Maisie looked slightly peeved at being interrupted from her deep discussion with her RAF man.

"It's fine. The boys can clear the runway tomorrow. They disappeared quick enough before the snowstorm today. I doubt we'll get anything out though; they forecast more snow overnight."

Joyce's expression shifted from joyful to concerned. "So we were lucky to get in today?"

Odette reached over and patted her arm. "No, you were skilful to get in today."

She continued leaning forward, and Charlie took his hand down from Odette's chair to cradle his beer. *Good.*

Maisie looked at her watch. "I guess we ought to make a move."

"Would you like us to chaperone you?" Charlie asked.

Judging from the gleam in his eye, his offer was more self-serving than chivalrous.

"No. We'll be fine, thanks. The local farmer has a contract to clear the snow to the airfield, which goes past our lodgings. He should be finished now. Maybe we'll see you here again." Maisie gave her full-dazzle smile to Rob, flashing her intent and attraction.

Rob whispered something in Maisie's ear, and she coloured

slightly. Beryl suspected there would be more trips to this pub in their future.

The men escorted them back to Maisie's car, and Beryl was relieved to see the road was clear. Rob kissed Maisie on her cheek, and Charlie did the same to Odette, but she didn't reciprocate, thank God. She and Mike shook hands awkwardly, and the men left.

The road was quite icy, so Maisie concentrated as she drove. Joyce turned slightly in the front seat to address Odette.

"Charlie had the hots for you. I thought you might go back with him."

So Beryl hadn't been imagining it. Odette sat beside Beryl, but she could be a mile away.

She gestured with her hand as if waving off an irritating fly. "I could have gone with him when he was my student, but I didn't feel it tonight."

Beryl cleared her throat, needing to know the answer but simultaneously not wanting to know. "Would you have gone if you did feel it?" There was no moon, and all the windows of the houses were shrouded in darkness, so she couldn't see Odette's face, but she could feel the warmth of her breath.

"Maybe? You English are such prudes. I don't know how you have continued your nation. We go to bed with a lover, you go to bed with a hot water bottle."

They all laughed, but Beryl's sounded more forced to her ears.

"If she didn't have to drive us back, Mairead might not have needed a hot water bottle tonight," Joyce said.

Maisie flicked at her in mock annoyance. "Do you still want that bed tonight? I'm sure it's pure Baltic under the wing of the plane."

"If by that, you mean cold, then yes. If you don't want the inconvenience of a visiting pilot dying of hypothermia, yes please, I'd like that bed. Thank you."

The journey back seemed much quicker than the outgoing

one, mainly because Beryl was now dreading facing Odette. It was going to be difficult to share a room and keep her attraction hidden. She knew it was stupid to be disappointed, to hope for something, anything, but mortification weighed heavily in her chest.

When they tumbled into the kitchen, shedding the cold with their overcoats, Maisie put her finger to her lips and whispered, "Do you need anything else?"

"A hot water bottle," Odette said, and they all stifled their giggles.

"Shush," Maisie said. "You'll wake up Mrs Parker."

Although their landlady was kind and motherly, Beryl didn't want to raise her ire. She had enough to contend with, with her husband and son both fighting overseas, doing war work at one of the local armaments factories, and tending to her chickens. The real bonus of that was fresh eggs every day.

After all four women had used the bathroom, Odette approached the bed in Beryl's room. Her long legs stretched out below the hem of her nightie, and Beryl's traitorous body tingled with excitement.

Beryl cleared her throat and pointed to the bed, not daring to look Odette straight in the eye. "You take it. I'll sleep on the floor." The rag rug should provide the most comfort, and she'd picked out a spare blanket and pillow from the airing cupboard, hoping that Mrs Parker didn't mind.

Odette patted her hand on the bed. "Sit here."

Beryl sagged on top of the quilt and tucked her feet underneath her body to keep them warm, careful to keep a distance from Odette.

"Beryl, look at me." Odette stared deep into her eyes. "You can barely make eye contact, and I seem to have upset you. I don't know what you expect of me. I'm sorry if you're hurt."

Beryl shook her head. She tried to speak but needed the courage. She inhaled deeply. "No, I'm sorry. You were my hero, pointing me towards flying, and here you were appearing in a snowstorm, and we almost kissed. Then you flirted all night with someone else, as if you're mocking me."

"No, I wasn't mocking you, Beryl, but I can't take life as seriously as you do."

"But life is serious. The war—"

"Will continue whether or not we are serious about it. Death is serious. Life is for living and should be fun. We need to make the most of every minute. We may be dead tomorrow. Look at your hero, Amy Johnson, and the pilot who sabotaged my fuel pipe."

"So you do remember?"

Odette took Beryl's hand and rubbed her thumb over her knuckles, setting her nerves sizzling beneath the skin. If only her hands were soft and feminine, not rough and calloused from pulling apart engines.

"How could I forget someone like you? Someone who is so passionate about flying and is so engaged and engaging. But that's not me. I don't expect to survive this war. Too many of my friends have died. The future is another land, but I can't tarry there. Too many pilots have lost their lives. Excellent pilots. Now we're not even allowed to use all the instruments available. It takes too long to teach, and we need people ferrying planes now. Besides, often they don't fit the instruments until after we've ferried them. They say we'll be tempted to fly in poorer weather, but they need the planes not tomorrow, not next week, but today, so we fly when we can, irrespective of the weather. There's constant conflict."

Beryl gave a humourless chuckle. "You aren't selling joining the ATA."

"Because there is only being at one with the air, catching the wind, and flying around the clouds. It's what I live for, what makes me come alive like nothing else can. I think it's what you live for too."

Odette was right. Nothing compared to that feeling of

freedom, using her skills and knowledge to beat gravity. She had never felt so seen or understood before. Beryl shivered.

Odette flipped the top sheet into a corner of welcome. "Please share the bed. Be warm and comfortable. You've already given up your bed to me once. Then you were too young, but now..."

Beryl didn't want to be used or made to look a fool. "You said you would have gone with Charlie if you felt it tonight. You were flirting all night with him, yet you seemed as if you would have kissed me earlier."

The bed springs creaked as she lay under the quilt. Deliberately keeping to her side of the small double bed so they didn't touch, Beryl turned to watch Odette, whose face glowed by the light of the electric lamp on the bedside table.

Odette smiled. She shuffled across to Beryl and drew Beryl's knuckles to her lips in a graze of a kiss. A brush-off kiss, yet still her nerves tingled at the touch.

"Don't be jealous of Charlie. He has no finesse. He forces the plane to do his bidding like a wild horse. Nor does he read the air, or the ground, or the weather. He doesn't notice the change of wind by the ripples on the water because he doesn't look for it. He is brave like a bull, but I do not want to kiss a bull."

Beryl cleared her throat, mesmerised, and even now longing for more than a kiss to her hand. "Does that make me a cow?"

Odette laughed again and stroked Beryl's face. "Non. You are a beautiful woman I am in bed with and who I would like to kiss, but it will mean too much to you. Sometimes a kiss is no more than a kiss. It feels good, and I like to feel good, but my heart is like a blackout curtain. There is no light, no love that gets in or out. Do you understand?"

Beryl nodded, her head rustling against the pillow. Part of her screamed to stop because she didn't want to be hurt, but the bigger part of her yearned to be touched, to be kissed, to be explored, and Odette could show her what she'd fantasised about for years. Her resolve to not yield melted when Odette pushed back a strand of hair from her face. Odette's gaze lingered on Beryl's lips. She swallowed. "I know it will just be a kiss, and it means nothing to you." Her head screamed at her to stop now. But this could be her one chance to fulfil her fantasy and she would take anything to have Odette look at her, kiss her, or more.

"May I?" Odette asked.

Beryl nodded again, and Odette pulled her closer until their lips met. A gentle sensation tingled in her nerve ends and opened her heart, however much she tried to shutter it closed. Odette ran her tongue along Beryl's bottom lip, and she let out a groan as she let her enter. Their tongues touched, and Beryl melted into the moment, her whole body responding in ways completely unfamiliar but delicious. This was everything she had hoped for, as life-changing as the first time she had flown with Odette.

Odette kissed with a fervour and passion that fired her up and stirred the certainty of who she was and what she wanted. Every cell in her body was alive, and she didn't want it to end. Life before was a sepia photograph and now it burst into technicolour like the *Wizard of Oz* film she and Maisie had seen. And she wanted to live in a world of colour with the enigmatic Odette. Odette's warning of not taking it seriously jarred in her head, reminding her not to expect anything beyond now. But how could she accept living in black and white when she was finally revelling in colour?

When they pulled back for air, Beryl whispered, "Thank you."

Odette stroked her cheek. "You just made my day, but I can't let my heart get involved with anything or with anyone."

"Is that anything to do with why you left France?"

Odette's eyes widened. "Yes, I suppose it is."

"Whatever it was seems to define you." A hand seemed to grip her heart, but Beryl refused to break. She needed to be strong.

Odette pulled Beryl close to her. The coarseness of her

nightie tickled her skin, and the lavender soap she must have used in the bath enveloped her completely. She wanted to stay there like this all night, and she snuggled against Odette's chest. Odette's heart beat fast, and her breathing shallowed. At least Odette wasn't as unaffected by the kiss as she was suggesting.

"It does," Odette whispered. "Now we should sleep."

No, we should kiss again and gaze at each other naked and fold in each other's arms and explore our innermost secrets.

Beryl bit her bottom lip so she didn't say what she really wanted, to take off their nightwear and lie naked, breast to breast. She had no idea how she was supposed to sleep with the woman of her dreams in bed next to her. She turned over and switched off the lamp. "Okay. Good night."

"Good night, beautiful."

Beryl knew she would always remember those words in the dark in a wonderful accent and had a feeling that the memory would keep her warm in nights to come. The bed was too narrow to allow two people to share it without their bodies pressing together. Her mind churned with the unfulfilled desire, but she didn't want to move and disturb Odette, whose breathing had evened out into gentle puffs of air in her hair.

Beryl's whole day had been a turmoil, from the snowstorm to seeing Odette again, from the evening in the pub to knowing she could try the ATA again, and finally from a kiss holding the essence of all that was wonderful. She touched her lips. Odette had kissed her making her week, her month, her year. If only it could happen again, but the thought was like catching a snowflake with warm hands, melting before she could grasp it. Everything was beautiful, life-changing, and ultimately ephemeral. But she had a promise from Odette to provide the details of the ATA flying tests, and that gave her permission to write to Odette. She would grab that opportunity with both hands. Odette had opened her world before and done it again now. Her world was unfurling, and she would do everything she could to fly her flag.

Chapter Four

THE LYSANDER SHORT TAKE-OFF and landing aircraft Odette was coaxing back from an airfield on the south coast was not her first operational plane, but it was the most damaged. Besides the holes in the fuselage from gunfire, the flaps were half stuck open, causing drag. Who knew what else was wrong or could go wrong as she landed? "I must not break the plane," she repeated as a mantra.

They had drilled into them that some men, including "high ups," were just waiting for the women to fail or bend an aircraft so they could insist they weren't capable of flying fast, modern aeroplanes. Not that this Lysander was either of those things.

There was a rumour the Lysanders were used to drop off and pick up special operatives. "So, you've seen France more recently than me," she said. "She hasn't treated you well. But is she still as beautiful as before?" She shook her head at her stupidity. No, her country was forever changed. It was under a fascist regime. Maybe she had a nostalgic view of France. Would she ever return? If the scare about an imminent invasion of Britain was true, then the answer was probably no.

She mulled over her conversation with Beryl when she'd admitted she didn't think she'd live through the war. Despite trying to forget her, Beryl had often been on her mind, and they had shared correspondence over the past few months, more sporadically in Odette's case. She tried so hard not to respond and sometimes resisted the temptation for days, but she felt compelled to reply. And when her heart gave a jump of delight when she received a letter, then that was just because letters were a novelty, wasn't it?

This morning, a letter from Beryl was nestled in her pigeonhole when she picked up her flying chits for the day. She hadn't had the time to read it, but she had tapped the envelope in her top pocket repeatedly to check it was still there.

By the time she'd delivered a twin-engine Airspeed Oxford to one airfield, a Tiger Moth to Upavon, and picked up the high-winged Lysander, she'd hardly had time to freshen up, eat, or read a letter. After she delivered this battered old lady to Elstree, she had another flight to make before sundown, though they hadn't seen the sun today. This was her life, day after day, and she loved it. To be paid to fly and experience the joy when a landmark appeared exactly as she expected warmed her with pride and gave her a sense of achievement.

She had to be more careful today. The clouds were lowering towards the ground in a dark grey curtain ahead. She had a choice: to go below the cloud and hope to find her way in the rain, avoiding high ground and barrage balloons, which is what ATA regulations required, or she could fly above the clouds, using dead reckoning calculations of time, distance, and wind speed, then pray there was a hole in the cloud where she could let down. The rattling of a heavy rain shower sounded like gunfire and obliterated visibility above and to the left. She could turn back, but she doubted this old girl would fly again without a major overhaul at Elstree.

"Can you climb above the clouds, ma vieille dame?" It would be tricky with the half-lowered flaps, but she trimmed the plane as best as she could and slowly eased up the throttle. Amazingly, the battered old thing responded, and she climbed through a hole in the clouds and popped out in bright sunshine. Up there, it was a beautiful day and the barrage balloons around London formed a puffy line as far as she could see. She checked her watch and glanced at the map. She needed to head north, keeping above the Chiltern hills which stood at nearly one thousand feet.

Judging by the clouds, the wind direction was slightly different up here. She mentally made some adjustments and shifted her heading in relation to the barrage balloons. She double checked the location of the markers she had highlighted in red pencil on her map and noted the time.

The cloud below was much thicker than had been forecast. It was like a fluffy white quilt, spreading as far as she could see. Towering above her were a couple of large, dark anvil-shaped cumulonimbus that notified heavy rain and possible thunderstorms. Despite that, everything seemed in control. As if she had jinxed it, the engine coughed and backfired but continued to run. Now she was alert, and her heart sounded as loud and fast as the rain had a few minutes ago.

If her reckoning was correct, she would be over the Chiltern hills. The ground would be covered in cloud—not the place to drop through, because she wouldn't be able to recover in time to land safely. The engine continued to run but sounded rough. Odette scanned the instruments and checked the trim, before she pulled back on the throttle a little, in case the mixture had been too rich. "Come on, Lizzie. You can do it." It was crazy to talk to the plane, but sometimes it helped to hear any voice in the cockpit, as though there was at least one rational person present.

She used to talk to Simone in the cockpit, but now she left her dead partner in peace. She touched Simone's scarf. At some time over the last seven years, she had switched to speaking to the planes in English, not French. Maybe Simone had now receded into the background, or had someone else intrigued her? Subconsciously, she patted the top pocket of her flying suit, and there was a satisfying crinkle of paper from Beryl's letter.

There was something about Beryl that reminded her of Simone. Simone was always glamorous in whichever guise she adopted. Beryl had not yet learned to be a chameleon. She still presented as her true self wherever she was, and Odette wanted to rush in and protect her to show her how to live another way.

And yet she admired Beryl for being herself. She admired her courage and determination. But why was she even thinking about Beryl? That was totally against her rules of no favourites, no flings, no falling in love. None of that *Work, Family, Fatherland* rhetoric for her. She had to protect her heart more than anything else.

Odette checked her watch again. She should be over the airfield, but the cloud was even thicker now. If she was out by just a few feet, she would crash spectacularly. That wasn't how she wanted to die. It would hold back the women's flying cause if she damaged the aeroplane.

"What are our choices, Lizzie? We can fly north and try to find a hole we can pop into and fly back to the airfield, assuming the cloud is above the ground. Or we can fly even further north and hope Hatfield is clear. Flying north is the logical choice." She definitely didn't want to continue flying east and land in the Thames estuary as Amy Johnson had done, or due south into London and the ring of barrage balloons.

Decision made, she gently banked the plane and wrestled with the trim to keep it straight and level. Fortunately, it had a large fuel tank behind her, and she twisted to see the gauge. Fuel was fine. One less thing to worry about. Up ahead, there was a glimpse of green where the clouds were thinner, enabling her to find a hole she could lower down through. *Parfaite*.

But when she arrived there, the hole had moved, and now there were signs of a town below. Which one? Depending on how low the cloud was, she might need to watch out for towers and church spires. It seemed the best option to come down there and pray that the engine didn't falter until she was in the countryside, where she had a hope of making a forced landing.

The great thing about the Lysander was the clear visibility and as she dipped the nose of the aeroplane, the flat tower of St Albans Cathedral appeared a mere hundred feet to her portside, the top almost brushing the bottom of the cloud. Sweat beads formed on her forehead. Too close. If she had been just a touch to the left, she would have collided with a building that had stood for hundreds of years. The powers that be would not appreciate her destroying an ancient monument.

Odette exhaled loudly and muttered a quick prayer as she circled the cathedral, exhilarated that she had escaped death again. The way south back to Elstree Airfield seemed marginally clearer in the rain. Visibility was sufficient that she could follow the glorious straight Roman Road towards the destination airfield.

"All praise Roman engineering," she said. "Who knew nearly two thousand years later I would use their roads as navigational markers?"

Odette followed the road, peering through the murk until she could see Aldenham Hall, with its polo grounds, and just over the hedge was the airfield itself. She had rarely been so grateful to reach a destination. The Lysander crossed the centre line of the runway to join the circuit. As she did, the engine spluttered again and stopped, and the nose tipped upwards. *Don't stall.*

A flash of memory of Simone's plane stalling seared itself into her brain but fortunately, her body reacted. She pushed down the nose and trimmed frantically to maintain airspeed, so she didn't just drop out of the sky. The sole noise was the wind whistling through the windows and the bullet holes in the fuselage.

Hoping no one else was on finals, she made a sweeping approach and lined up, knowing she had no engine to make a go-around. She shouted out her pre-landing checks to convince herself it was just a normal landing and to calm her drumming heart.

Flying low over the hedge reminded her of the first time she met Beryl when her fuel line had been cut. What a strange thing to pop into her head when her life was on the line, while time stood still as the end of the runway rushed towards her too fast. She pulled the nose up to stall at the last moment, and the old bird creaked and sagged on her undercarriage. Miraculously, it remained upright and rolled to a stop just at the end of the runway. If she hadn't stalled, she would have hit the trees at the far end.

She let out a whoop of delight. The rush of blood to her head gave her the buzz of surviving by her skill and good fortune. Again. When she was safe and her adrenaline level dropped, her teeth started chattering and wouldn't stop.

It took ages for the ground crew to arrive with a tractor, and her hands trembled so much she couldn't even apply her lipstick.

"Are you okay?" a young man asked. "Wow, she's a mess, isn't she? I'm surprised she flew at all. We're going to cannibalise parts from her."

Something snapped. Perhaps it was the fear that had built throughout the flight, that she'd had a close shave with St Alban's Cathedral, the poor weather, and an engine out in the circuit that made her release a torrent of swear words. It took a few seconds before she had control of herself, and she inhaled sharply and spoke as evenly as she could manage. "You mean I risked my neck for something you plan to scrap?"

The young man shrugged. "Sorry, lady, but that's the war for you. I hope you can get a car to take you back. We're closing the airfield. We'll sort the plane out, and you can fill out the snag sheet while we get you a brew."

Technically, she didn't need to complete a snag sheet for an aircraft that would be scrapped, but she would ensure she did, to prove to herself that she'd cheated death. She grabbed her parachute and overnight bag and let him help her down from the cockpit.

"Hop into the truck to take you back to the control tower," he said.

Odette complied, glad to let someone else make decisions for the moment. She leaned against the greasy old leather seat and closed her eyes. This wasn't like her. Normally she volunteered for the difficult flights or the rust buckets and flew in all weathers to get the job done. She got a thrill from doing what others couldn't, of pitting herself against the air and her machine. Better she died than some of the young women with husbands and boyfriends. She had nothing to live for, so it didn't matter what happened to her.

As if her subconscious tickled her, the unopened letter from Beryl rustled in her top pocket. She patted it, deciding to read it after the commanding officer had signed the chit and she'd completed the snag sheet. It would be a long one. At least the aircraft was mostly intact from the landing, so she wouldn't have to face the accidents' committee where they acted as judge and jury. They really didn't need a woman pilot to be found at fault for crashing a plane.

The operations office, which also doubled as the control tower, was cramped, and the commanding officer looked over his spectacles at her as she entered.

"You were lucky. All the other airfields around here are closed for the weather. Two massive thunderstorms are coming in."

Odette stared at him. That certainly hadn't been forecast. Almost immediately, the dark clouds lit up with a crack of lightning, and thunder roiled around the sky. The first drops of rain rattled on the tin roof and within a few seconds, the tattoo was so loud they had to shout to be heard.

"Can I check in with my base?" she asked.

The commanding officer signed her chit and nodded to the telephone before exiting. He obviously wasn't one for idle chitchat, or maybe he was peeved an aeroplane was cluttering up his runway and they couldn't close the airfield until it had been removed.

Odette blocked her ear with her index finger against the noise of the rain and called control at Hatfield.

Their operations officer, Amelia, answered.

"Odette, I am so glad to hear you safe and sound. We were worried because the weather report changed after you left. A car has gone to White Waltham to pick up a couple of pilots. I'll call there and ask them to pick you up on the way back here. Make yourself comfortable; it could be quite a wait."

Amelia sounded relieved. Her job of trying to sort out the logistics of flying different aeroplanes with pilots with a range of skills to different places was incredibly difficult. To add more complications, she had to amend the programme on the go when aircraft became unserviceable or pilots had to divert because of the weather. Odette didn't envy them their task, especially on a difficult flying day like today.

"Thanks. See you tomorrow." As Odette drank her cup of tea, she realised they would drive back up past St Albans on the Roman Road that had been her navigational lifeline. She could just imagine the newspaper reports if she had crashed the Lysander into the cathedral. Maybe she'd used up three lives in one flight. That had to be a record. She probably only had a couple of lives left.

Odette pulled out the rather crumpled letter from Beryl. If she had a smile on her face as she did so, it was just the relief at having escaped to fly another day. Wasn't it?

Dear Odette,

I thought I'd send you a quick letter to say they accepted me in the ATA. Hooray! Thank you so much for the tip-off and for encouraging me to apply. The flight test was fine, and of course the technical questions were really basic. Phew. The great news is that Maisie also passed, so we can join together. We'll be reporting for training in three days. I can't wait to fly every day. Heaven. Hopefully, I'll get to see you as well.
Thank you again for encouraging me to apply.

Yours gratefully,
Beryl.

Heaven? After just being scared halfway to the heavens, this job seemed more like Hell. She traced her fingers over Simone's lucky scarf. The difficult flights were always the ones that replayed in her head in the early hours of the morning, robbing her of sleep and posed the searching questions. For all her bravado sometimes she seemed to be tempting the fates.

Odette shook out her legs and realised just how hard she'd been tensing them when she was flying. The muscles ached from her calves to her buttocks. What she would give for a massage, but that was another thing she'd never seen in England. Perhaps Joyce would know where she could get one. She folded the letter, replaced it in the envelope, and carefully returned it to her top pocket and fastened the button.

Part of her was worried for Beryl. Often, they had to fly in poor weather using just a map and compass, with no instruments and no radio. Beryl was an instinctive pilot but had little navigational experience. What if anything happened to her? Would Odette add guilt to her feeling of malaise, especially since she had encouraged Beryl to join? She had got along fine for the last number of years being closed off emotionally and didn't want to have to consider anyone else.

Yet, it would be good to see her regularly. Beryl was kind and modest, with a real aptitude for flying and absolutely no idea how stunning she was. It was the first time in many years that Odette had even thought about someone else in anything but a platonic way.

For all of her chatter and banter with her fellow pilots, she had not been physical with anyone for a very long time, and the last kiss she'd shared was with Beryl. That should have been as meaningless as she had claimed, but it had played over and over in her mind. How soft Beryl's lips had been, how they seemed to communicate physically without words, and the passion with which Beryl committed to the kiss. There was no holding back. It had surprised Odette and stirred emotions and physical reactions she didn't want to acknowledge. That would be a slippery slope.

She was glad that Beryl's friend Maisie was joining too, to keep each other company. Maisie had the advantage that she already knew several ATA women in the highest social standing who could help with acceptance and assimilation. People like Joyce.

Beryl, coming from a humbler background, might feel daunted by the opulent wealth. Or maybe she wouldn't. She seemed happy to hold her own. Underneath her concern though, Odette realised she felt something she hadn't felt for a long time: excitement and anticipation. It was good for the ego to have someone admire her, although it was more than that. And Beryl wouldn't be her first student with a crush on her. What was it about Beryl? Was it because her enthusiasm for flying was contagious or because, despite everything, Odette's body responded to her in a way it hadn't since Simone? Whatever it was, it was imprudent for her to take anything further. And she was happy with that. And if she kept telling herself that, she might actually believe it.

Chapter Five

AFTER THEIR FIRST WEEK at the ATA flying school, all the new recruits sat in a crowded, noisy pub on the Friday night. Beryl couldn't believe she was there. Thank goodness Maisie was there too. She always knew something or somebody who could help get them nice lodgings, bikes to get to the airfield, and umpteen items that made life easier.

"What is top dead centre? It sounds like a hill in a cemetery. Why does it matter? I don't understand. You can tell Watkins hates having to teach us nincompoops," Edna said and took a sip of her drink that was something red, in a dainty glass. A bit like she was, although her hair was more auburn than red.

Beryl liked Edna. She wasn't afraid to say she didn't know something. Perhaps because she was Canadian, she had to ask many questions to weave her way through the peculiar English culture and bizarre regulations. Beryl smiled. "Would you like me to explain it?" She pushed her beer out of the way and reached for a napkin from an adjoining table. She sketched out the Otto cycle of a piston engine with a pencil she carried everywhere. "It starts with the intake."

Edna listened and asked questions as Beryl explained. When Maisie leaned over and wanted to clarify about valve overlap, Beryl's heart expanded. She had never been accepted before, nor had anyone take note of anything she said. Her dad and brother already knew it and didn't ask for her contribution. She was so proud to be part of the group of ATA cadets celebrating their first week of training and getting envious glances from the civilians. Some cadets had escaped to London to the nightclubs, but most couldn't afford the petrol coupons, or, like Beryl, didn't have a car and had little inclination to push their way onto an overcrowded train to be jostled in a way too noisy nightclub that might be disturbed if there was an air raid anyway.

Pauline put down her drink. "I've already sat through a week of this. No offence, Beryl, but I want to relax on our days off. Shall we get those RAF boys to buy us a drink? Come on, Hetty. Let's see if they'll come and join us."

"Are you sure it's just a drink you want, Pauline?" Dorrie asked and gave a wry smile.

Edna laughed.

Pauline smoothed down her skirt. "Well, I'm not going to say no if a handsome man asks me to dance and maybe more."

"Do you think they're handsome?" Hetty pushed back her chair to inspect the men.

"Who cares? They're officers, aren't they? Ooh, wait, more people are coming in. Let's see what we have here."

They all looked at the mixed group entering. Pauline and Hetty muttered and pointed, acting like they were choosing their favourite treats from a sweet store.

"They're more ATA pilots flying from White Waltham for upgrades to a different class of plane," Edna said and resumed her quiet conversation with Dorrie.

Beryl's heart picked up pace, because among the gaggle of people entering was Odette, who was laughing. Beryl tried hard to squash down the spike of jealousy and not gawp as she followed Odette's path to the bar. Not that she was looking over. Odette hadn't responded to her last letter saying she had got into the ATA. It had been nearly two weeks ago now, and those days had dragged. She kept telling herself it was because Odette was really busy ferrying planes every day.

As time passed, it seemed Odette was giving her the message that she wanted nothing to do with her. Beryl had to get over her, or maybe have a conversation to clear the air. Seeing her there just across the room, she couldn't help but stare. *Stop it.* Deliberately, Beryl forced herself to look at Pauline.

Disappointment spilled from Pauline like oil from a sump. "Oh, they're just girls and ancient men. Now they're crowding the bar too, so we'll have to wait."

Dorrie eyed Pauline, a look of amusement on her face. "What sort of men do you fancy?"

Pauline batted her eyelashes. "Rich."

They all laughed.

"It isn't all it's cracked up to be," Maisie said. "Trust me, I've seen some absolute bounders who were rich."

Pauline rubbed her finger and thumb together. "But given the choice, I'd prefer a bounder who's rich than a pauper."

Maisie raised an eyebrow at Beryl, and she knew she was in trouble.

"So, Beryl, what sort of man do you like?"

Really? Maisie was doing this. She could feel the blush starting from her neck upwards. She couldn't explain that she didn't like men at all. Not in that way, anyway. She was quite happy to have them as friends but no more, thank you. But seeing Odette in the bath—that had been something else. Not daring to cast a glance at Odette, she glowered at Maisie, who grinned.

"Seeing someone's spanner collection would probably turn Beryl on," Pauline said, and they all laughed again.

The laughter shut a door on further conversation and cut her out. There were so many more interesting things to talk about than men. Fortunately, Hetty prodded Pauline that the airmen were looking this way. They waved, and the men smiled.

Beryl sipped at her bitter shandy, hoping the conversation would drift off to another topic. Even her drink set her aside from her peers, but she wouldn't change it to some disgusting sweet concoction just to be like the rest of the ATA cadets. She wished she was in their lodgings reading up on everything they had to learn, not spending the evening in the pub, but Maisie could be very persuasive. She was being unfair; Maisie had been wonderful and smoothed the path for both of them. Money and contacts could do that. As if Maisie knew Beryl was watching her, she caught a glance and flashed Beryl a wicked grin. What was that about?

"Come on, Beryl. We don't know much about you," Dorrie said. "Who do you fancy?"

Without being conscious of it, Beryl cast her gaze across at the group of experienced ATA pilots and pivoted back to the faces at her table, not wishing to give away that she was infatuated with Odette. She wiped her clammy palms on her uniform skirt.

She cleared her throat. "A pilot."

"Och, tell us something we don't know," Maisie said with a grin. "That's probably a prerequisite, so you can share notes on Otto cycles."

Even Beryl laughed. Being teased meant they accepted her, right? Even if she was an oddball. And with Maisie, she knew there was no malice behind the comments. If she could keep it neutral, she might get them off her back. "Brave, dark-haired, striking good looks."

"Rich?" Maisie asked, grinning at Pauline, who just quirked her eyebrow.

Beryl shook her head. "No, I don't care if they weren't born to the nobility or have a huge stash of cash."

"Ah. I might know the right person for you," Maisie said.

Beryl swallowed hard. Was she so obvious? She didn't dare look over at Odette and her friends, although the laughter drifted over from that table. She would love to be the one making Odette laugh.

Maisie looked at her watch. "Good. They should arrive about now."

Odette's already here, Beryl wanted to shout, but of course that wasn't what Maisie meant. As if on cue, the door to the pub opened, and Rob and Mike strolled in. When they caught sight of

Maisie and Beryl, they smiled and made their way to their table.

Ah, she knew there had been a purpose to Maisie's questions. Beryl prodded Maisie with her toe. "You set this up."

Maisie winked and turned to beam as Rob approached the table.

"Good evening, ladies. May we join you?" Rob asked.

Pauline leaned forward, displaying her ample breasts, prominent even in her uniform. She really wasn't subtle.

Pauline patted the empty chair beside her. "Please do. We were just saying that we really look forward to spending time with you flyboys. I'm Pauline."

She held out her hand. Rob shook it and introduced Mike before asking if anyone wanted a drink.

"I'll come with you," Maisie said and linked her arm through Rob's in a territorial manner. "Same again, everyone?"

Maisie wasn't being subtle either, but it didn't irk Beryl in the same way.

Mike stood beside Beryl so close she could smell his strong aftershave. "How are you? So glad to see you actually got into the ATA."

Beryl smiled, realising Mike could fit the same description as she had given about Odette. Well, a bit of deflection wouldn't harm.

"I hear they're letting the ATA women fly Hurricanes now. That's great news. Anything to relieve the pressure on the frontline pilots." Mike drew up a chair to sit beside Beryl. "May I?"

Pauline blinked when she heard Mike's accent, which indicated he was clearly not from the upper classes, so she leaned back and sat up properly to finish her drink, her gaze seeking the whereabouts of other RAF officers.

Mike rubbed his hands together as if he was cold from being outside. "What have you flown so far?" he asked.

"A desk. We're just cadets-in-training. This is our first week."

Edna leaned over, and her red hair trailed over Beryl's uniform.

"Except Beryl knows it all already. She was explaining to me how a piston engine works. I couldn't make head nor tail of what the lecturer was saying. Sometimes they forget that we women are not taught anything about cars or anything mechanical. Except Beryl."

Mike nodded. "And is it true you have to jump into any plane and take it anywhere in the country?"

Edna was warming to the subject, and she patted Beryl on her thigh as she leaned across her. "Yes. They give us pilot's notes, which have the key characteristics of a plane, landing speed, cruise speed, etcetera, and off we go."

Mike rubbed his forehead as if the thought made his head hurt. "Wow, I couldn't do that."

"It isn't any plane." Beryl felt obliged to clarify. "All the planes are allocated into classes, and we're taught to fly an example of that class of plane. Obviously, we're starting on the slower, single-engine trainers."

"But you've got over a hundred hours."

That he remembered surprised Beryl. She was touched and warmed to him even more by his surprise and concern. She smiled. "I haven't flown for over two years, and I'd be rusty by now. I'm looking forward to the navigation flights, because I did most of my flying in the circuit."

"True. The group over there are celebrating because the women have just been signed off to fly the Hurricanes." He nodded towards Odette and her group and waved vigorously. Odette waved back, and Beryl raised her hand, unclear if she was waving at her, Mike, or in general. At least she wasn't ignoring her.

On her first day at the training school, they'd been informed the more experienced pilots didn't mix with the newbies. They were referred to as the sprogs, not too unkindly, and that suited Beryl just fine, although she was eager to pick up any tips experienced pilots might have.

But she could ask Mike about the Hurricanes. "Is it true that the Hurricanes are nose-heavy, and the undercarriage is a pain to get down?"

He nodded. "Yes, but my undercarriage is as smooth as silk, because she's been up and down so many times."

She listened intently when Mike discussed the handling of the Hurricanes, absorbing any detail that might help her master her piloting skills.

Rob and Maisie returned with the round of drinks. Rob grinned at Pauline as he set down the beer, and gin and tonics for the others.

"Maisie asked the RAF chaps at the bar if they wanted company, and they said they'd be delighted, so your drinks are with them. They're already paid for."

Pauline flung her hand to her chest. "Oh, I didn't think they'd noticed us."

She wasn't fooling anyone.

Maisie pushed a small beer in front of Beryl but kept her face towards Pauline. "They noticed all right. They said they were particularly keen to meet you and Hetty, Pauline."

"They are? How could we say no then?" Pauline and Hetty rose, picked up their belongings, and wiggled their way through the packed tables to the bar.

After they left, Mike cocked his head and turned to Maisie. "Did you say that just to get them out of your hair?"

Now it was Maisie's turn to clap her fist to her chest. "Mike, don't you know a girl never reveals her secrets? But we will take their seats."

She winked at Beryl again. This situation was clearly being manipulated. She was surprised Maisie hadn't sent Dorrie and Edna away, but they were deep in conversation, their heads close together and speaking at a whisper so Beryl wouldn't have overheard even if it hadn't been really noisy.

Maisie drank a little of her G&T, then turned to Beryl. "Joyce and Odette are over there and said they might come over and join us in a minute."

Beryl almost choked on her drink and had to put her hand in front of her mouth to stop the beer from spraying out. "They did?"

"Don't choke. We need you for our extra-curricular principles of flight lessons if we have any chance of passing," Dorrie said, looking up from her conversation. "We'll let them have our seats. We're going back now. We're up early tomorrow, because I'm taking Edna back to my house so she can see a typical English home."

"That's kind," Beryl said, feeling her cheeks burn. She should have done more to welcome Edna.

Edna leaned into Dorrie and squeezed her shoulder. "Oh, she is." Her lips quirked as if she was disguising some private joke. "We'll see you all back at the airfield on Monday, so Watkins can bamboozle us. Beryl, I may come to you for extra lessons again."

Beryl raised her glass to them. "Any time."

Edna blew a kiss at them all, and Dorrie pushed her forward. "See you on Monday."

They left, and almost immediately, Joyce and Odette joined them.

"They looked cosy," Odette said, watching the women retreat.

Maisie pulled the spare chairs closer so they could sit down. "Dorrie's invited Edna back to her home for the weekend."

Odette gave a rather enigmatic smile. Joyce sat by Maisie with Odette on Beryl's other side. Her heart fluttered, and she inhaled deeply to contain her delight.

"The weekend? What's that?" Joyce said. "We're back on ferry duty tomorrow. We're all placing bets on who the first person will be to fly a Hurricane. My money's on Odette."

Maisie shook her head. "No bet. She's probably the odds-on favourite."

Odette smiled. "Nonsense. It depends on who's sent where.

I'll probably have a delivery up to Scotland tomorrow, or I'll have to fly the taxi ferry."

Beryl turned to Odette, whose hair was perfect and lipstick pristine as before. She was always so glamorous in a way Beryl could only aspire to. Except she didn't aspire to look like that, just to admire that and appreciate and... She had to stop this. She turned to Mike. "Odette is a very experienced pilot."

"I know," Mike said.

Odette was sitting so close, her legs brushed against Beryl's under the table, which made her body buzz with delight. It would be so easy to lean into the touch, to delight in the thrill of it, but she really shouldn't rub her leg against Odette in case she put a ladder in her stockings.

Still, she glowed with pride at being able to wear the uniform. Soon, they would take to the skies, and she really didn't care if they had long days and no weekends. She would be flying again for the first time in two years. She couldn't wait until she earned her embroidered wings with the ATA letters in an oval in the centre. Sitting here with the woman she was attracted to, talking about flying was heaven on earth, and flying the planes would be heaven in the skies. She was so lucky.

"Would you?" Mike asked.

Had he been talking to her the whole time? Beryl's cheeks burned. "Sorry, what did you say?"

"Will you come up to London tomorrow and go dancing? Rob and Maisie are coming too. I promise we'll accompany you home."

Maisie clapped her hands together. "Oh, yes, please come. We can both stay at my father's wee house in Chelsea."

Her father had another house? Beryl thought he lived in some old hall in Scotland, and she doubted anything in Mayfair could be described as tiny. She leaned over the table to Maisie and whispered, "I have nothing to wear." With the new clothing rations, she wouldn't be able to buy anything even if she did have the spare cash.

"No problem. I'll lend you something. We're about the same size," Maisie whispered. "Please come. I need a chaperone to satisfy my over-protective father."

An evening dancing was not her idea of fun. "Can't you ask someone else, like Joyce?"

"She's working, and so is Odette. Please, Beryl, I really want you to come, and I know Mike would too."

She grinned, probably thinking that would be the clinching argument. All Beryl wanted to do was run and hide under her bedclothes at the implied expectation that she would pair up with Mike.

She felt a hand on her thigh. She turned to face Odette. Did she have any idea what her hand was doing to Beryl's body?

"You should go," Odette said. "It will do you good to get out and be seen."

Beryl frowned and slumped back into her chair. Seen? By whom? Why?

Odette must have read the confusion on her face because she leaned towards Beryl and whispered, "You need to be seen going out with men."

Her breath was hot and sweet from whatever she was drinking. Vaguely, she wondered where they got the sugar from to concoct such a drink. The hairs on the back of Beryl's neck rose. What was Odette suggesting? Mike, Rob, and Maisie were deep in conversation about where they should go, so Beryl could give her full attention to Odette. "Why?" she whispered.

Odette lowered her head so only Beryl could hear. "Decoy."

Beryl gawped, wondering if Odette had had too many of those disgusting-looking drinks she sipped so daintily. "What am I, a duck?"

Odette's thumb stroked Beryl's thigh, and it was all Beryl could do not to squeak. What was Odette trying to do to her?

"If you want to nestle in swan's feathers, you need a different narrative."

Beryl stared some more then closed her mouth. Was Odette suggesting what she thought? Had that kiss they shared meant something to Odette after all? Did that mean she wanted to explore something with her? Or was she talking about general appearances?

Odette squeezed her thigh before she let go. "Relax. Not now, and not here. Go out with them tomorrow."

Beryl nodded as understanding dawned. It wasn't a promise, just a hint of potential, and she wanted that. She would take anything on offer. Also, Maisie had been a great friend, and Mike was kind, so it was churlish and selfish not to go. It could be fun. She turned to Maisie. "Okay, I'll come with you."

The dazzling smile on Maisie's face was worth all the discomfort Beryl would endure, and as Odette suggested, she had a decoy.

"That's great," Mike said, and he glanced across at Rob.

They all raised and clinked glasses.

"What magic did you weave, Odette, to persuade Beryl to come? I've been trying to get her out for weeks whenever we've had a spare evening." Maisie said.

Odette stole a wink at Beryl and sipped her drink. "What can I say? I bribed her with a flight in an Anson."

"She'll get that when we start ferrying."

"I know, but there's nothing wrong with giving people what they want."

Maisie positively bounced in her seat, and Rob seemed relieved as they shared a look that was definitely not for company. Beryl panicked she was being set up with Mike and hoped Maisie wouldn't abandon her, but she couldn't believe Maisie would do that to her. She knew Beryl was shy and inexperienced, didn't she? What had she agreed to?

Mike gave Beryl a genuine smile. "I'm glad you're coming."

It felt like a trapdoor was snapping shut. She didn't know how long she could keep Mike dangling. "I might need instruction in dancing though. I'm not very good at it."

"We'll have a wee practice tomorrow," Maisie said. "In fact, if you men are free, why don't you come over, and we'll practice at my dad's place?"

Beryl wondered if that had been part of the original plan too, as it seemed to roll off Maisie's tongue so smoothly. Rob was already nodding. Beryl wiped her palms on her skirt. They seemed to be uncomfortably clammy. There was no backing out now.

"Where are you planning to go dancing?" Joyce asked, looking rueful. "I'd love to join you, but we have a full day's ferrying tomorrow, and the only thing I'm fit for when I get home is to collapse in a heap with a gin. If I had the energy, I'd join you."

"The old jazz club off Leicester Square. Because it's down in the basement, it should be immune from any air raids, if there are any," Rob said.

Instinctively, they all touched the wood of the table superstitiously. So Beryl was going to dance the day away tomorrow. She would have preferred Odette show her how to dance. She could almost imagine how it would be if they danced together, nestled in a close hold, feeling the warmth of Odette's body pressed against hers. Beryl mentally chastised herself for going down this path and smiled at the others. Being accepted as part of the group was a novelty and she basked in the sense of belonging. And if dancing with Mike was the cost of whatever Odette was offering, she would gladly pay the price.

Chapter Six

THE FOLLOWING DAY, ODETTE had wonderful visibility as she flew along. Even the smog seemed less today, probably because there was a strong crosswind. She preferred to fly through the narrow balloon corridor rather than over the water. With the sea, there were no landmarks, and it was easy to get disoriented, as Amy Johnson found to her cost. Today, the heading was easy to keep, and she could see her next turn point ahead in the distance.

Should she have made a move on Beryl last night? Odette was lonely, and if this war was teaching her anything at all, it was to make the most of every moment, to snatch a lifetime's experience when she could, because life could be cut drastically short.

Beryl was charmingly naïve, with a shyness that radiated from her. More callous souls would take advantage of her, and Odette felt a strong need to protect her, to wrap her arms around her and encourage her to blossom. Beryl had no idea how gorgeous she was and had seemed surprised when Odette had mentioned it, waving away the compliment as if it was ridiculous. The sad thing was that rather than glory in her not being feminine, Beryl would be watched and treated with suspicion. The ATA would try to soften her up and glamorize her for the newspapers. Beryl wasn't sophisticated like most of the people Odette had been with. She was open and guileless and unashamedly enthusiastic about flying. Who wouldn't want to be surrounded by that, be engaged and entertained by her? Beryl was unique. Suddenly, unbidden, a vision of Simone flashed in her memory, and the parallel became obvious. In the joy of flying, the sensitivity with which Beryl finessed the plane, reading the air, Beryl was similar to Simone: a gifted pilot. She would do what she could to nurture that and help Beryl blossom.

Odette was still smiling as she landed at St Athan in Wales to hand over her plane and wait for the ferry taxi back to her home base. She checked her watch and settled down in the lumpy armchair to eat her precious chocolate bar. With any luck, they would be back by eight, and she could relax in a long bath.

The Anson ferry pilot, Piotr, an ex-Battle of Britain Polish pilot, entered the dispersal lounge. "Anyone for White Waltham and Hatfield?"

Where was Joyce? She said she was due for pick-up here this evening, and she would hate to take a cold, packed train back to London.

"Has anyone seen Joyce?" Odette asked but was met with head shakes.

"No, and we need to get going. I have a date tonight," one of the other pilots said.

Odette settled herself in the plane. She sat on her parachute, which was bulky and uncomfortable and chafed at the top of her thighs but was needed if there was an emergency. Now it was like a second skin—a forty-pound skin. She wriggled on the leather seats to ease the discomfort. It had been a long day, and she still had a one-and-a-half-hour taxi ride home.

As she peered out of the window, she caught sight of Joyce running towards their Anson.

"Piotr, we have another passenger," Odette called out.

Piotr, who rarely spoke, looked up from his pre-flight checklist and nodded before returning to the instruments. If Odette didn't know better, she would assume he hadn't heard.

The ground crew opened the cockpit door, and Joyce squeezed herself inside.

"Thanks so much for waiting," she said to Piotr.

He nodded again and resumed his deliberations, touching

each of the instruments and gauges as if each were a holy relic, while his lips moved in an incantation.

Joyce slipped into the seat across the narrow aisle from Odette and clipped on her seat belt. "Phew, I'm so glad I made it. I had to make an extra stop at Tern Hill with a faulty fuel gauge."

As the plane taxied towards the runway, Joyce tapped her fingers together and said, "I might go along to the old jazz club tonight and join Beryl and Maisie."

Odette raised an eyebrow. "You want to play raspberry?"

Joyce laughed. "You mean gooseberry."

Odette shrugged. She knew the idiom, but Joyce looked as though she could do with relaxing. She was all spiky energy. Odette suspected the extra stop had been traumatic and frightening, although she doubted Joyce would discuss it. "And it's not because you're hoping a certain pilot will be there?"

Joyce's rose-coloured cheeks indicated Odette was right. "Maybe."

"Oh, yes? Who are you meeting?" Odette asked, shouting above the noise of the engine.

Joyce frowned. "Pilot Tommy Evans, of course. He said he would be there if he can get off early, and I really want to meet up with him. He hinted they'll be posted abroad somewhere soon."

It really didn't concern Odette who was going out with whom. She pulled her scarf tighter and wiped the condensation from the side window. Although it was officially summer, the interior of the plane was cold. Now she was no longer pilot-in-command, fatigue flicked at the edges of her consciousness. Selfishly, she wished she hadn't encouraged Beryl to be seen with men.

They all had to keep secrets about who they were and how they presented themselves to the world. The newspapers seemed to have an unhealthy interest in "our brave Attagirls" and would consider it a scandal if it ever got out. Odette never read the newspapers anymore; they were all lies and propaganda, and it was a long time since she'd done it to improve her English. If maintaining the image and keeping secrets meant she continued flying, she would do whatever it took.

Later, Odette was in her lodgings when the phone rang. Before she had even tucked in the bookmark and put down her novel, Joyce had run to the hall and picked up the receiver. As the door closed behind her, Odette resumed reading to give Joyce privacy.

A few minutes later, Joyce slunk into the room and flopped onto the other armchair beside Odette. Her face was the picture of misery.

"Tommy can't make it to the club. He has to do something with the boys, whatever that means."

Odette put her book down to give Joyce her full attention. "Will you be able to see him before he goes abroad?"

Joyce picked at the peeling leather on the old armchair. "I hate this. I have no idea if I'll ever see him again. He's being transferred to North Africa next week, and we're not supposed to know, but it's not going well. They're flying obsolete aircraft out there, and they're being picked off like flies. It's ridiculous, sending them to slaughter. I'll probably fly a Spitfire before he does, if I don't kill myself first."

Odette placed her hand over Joyce's to still them, willing her not to spiral down, which would help nobody. "Do you want to talk about it?"

Joyce ducked her head, then huffed a deep sigh. "I panicked when my engine failed today." She spoke into her lap. "I had to turn the fuel to the other tank, and the engine coughed and died."

Odette could imagine Joyce's panic; she was such an anxious pilot. "Well, you're still here, so you must have done something right."

Finally, Joyce raised her head to meet Odette's gaze. "I

pushed the nose down, turned back to the other tank, and diverted to Tern Hill. The gauge was wrong. I don't think they filled the second tank properly."

Odette squeezed Joyce's trembling fingers. "Perfect. You went through it logically, which is what you need to do. Well done."

Joyce looked at Odette earnestly. "I kept on thinking, what would you tell me to do?"

Odette smiled. "And you did brilliantly."

"But I was so anxious. Don't you get worried?"

Odette inhaled and closed her eyes, wondering how to thread her way through this minefield. She could hardly say she loved the buzz of an interesting or challenging flight, that being so close to death made her feel alive. "I'd be lying if I said I didn't, but as you get more experienced, you deal with what comes up more easily. I push my anxiety into my forgetting box and talk aloud as I fly. I did that the other day when I was flying the ferry taxi, forgetting I had passengers, and they all teased me about it."

Joyce huffed and held her head in her hands. "I'm not cut out for this. But I can't just sit around doing nothing."

"From what I've seen, you're a careful pilot, and you think about what you're doing, so that makes you a safe pilot too. The ATA trains us well and gives us the authority to refuse a plane—"

Joyce slammed her hands down on the arms of the chair and shot up. "Don't give me that tosh. You know some men are expecting us to fail, and they'll use any excuse."

"Where's all this anger coming from? Are you sure it's not your anxiety about Tommy being posted?" Odette asked gently. Joyce scowled at her, and Odette smiled. Time to resort to the standard British answer. "How about a cup of tea? We've got some oaty biscuits left that you brought back from your trip home."

Joyce strode out of the door. "I'll make it."

There followed much clattering of teacups and plates. Joyce had insisted they should have the silver tea service as though she were clinging on to her pre-war life as a debutante. Heaven knew what she thought about the way they served tea at most of the aerodromes they visited. Enamel or grubby chipped cups were not uncommon, with strength ranging from strong to paraffin.

Odette put out the backgammon set, their go-to pastime. Although it was a game of luck, over time, the better players were more successful, and Odette strategized playing backgammon as much as she did flying a plane. Consequently, over the months, Odette was way ahead of Joyce, even at a penny a game.

When Joyce returned with the tray and caught sight of the board all set up, she shook her head. "Do you mind if we don't play tonight? I might just have this cuppa and head to bed. As shattered as I feel, I'll end up losing my shirt."

Odette grinned. "Poor loser?"

Joyce grimaced as if she couldn't cope with teasing just now.

Odette picked up some of the pieces and placed them back in the box. "Sorry. Are you all right?"

Joyce poured the tea. "I will be. Thanks."

Over tea, they exchanged only the logistics of getting to the airfield the following day. For the most part, Joyce stared at the fire burning in the grate, seemingly absorbed in the lick of flames and the shifting of the coal.

Joyce replaced her cup on the saucer.

"Leave those. I'll wash them up in a minute," Odette said. Joyce left and Odette picked up the newspaper but couldn't settle. Was Beryl enjoying her evening with Mike, or was she as listless as Odette felt? It was selfish of her to push Beryl into going out as a smokescreen, but Odette didn't want to examine why it bothered her so. She didn't want her name linked with Beryl because if anyone looked too closely, they'd see that her feelings for Beryl were written all over her face. Feelings she should not be entertaining but that were bubbling up anyway, like desire and admiration.

She tossed the paper down, unread, and finally, just before

ten, she retired to her room.

Later Beryl unpeeled an orange deliberately and presented Odette half. Odette's mouth watered and the acidic scent clung to the inside of her nostrils. "Where did you get them from? I haven't seen an orange in years," she said.

"What's that alarm?" Beryl asked.

It wasn't an alarm. Odette awoke with a start at the telephone ringing. How strange, the dream had been so vivid, and it didn't take a genius to work out that Beryl was offering her something she desperately wanted but couldn't have.

Joyce ran down the stairs first and snatched up the phone in the hall. "Odette, come here."

The panic in Joyce's voice was enough to have Odette grabbing her dressing gown and following her down. Joyce trembled. Her hand covered her mouth, and her eyes were wide. She held the receiver in one hand and a disembodied man's voice echoed down the line. "Joyce, are you there?"

Odette took the phone from Joyce's grip. "Hello, this is Odette. Who am I speaking to?"

"I don't know if you remember me, Tommy Evans? Sorry to phone so late, but we've just heard that a bomb has gone off in the Old Jazz Club. Went down the air vent. Lucky shot, really."

Odette's emotions numbed as they did when she was dealing with a flying incident. Typical man talking about the irrelevancies, or maybe that's how he dealt with shock. Logic kicked in and she asked, "Casualties?"

"Not known at this time. Some of my boys were there, but they escaped and called me. I didn't want Joyce to worry if she saw it in the papers tomorrow. Wasn't she meeting friends there?"

Friends. Now the fear came rushing in like a storm, crushing her chest and throttling her. "Yes, Maisie and Beryl were meeting some RAF friends there," she said, barely able to form the words.

"Oh. I'm sorry to hear that. If I hear anything more, I'll keep you posted."

"Thank you." Odette replaced the receiver and sunk onto the floor. She'd lived in England too long—she was beginning to sound as polite and stiff as the natives. She wanted to wail, and her teeth began to chatter. The stone floor was cold to the touch, grounding her. Or maybe it was the shock that was making her shiver. If anything had happened to Beryl, she'd never forgive herself. She'd practically forced her to go. She couldn't lose Beryl too. Not now. They had just met again, and despite trying desperately not to obsess about her, Beryl had prised apart the shutters around Odette's heart and she was exposed and vulnerable. Fear ripped open the shutters, and they flapped in the wind. Odette stood to calm herself. *Keep it together.* Despite feeling raw inside, Odette went over to Joyce, who sat on the hard chair beside the telephone table, staring at the phone as if the scary news was its fault.

"A bomb. They could be..." Joyce's Adam's apple bobbed up and down.

"Let's not jump to conclusions. We need to gather the facts."

"How can we do that?"

Odette put her hand on Joyce's shoulder. "We can phone Maisie's house."

"I feel so guilty because I'm relieved Tommy wasn't there, but what if something's happened to Maisie and Beryl, or Rob and Mike?"

Odette squashed her feelings back into the forgetting box, tamping down the lid with all her emotional strength. She needed to be rational. "Let's call Maisie's number. Maybe they left the club early."

Joyce nodded dumbly and pointed to her address book at the side of the telephone. "It's under Stewart."

Despite her placating words, Odette's hands trembled as she

dialled. Glad to have a distraction so her mind couldn't spiral, she asked to be put through.

The receiver was picked up at the other end, and there was giggling and shushing before Maisie's voice came on the line. "Hello, Maisie Stewart speaking."

The tight rope around Odette's chest loosened. "Maisie, thank God. It's Odette here. Are you with Beryl, Rob, and Mike? You decided not to go to the club?"

Maisie giggled. "Stop it, Rob. Yes, we're playing cards instead. Rob didn't want to use his petrol ration this evening because he's driving home tomorrow. Why, what's happened?"

Odette leaned against the wall and closed her eyes. She took a few seconds before she explained about the club. Beryl was safe. They were all safe. But the giggling implied there was more than just cards going on. Relief morphed into a pang of jealousy. That wasn't fair. Beryl had made it clear she was only interested in Odette. Or was it Maisie and Rob who were constantly seeking chaperones under the guise of respectability?

Joyce virtually snatched the receiver from Odette's hands. "Let me talk to her."

Joyce vibrated with excitement as she talked to Maisie. Odette went into their small lounge and sat in the armchair, pulling her robe around her in an attempt to stop her teeth chattering. The fire had gone out, and it was very dark with the blackout curtains.

A few minutes later, Joyce called Odette into the hall and handed the receiver to her. "Maisie wants a word. I'm going to make another cuppa. I won't be able to sleep just yet."

Joyce slipped into the kitchen with a lightness to her step.

Odette cleared her throat. "Hello, Maisie. I'm so glad you're all okay."

"We're fine. I wanted to ask if it's true that you and a group of experienced pilots are going to set up a new ferry pool in Hamble?"

By now, Odette shouldn't be surprised that Maisie and

Joyce seemed to know all the changes. They had connections everywhere, but it still caught her off guard. "That's my understanding."

"Oh, no. Just as Beryl and I are going to be in Hatfield, you're moving on. That's so disappointing. Great for you, but I know Beryl's disappointed. She's just here. Let me pass you on to her."

"Hello, Odette. It's lovely to hear from you. Thank you for checking up on us. We're all fine, but how awful for those poor people in the club. Is it true you're going to Hamble?"

Beryl's excitement was palpable and she needed to be less obvious with her infatuation. Odette hoped Maisie hadn't noticed.

"Hello, Beryl," she said, without letting fear choke her.

"I'm sorry you were worried about us. Are you okay? Have you flown any Hurricanes today?"

"A couple."

"It's good to hear your voice," Beryl whispered.

Odette willed herself to ungrit her teeth and hoped Maisie had moved away from the telephone. They could not be seen to be too close. "Are you having a pleasant time with Mike?"

There was a pause on the line, and she could hear the puffs of air as Beryl breathed out.

"Is that what you want?"

Why did she have to question everything? Odette closed her eyes, trying to stop herself from imagining the hurt on Beryl's face. "Yes, of course. Mike's a nice guy."

Why was Beryl making her hurt her? Couldn't she see they had to maintain the façade, maintain their distance, if they wanted to be safe to continue flying? So much for it just being a kiss. She rued the day she thought that a kiss could mean nothing.

"Yes. He's kind." Beryl sounded clipped and distorted like she was talking down a Gosport speaking tube. "I must go back to him."

Odette replaced the receiver in the cradle and faced the wall, trying to steady her breaths. Why couldn't Beryl accept she had to be careful? That they risked losing it all? But the truth kept slapping at her heart. Beryl had cracked her armour and left her vulnerable—something she hated. She couldn't be weak.

Odette walked back into the sitting room, switched on a table lamp, and waited for Joyce to bring in the tea. They would be tired tomorrow, but she couldn't begin to think of sleep now.

She raked at the fire, poking some embers into life. Her response to Beryl was ridiculous. She had been able to control any desires or fantasies for years, but she was entranced when Beryl entered the room. Beryl said what she thought, which was so refreshing. Beryl was passionate and enthusiastic, so unlike most of the English people she'd met, who would prefer to crash a plane than admit they had feelings. Maybe that's what it was; Beryl was as much an outsider as she was. Add a bit of hero worship into the mix, and it wasn't surprising Odette was stirred up.

That Beryl might be canoodling with Mike made Odette feel nauseous. Odette never got attached emotionally, and she had pushed Beryl to be seen with a man. She wanted to protect her, because they couldn't be caught together, or they'd be dismissed from the ATA. That was all it was. Better to keep her head down and push her feelings for Beryl into the forgetting box.

She'd sealed off her heart and long may that continue. It kept her safe and able to take on the riskiest of flights because she had nothing to lose, and no one would miss her. Why did it feel like that might no longer be enough?

Chapter Seven

"CHANGE PLACES, TOMMY, SO you can stretch your legs out," Odette said as they took their places in the cinema.

Beryl's ears buzzed at the implications of the seating rearrangement. Did that mean Odette wanted to sit beside her? The cinema was packed, noisy, and very smoky. Beryl had worn lavender water, but there was no way Odette would be able to smell it with the cloying stench of cigarettes.

Beryl blinked and tried to stop her heart thumping so hard. She would probably be heard by their whole party. Mike waited until Beryl sat before taking his seat. He was the perfect gentleman, and she appreciated his kindness, but her pulse didn't quicken when he spoke to her, nor did she dream of him at night and wake, disturbed and wet and feeling very aroused. It was always the woman sitting beside her that triggered such a response.

Odette's thigh pressed lightly against Beryl's, sending heat under the skin where they touched. Mike's leg drifted against Beryl's other knee, but she had no visceral reaction.

The lights went dark, and the Pathé news came on. When there was a mini feature on the RAF, there was a big cheer from their party and booing from the other armed forces in the cinema. It reminded her of the rivalries of a football match that her dad and John used to go to. They'd explained it wasn't a place for women, because there was foul language and pushing and jostling. She was intrigued, but it was another experience denied to her because she was a woman.

The main feature came on, some comedy that Beryl hadn't even heard about. For just a few hours, they could forget the war, the rationing, the worry, and the hunger and believe they were living in a Hollywood happily ever after. But they weren't really here for the film. This was their joint outing to say goodbye to Odette and Joyce before they left the following week to the all-women ferry pool in Hamble, near Southampton and more importantly, close to the Spitfire factories.

"I wish I was coming to Hamble too," Beryl whispered to Odette. She caught the whiff of Odette's exotic perfume, and it made Beryl want to swoon. As expected, they were out in uniform, with her and Maisie in their ATA cadets' uniforms, newly fitted at Austen Reed in London. Odette looked pristine in hers, of course, and her makeup was subtle but sexy. Beryl had permitted Maisie to slap some lipstick on her lips but refused to wear foundation or make any other concessions to looking glamorous.

Odette leaned forward, and Beryl caught a flash of red from the multicoloured silk scarf tucked under her uniform so it was out of sight.

"Are you cold?" Beryl asked, having noticed the scarf seemed to be a constant with Odette.

"No. This is my lucky scarf."

Why would Odette need a lucky scarf? She was a brilliant pilot. All pilots seemed to have their superstitions and foibles, and if that's what they needed to do to believe in themselves, then she wasn't going to judge. Her ritual was to go through the checklists twice to ensure she didn't forget anything and call the answers aloud. Which was fine when she was flying solo, but at some point, she may take passengers.

She could feel Odette trembling. Beryl stretched her fingers below the arm of the seat and gently touched Odette's thigh. The intention was to express her compassion and empathy, but excitement radiated back to Beryl through the touch. Even more so when Odette, who was still staring at the screen, encased Beryl's fingers in her own. Odette held her hand, and her whole body tingled in response.

"Can I hold your hand?" Mike whispered and placed his hand palm up on the arm of the seat.

No, Beryl wanted to scream aloud, but even she had gathered she needed to be discreet about her preferences, so she complied. He didn't squeeze or hold her close but just lay there like an old fish.

She glanced back to Odette to see if she had noticed. Perhaps Odette felt Beryl's gaze upon her as she turned her head away from the screen and raised a single eyebrow. A slight smirk played on her lips. Meanwhile, she stroked Beryl's fingers, palm, and knuckles, and everywhere she touched, goosebumps followed. Every single cell in her body wanted to get as close to Odette as she could, wanted to breathe in her scent and be surrounded in her aura. She wanted to laugh out loud, to dance and sing. This was heaven and also purgatory. There was so much more she wanted to explore with Odette but doubted that she would ever get the chance, so there was this now, their tentative touching of fingertips. No more than a whisper of what could be if the world was different, and life was easy. Her belly fluttered with nerves, and she willed her heart to slow.

But was this all she would ever have? The promise of something, the brushing of fingertips in a darkened room while having an overt display of affection from a man she liked but felt nothing for?

As if on cue, Mike squeezed her fingers, dragging her attention back to him. Beryl shared a rueful smile with Odette and leaned back to Mike's side of the seat.

"Can I ask you out, on a date?"

Her elation dropped into a ball in her stomach. She had been lucky to avoid this so far. Mike had been respectful and funny. Now their tentative friendship would be altered by the awkwardness. "We're much better off going out as a group." She nodded towards Maisie and immediately averted her eyes when she saw them doing more than holding hands. She caught sight of Rob's hand somewhere it shouldn't be in public. Her blush was probably visible even in the darkness of the cinema. Mike glanced around, and he seemed uncomfortable at the sight too.

Mike's lips tightened into a thin line, as if he was holding onto his feelings. Wasn't he happy for his friend? Maisie was a great catch: bright, beautiful, and an heiress. What more could a man want? Surely, he didn't want Maisie for himself. He seemed too self-deprecating and aware of his ordinary background. On paper, Beryl and Mike were much better suited.

Mike half-smiled. "We don't need to worry about chaperoning them. They'll find their own way to each other," he whispered.

Beryl needed a distraction to ensure he didn't repeat his question. "Did I say I've been slotted to upgrade onto class two planes? I'll be getting my first flight in a Hurricane soon." She didn't need to hide her excitement; it was evident for anyone to see by the lightness of her energy.

Mike's expression softened into a genuine smile. "That's great news. Maybe we should all have a celebration when you do."

"That's great. Let's do that."

He seemed to have taken the hint and didn't seem offended, fortunately. Her heart slowed to its normal rhythm, and she looked back at the screen, realising she had no idea who any of the characters were or what they were doing. For a comedy, the audience weren't laughing much, but maybe being here was just an excuse to stop the world for a couple of hours and for people to lose themselves in each other under cover of darkness. Half the audience seemed to be having whispered conversations, furtively holding hands, and more.

Odette had removed her hand when Beryl was talking with Mike, and Beryl's fingers felt cool at the loss. She reached out until her fingers met Odette's again, then she turned her head to watch Odette, who was staring at the screen as if she was unaware of anything else happening.

All the while, Odette's little finger made circles on Beryl's thigh. She gradually hoisted Beryl's skirt up her leg. Now her body was thrumming in anticipation, in a way she had never felt before. Her heart fluttered, and her mind unspooled like a broken film clattering and loosening. Odette's fondling caused her body to stir into life. The exploration was provocative and so frustrating because they could do nothing more. Tonight, Odette would go back with Joyce, and soon they would both transfer to Hamble. Beryl didn't know when she would see her again. And Beryl wanted to see her again, for Odette to explore her body fully. But this was torment: to be teased and never have the satisfaction of release. At home, if she was quiet, maybe she could provide herself with that. But now, it was all too much, and she was close to overload. She grasped Odette's fingers to stop her. "Please," she whispered. "I want this, but we can't do anything about it."

Odette withdrew her fingers immediately, triggering a longing so sharp and intense, Beryl stiffened and stared at the screen, fighting to maintain her equilibrium.

A second later, warm breath fluttered over her cheeks as Odette skated her lips over Beryl's ear, so casual as if Odette was whispering to her, not kissing her.

"I want this too, but you're right. We need to wait, to be careful. Now go back and give some attention to your boyfriend or watch the film. I don't know why it's a comedy; it's not funny."

And then, just as Beryl was gathering her senses, Odette pressed her lips to Beryl's cheek, exploding various sensations of desire, want, and craving. Hoping Odette had not left lipstick smears, she turned back to Mike.

"What was Odette saying?" he asked.

Had he heard? Cold dread squeezed a tightness in her chest. She smiled up at him and tapped her fingers on his hand. "She was just saying she couldn't believe it was a comedy because it isn't very funny."

He laughed, and the person behind them tutted and told them

to be quiet. Mike turned and tipped his cap in apology before taking Beryl's hand again and leaning into her. But whereas with Odette, her body had felt on fire, with Mike, it was a slight irritation that he was encroaching on her space. She sighed. She was going to have to deal with the absence of Odette and the persistence of Mike. She didn't know how long she could keep going as she was. She detested secrets and lies, and she was being split in two because of them. Life would be so much easier if she wanted men, but she couldn't give up on the hope of a possibility with Odette, not now she knew that Odette was interested in her. However much she had yearned before, the possibility of reciprocation warmed her to her core. And she was boiling.

At the end of the film, before they all filed out, Tommy said, "We have something to tell you."

They all looked around from picking up their belongings to stare at him. Tommy was a man of few words, but when he did speak, he had a natural authority that made everyone want to listen.

"I don't know if you can all rearrange your schedules and come down to Surrey for the day on the thirteenth of September, but Joyce and I are going to get married before I get posted. We'd love you all to join us. I know that doesn't give you much time, but it's the only time we can squeeze it in and still have a couple of days honeymoon. It won't be a big affair. We'll have a big society wedding to satisfy Joyce's mother when the war's over."

"Congratulations, both of you," Odette said.

She shook Tommy's hand and kissed Joyce on the cheek. It was so innocent, and Beryl wished she could be the recipient of the kiss. The throbbing of certain parts reminded her that her arousal had not completely abated.

Belatedly, she added her congratulations.

Joyce was too young to get married. What a waste of the pilot training. "Will you still fly in the ATA?" she asked.

Joyce smiled. "Yes, I may as well do something useful while Tommy's abroad."

Joyce was a year older than Beryl but was clearly so much more experienced. Beryl had only ever been kissed by Odette— she didn't count the slobberings of the boys at school—but she dreamed of so much more. Getting married was something that could never happen for her. Not that she wanted the attention, but she would love it to be a possibility. She stole a glance at Odette, who was all smiles as she gently teased Joyce and Tommy, asking if they needed instruction. *No, they don't need instruction. I do.*

Chapter Eight

BERYL ROSE WHEN THE commander entered the Ops room, eager for a job to do. She'd hoped she'd have her check flight on the operational planes soon and had convinced herself it would be today.

"Edna, come with me, please. Wait here, Beryl," Amelia said.

Beryl dropped back into her seat. Disappointment gnawed at her gut. She opened the pilots' handling notes, but even that didn't hold her attention. Each of the other cadets were taken out with their pilot trainers for their various flying lessons, but no one came for her. Her spirits sank as she sipped the last of her tea, leaving only the dregs behind. A bit how she felt. It was Odette's last day before she transferred to Hamble, and Beryl hadn't seen her at all. She needed the distraction of a busy day's flying.

Alone in the cavernous room, she tried not to glance up at the large brass clock. Maybe the minute hand needed a little oil. It hadn't moved for the last two minutes, she was certain. She paced up and down. Her name was up on the blackboard, but there were no comments beside it.

Why wasn't she flying today? Was she in trouble? She mentally reviewed her latest flights. They'd all gone well. She had complied with all their ridiculous rules about dress code and had even worn skirts and makeup when going out. They didn't know about her feelings about women, did they? She swallowed. *Don't be silly, Beryl, they can't see inside your head, nor are they measuring your heart rate when a certain French pilot comes into the room.* She cracked her knuckles and stretched out her back, but that didn't settle her. Had someone said something?

A few newspapers lay discarded by the chairs, and someone had abandoned a cup of tea. She picked it up and carried it to the kitchen to wash, given there was nothing better to do. Five minutes later, she returned, but the ops room was still empty. The notices on the noticeboard needed straightening, which occupied another few minutes. She even lined up the spare tin tacks on the top right of the pin board, ready for whoever needed them next.

She resumed her seat by the desk, opened the detailed handling notes, and skimmed the surface of the words, neither registering nor absorbing them.

Finally, an hour later, the door swished open, and Odette walked in with a huge grin on her face.

Beryl's entire body thrummed in surprise and delight, and she shot up to greet her. She caught the scent of expensive perfume and was intoxicated by her warmth and closeness. It would be so easy to stretch out and kiss her, but someone could come in at any moment.

Odette must have thought the same thing as she stepped back and folded her hands together in front of her. "Sorry for the delay, Beryl. The chief flying instructor is caught up with a VIP visit today, so he asked me to do your check flight this morning. But I had to take another flight first thing."

Beryl's heart skipped, and it seemed to have lodged itself in her throat, making it difficult to speak. "Did you just say check flight?"

"I did. Congratulations, Beryl. You're the first of your intake to get to this stage. Are you ready to go?"

Was she ready to go? This was what she'd been waiting for since she joined the ATA. It was her chance to be checked out on flying fast, operational aeroplanes, from the Hurricane to the Spitfire. She tried to keep her grin in check and appear professional, but she wasn't succeeding.

"Yes, of course. I thought you were going down to Hamble

today?"

Odette signed out on the blackboard with white chalk and hitched her parachute onto her shoulder. "I am later, but I happily agreed to do your check flight."

Wow. She didn't know Odette could take a check flight, but she wasn't about to complain. Her heart was racing like a Merlin engine. She so didn't want to make a fool of herself. Not with Odette. "I'll just go to the bathroom quickly. It must be that extra mug of tea I had." Nothing to do with the nerves that suddenly overcame her. It was a toss-up which was more nerve-wracking: her check flight or flying with Odette.

"Okay. Meet me at the plane. We'll go dual in the Harvard trainer first, then if everything goes well, which I'm certain it will, you can take out the Hurricane."

She almost skipped as she made her way out to the radial-engine Harvard and mentally revised the characteristics of the plane.

When she met Odette by the plane, Odette's smiles had gone. This was serious. Odette had to determine whether Beryl was safe to fly. She went through the pre-flight checks she'd done a hundred times before with great care, while still trying to be efficient. Now wasn't the time to mess up.

She started her up and the excitement rushed through her at the roar of the engine. This was her way of entering her element, where she became one with the plane. She was a mariner of the air, riding invisible waves and harnessing petulant winds to progress and guide but never to conquer. To fly and be able to share this with Odette was her greatest dream. Her family-friendly dreams anyway.

"After take-off you can take her up to nine thousand feet," Odette said.

What? Beryl attempted to get moisture in her mouth. "Nine thousand feet?" She'd heard that others had only done a few circuits and bumps.

"You're going to do a few stalls."

It wasn't just a few stalls. At first, Beryl over-corrected slightly, and the plane was so responsive, it was easy to see how a pilot could get into trouble, but she picked it up quickly.

"Okay, now you are going to spin it."

"Really?" This was more than others had done, but it was a great opportunity to play with the plane.

"That's why we've come so high. It takes longer to come out of the spin than some of the other planes you've flown."

This is living. Beryl couldn't help but grin as Odette put her through her paces, and she recovered and reverted to straight and level each time.

"Do you want to do something we're not supposed to do?"

Beryl grinned widely. "Silly question. What?"

"Check you've got nothing on the floor and button up your chest pocket. You don't want your lipstick or compact to drop out."

Beryl laughed and checked her button. "I don't wear lipstick unless I have to. Are we going to fly inverted?"

"Maybe. Is it clear?"

The sun was shining, and there was hardly a cloud in the sky. Beryl scanned the sky and flipped her wings to check no one else was in the vicinity. "All clear." Her voice had a slight wobble to it, but it was just excitement. She hoped Odette didn't think she was scared.

They weren't supposed to do aerobatics, nor were they allowed to fly at full speed, but the temptation was too much. If they were going to break ATA regulations, they may as well do it today.

"Ready?" Beryl flipped her ailerons to check their responsiveness. A thrill ran through her. Should she? Yes, she was a pilot. She tipped one aileron down fully and rolled the plane around its axis until they were flying upside down.

"Woo hoo!" Beryl called, and she heard Odette laughing

behind her. Looking through the canopy, she could see the railway line now above her. Her shoulders pulled against the straps, her notebook and pencil strained against the buttons of her flying suit, and the blood pounded in her head. She was probably turning bright red now, but she didn't care. The world rushed past upside down in a blur at nearly two hundred miles an hour. If she didn't live to see another day, this happiness would have been worth it.

"D'accord. Time to be good. Come back to straight and level and return to base now." Odette said.

Beryl rolled the plane around so she was upright again. The blood drained from her head, but the smile was branded on her face.

"You have an engine failure. Where will you land?"

Beryl faced into the wind with the airfield just ahead. There was an alternate field to the starboard, but it looked tight. "I'd land on the airfield."

"Bien. Do it."

The landing was smooth, although on touchdown, the plane snaked left, so she had to pounce on the rudder to counteract the movement. Embarrassment burned a blush on her cheeks. *Damn.* Had she blown it at the last moment because she'd lost concentration. "Sorry. It almost caught me out."

"But you corrected. It's a useful lesson that the more powerful aeroplanes need to be flown and taxied with care until the plane is shut down and post flight checks are completed."

When she taxied to the refuelling point and cut the engine, she didn't know whether she would fly the Hurricane sitting a few feet away. Odette said nothing. Had she not been good enough? They climbed out and handed over the Harvard to the ground crew, with Beryl feeling more anxious with every step she took towards the Hurricane. "Sorry. Did I blow it?"

Odette looked at her, eyes wide. "No, Beryl. You're a natural pilot. I threw more complicated manoeuvres at you to see if I could catch you out. I couldn't. You read the sky and the machine as though it's an extra limb. I love flying with you, and it's a flight I'll remember forever."

The breath caught in her throat. "Me too."

"Good. Now take the Hurricane up. Just four circuits and bumps then come in to land. No aerobatics, which of course, none of us are cleared to do. I'll be watching every move." Odette winked.

Beryl almost saluted. "Of course not. I wouldn't dream of it."

The roar of the Hurricane's engine thrilled her to her core. This was what she had wanted; to make her living by flying, having to concentrate on the wind and the weather, making the tiniest of corrections. What a perfect day to fly and be checked out. How amazing that she was born only fifteen years after the first flight by the Wright brothers, and now she was flying at hundreds of miles an hour in a plane as sensitive and sexy as any beautiful woman. And she had a sensitive and sexy woman in mind she would love to fly with again.

Chapter Nine

A COUPLE OF WEEKS later, Odette, Maisie, and Beryl arrived at Joyce's home in Surrey. A chauffeur in a Rolls Royce saloon had collected them from the station to take them for Joyce's wedding.

Beryl openly gaped at the deer park and the grand house they were approaching. "Wow."

She articulated what the others were probably thinking but were too polite to say aloud. Even Maisie looked impressed, and she was from a wealthy family. Joyce was from old money though, and that was reflected in the age of the buildings, designed to impress, with their symmetrical wings and Palladian portico.

As they bumped down the long drive, the chauffeur, Ben, spoke. "I'm very sorry about the state of the road, but all but one of the gardeners are fighting abroad."

Odette didn't mind Beryl leaning into her as they were jostled on the back seat. She inhaled her lavender soap and enjoyed the warmth of Beryl's body pressed against her own. They shared a glance that promised so much. If she leaned a little closer than was necessary, then who could blame her?

Beryl's full lips fascinated Odette as Beryl chatted to Ben and Maisie. She wanted to kiss those lips, to cover them with her own and devour them. Odette shook her head to clear it. That was not supposed to happen. It was what Beryl did to her. She cut through Odette's charm and joking, the trivialisation of her attitude to life and death. She peeked below the surface, not satisfied with the superficial. But Odette cowered behind a flimsy curtain; she wasn't some magical wizard. She was just a raw and vulnerable woman scared to commit. Beryl saw Odette for who she was, yet she stayed and was still interested. And that filled Odette with warmth and joy, feelings she hadn't allowed herself for years, and they bubbled to the surface, in danger of overwhelming her. She didn't just want Beryl, she needed her. And she hated being so weak.

Beryl pressed against her, causing goosebumps all over her body, but it wasn't the cold. Now clothes were rationed, Joyce said she would wear her mother's wedding dress, which had been altered to fit her, and everyone else would wear their uniform. Odette stroked the back of Beryl's jacket and admired the broad shoulder stripe of the third officer. Within months, they had almost caught up with the original pilots in the class of planes they could fly, and Beryl led that charge.

The stately car pulled up to the family chapel, and they shuffled along the wide leather seat to exit the car. There were just a few steps until they made their way into the cool of the church. Around the chapel were tombs and memorial plaques of Joyce's family through the ages. They sat in the back pews, but Tommy signalled them to come forward. He looked uncharacteristically nervous, as though he'd prefer to face a Messerschmidt than marriage.

Joyce's mother had a pinched expression. From what Joyce had admitted late the other night, her parents didn't approve of the wedding. Even though Tommy was now a squadron leader, he wasn't the right class or thought to be good enough for their daughter. Odette didn't blame them trying to snatch a little happiness when they could. Life was too precarious to believe they'd survive the war or flying.

Eventually, Joyce's parents had relented and agreed to the rushed timetable, especially with so few attendees. Apart from a few family friends and members of staff from the household, the rest of the congregation were people from the RAF or the ATA. Rob and Mike couldn't attend because their squadron was on call, and Joyce and Odette had pulled in a few favours to be on leave at the same time.

The rather scratchy organ played the wedding march, and Joyce entered on her father's arm. The vicar asked them to stand. The encouraging smile Joyce and Tommy gave each other was warm and affectionate. Joyce's mother may not approve, but they were clearly in love. *In love*. It was not something Odette had experienced for years and never expected to experience again. She snapped shut her forgetting box and paid attention to what was going on.

"Dearly beloved, we are gathered here today..."

Odette half listened to the vicar droning on about their war effort and how wonderful to welcome a hero of the Battle of Britain into the bosom of the community. Tommy's ears took on a tinge of red. He hated being called a war hero. He'd said he was just lucky to have come back in one piece and no bits missing.

She and Beryl shared a hymn sheet, and she had to smile at Beryl singing off key at full volume. It amused her that Beryl knew she couldn't sing but didn't care what people thought and sang loudly anyway.

She was so much more emotionally courageous than Odette would ever be. Give her a difficult flight in a tattered old plane, and Odette was happy, but any chance of being vulnerable, and she would flee as fast as she could. So it made little sense that she was craving time with Beryl and wanted to get to know her better.

Normally, she was happy with the superficial interactions and chit-chat around flying, being friendly with everyone but close to no one. She knew some of the ground staff thought she was stuck up, but that wasn't the case. Before a flight, for all the adrenaline pumping and the bravado, she wanted to double-check what had already been covered by the ground staff. Having her fuel line cut when it was supposedly flight-checked was something she would never forget.

Why did everything come back to Beryl? She'd hoped that

kissing her would dissipate her attraction and her obsession would fade, but it had become stronger. She was being pulled in, like a strong crosswind blowing her towards a specific destination. It didn't matter how much power she pushed against it. Couldn't she just accept the feelings and let herself yaw with the wind and drift?

Was she just jaded and lonely? Maybe she was ready to move on, to break down more of those walls and let Beryl in. Fear gripped a tight band around her chest.

Beryl coughed, and she realised she hadn't heard a word of what was being said. The congregation had all slipped forward onto their knees to pray, so she hurriedly followed suit and placed her hands together. But she felt no connection to God in an English chapel built to service a particular household for hundreds of years. She felt closest to God when she flew in the bright blue sky, where clouds were fluffy and white, and she almost felt she could stretch up and touch the heavens.

She stared at Beryl's hands clasped in prayer. They were slightly calloused, with close-cropped nails, unpolished and natural. Beryl was unapologetically her own person, an individual both intriguing and engaging.

Beryl was passionate about flying, which was Odette's lingua franca and her comfortable place. But a lot of pilots loved flying, so it was more than that. As if Beryl had caught her watching, she turned her head and their eyes met. Beryl smiled a full-dazzle smile, and Odette melted a little inside.

With her came hope of Odette being someone else again, someone she'd once been: fun, brave, and happy. But that Odette had died in a plane with Simone. It couldn't be. She craved another touch, another whisper of comfort and potential, and it took all her willpower to straighten in her seat and leave a gap between them. She needed to get a hold on herself before she fell any further, before she was sent into a flat spin from which she couldn't recover.

Chapter Ten

Piotr did his usual routine of tapping the instruments on his approach to land. Beryl wondered if it was because he only had one eye and his sense of depth perception had gone.

He had probably been handsome before he'd escaped his burning Spitfire but now, one side of his face was distorted and scarred. He'd never talked about it. He didn't speak much at all, as though it was all too much effort. But the ATA pilots felt safe flying with him, because he didn't show off to the women he was ferrying. It was ridiculous that some men still tried to impress them. Some of the women pilots were more experienced than they were.

Beryl was always happy to sit in the co-pilot seat when flying in the Anson and help wind down the undercarriage—one hundred and fifty turns of a crank handle—which wasn't feasible as a solo pilot. It also gave her an opportunity to observe and understand the procedures on a more complex twin-engine plane. Besides, she was never really interested in the conversations about men or makeup from the other ATA pilots who sat in the back. On the morning ferry flights to the pilots' first destination, there was usually an eerie silence as people studied their notes, refreshing themselves on a plane they had flown before or examining the particulars on a new marque or new type of aeroplane. It was incredible to have all the vital information in a small blue binder. Beryl didn't let on she had studied not just the "blue book" pilot notes but also the more detailed handling notes and the engineering manuals of the planes she hoped to fly one day. She hoped she might be able to transfer to Hamble and join Odette and Joyce, though her ferry pool commander had said there were no vacancies, and she was needed where she was.

Beryl should be grateful she flew for thirteen days out of fifteen, and she was, especially as she was learning every day, but she was disappointed that Odette had moved out. Her heart ached for her.

"Undercarriage down," Piotr said.

Beryl jumped to action and cranked the handle to unwind the undercarriage. If nothing else, she would keep the muscles in her arms. She'd been ferrying planes a few months and felt as if she had lost a lot of her strength. She was haunted by the anxiety of not wanting to prang the aeroplane, and so far, she hadn't been caught out with any engine failures or difficult flights. To start with, she and her group of "sprogs" had been assigned to flights from an airfield with a proper runway to another airfield with a proper runway, none of them too far from base. And she loved it. Her heart pounded with excitement when she lifted off the ground and set course, keeping to the strict height limits and speeds. It was what she was made for.

Piotr made his usual daisy-cutter, smooth landing. There was so much Beryl could learn from him.

He turned and grinned at her. "I hear you've been signed off on the Hurricane. A Hurricane's a bit like a man; it needs to be bossed around. But a Spitfire is a woman and needs to be flown with finesse. I think you will love flying the Spitfire."

She blushed. He couldn't know she preferred women, though she dreamt of only one. Everything came back to Odette. They hadn't seen each other since Odette had moved, and Odette hadn't replied to Beryl's letters with anything other than the occasional few lines with facts and general enquiries. It was amazing that such a passionate woman wrote such prosaic letters. Perhaps she was too busy. The ATA was all-consuming, flying from morning till night, often arriving home just in time for a snatched meal, bath, and bed, before starting all over again the following day. Still, she hoped there would be a letter this evening when she returned home.

Her first flight of the day should be simple but a long one, flying an old Miles Magister trainer plane from Oxfordshire to Cambridgeshire. The weather was a bit iffy. A fog had lifted quite late in the day, so the whole schedule had been put back by about three hours.

Half an hour later, she was in the Maggie, singing as she headed due east after setting her time to the next waypoint. The clouds were thickening in the east, but everything seemed okay for the moment. It was just as well no one could hear her as she sang out of tune to the latest Glenn Miller record Maisie had imported from the US. It was getting more difficult to get anything from the States. So many ships weren't getting through the North Atlantic, but magic Maisie seemed to find a way to get her hands on the unobtainable.

A bitter wind blasted her in the open cockpit, and she glanced down at her flying suit to pull it closer to her body. Then she noticed the compass needle swinging wildly. The hairs on the back of her neck raised and sweat beaded on her forehead. How had she missed a problem with the compass? It had been fine a few minutes ago. Or had it? She hadn't been paying attention, just worked out her heading and viewed the next turning point, which was coming up. She looked down at a knot of railway lines converging on a town. But which town? From the air, it could be anywhere in England. An indistinguishable set of houses with a station, a river, and a barrage balloon to the south. Or was it the west?

She traced where she had last marked her time down. Twenty minutes ago. How had she been so stupid and arrogant? Just because she knew about aeroplanes didn't mean she could navigate. Talk about pride before a fall.

Beryl sketched out an arc from her last checkpoint, but her map flapped in the wind and her goggles steamed up, making it difficult to do accurately. What had the trainers said? If you're lost, go from ground to map. Check for features on the ground and find them on the map. She stared over the side of the plane and tipped the wings slightly, but she was flying over East Anglia—there were no features. She was also looking for a grass airfield, which could be anywhere in this patchwork of green. *Don't panic.*

Her heart was banging as loud as the engine. "Think through this logically," she said as if she was an instructor. What would Odette do? She would establish what information she could.

In the distance was an airfield, but it had hard runways. It definitely wasn't the one she was looking for. Did she dare land there? How embarrassing to admit she was lost. Sweat beaded on her forehead and she swiped it away. Better embarrassed than dead. How she wished she had a radio to confirm her position. If only the ATA could have access to an emergency channel for incidents such as this, but the radio frequencies were jealously guarded by the RAF and admiralty. And they would probably be derisive of her getting lost because of her arrogance. No, she was alone and would have to get herself out of the mess she'd flown herself into.

She would get a better idea of the airfield when she flew overhead. According to the map, it could be one of three possibilities, but they were spread out over the area.

She flew over the airfield and circled at twice the circuit height, just below the clouds. As she banked, with the intention of dropping to join the circuit and request assistance, she caught sight of a large grass field by a railway line about three miles behind her. She scanned her map. Yes, her destination was by the railway, and there was another bigger airfield within three miles.

Maybe, just maybe, and by sheer good luck, she had chanced on the correct airfield. She would go over the grass field and if it didn't have a windsock, she'd return to the larger airfield.

It took a few minutes to get there, but when she did, she saw a windsock and a hangar with a Tiger Moth sitting outside. Her shoulders relaxed. That was her ride back. She whooped with delight – and relief. How arrogant to think she could fly without paying attention. At least her hubris had not resulted in disaster.

A Very flare was shot to signal she could land, so she joined the circuit and satisfied herself with a perfect landing. She taxied up to the dispersal hut, still not entirely convinced she was at the right place, but her heart was gradually returning to normal.

It wasn't until she was inside waiting for the commanding officer to sign off her chit that she saw a notice confirming she had indeed landed at the correct airfield, despite having previously flown straight over it. It just showed that timings were critical.

Her legs turned to jelly, and she was glad to sit down and recompose herself before she flew the Tiger Moth on to one of the maintenance units. She would need to nab herself another compass though, especially as the weather was closing in.

Probably because she had frightened herself silly in the first flight, in the second, she was hyper-vigilant. As she flew along, she couldn't help but remember her virgin flight in a Tiger Moth with Odette in 1934. She had been so naïve and young then. Now she was left dangling by Odette, unsure if they were anything to each other. Her focus had to be on flying and navigating and not on yearning, wishing life was different.

Her landing was smooth, and she snaked from side to side to see her forward progress and taxied to the dispersal office.

In the Ops room, the commanding officer signed her chit and nodded to another room. "Your carriage awaits, and he's been waiting a while."

"Oh, dear. I'll just finish the snag sheet then." She was glad to hand over the rather battered and unresponsive Tiger Moth, which was definitely in need of an engine overhaul. She hoped that whoever was waiting for her wasn't in a bad mood because it was late in the day, and they'd have to take off immediately to guarantee they landed before dusk. No one enjoyed having to stay out for the night or take a boring train ride home.

Although she would have loved a cup of tea before she left, she used the bathroom and splashed some cold water over her face before returning to the room to find the pilot for her ride home. For the first time ever, she would be glad to see the end of a day's flying. The long flight had spooked her more than she thought.

She steeled herself before opening the door. When she caught sight of Piotr reading the paper, she blew out a breath of relief. He nodded to her, rose without a word and hurried to the plane. Judging by the cursory look he gave the plane, he had already done his pre-flight checks.

He settled himself into the pilot's seat, crossed himself—his first action whenever he flew—and started on the internal checks.

Beryl looked around but no one else joined them in the cabin.

"Clear," Piotr said and started the engines.

Beryl knew that he would need to concentrate until they were up and flying, so she waited until after they had taken off before she turned to him and gave him her warmest smile. "I'm so glad to see you. Did you come here 'specially for me?"

"I had to drop off two pilots here and wait for you," he said as the plane lifted up, and he trimmed it for the climb.

"Yes, sorry I'm a bit late. I had a problem with my compass," she said as she wound up the undercarriage.

Piotr touched a small round medal around his neck. "I'm glad you're okay. I've been asking St Kristof to look over you. I also say a prayer for you every time you go up."

Beryl sat back onto the hard leather seat, the wind knocked out of her lungs. "You do?"

He looked over at her and gave a lopsided smile. "Yes. You're kind and fun, and you're really interested in flying. We get on well together, yes?"

He turned back to check the cockpit, but he had the plane trimmed so expertly he didn't need to make any corrections. Beryl shuffled her bottom back into the seat. It was still hard and uncomfortable, but it gave her a few seconds before she responded. Was he being friendly or more? She had no manual for such an interaction. "Yes, of course. I can't tell you how grateful I am that you picked me up. I really didn't fancy having to catch a train back to Hatfield this evening. Especially after the day I've had." She hoped she would be able to divert the conversation onto the safe topic of flying. "My compass went unserviceable on my first flight to East Anglia, and there was nothing there to give me any clue as to where I was."

"Didn't you do dead reckoning?" he asked, not looking at her.

A blush burned her cheeks. She didn't want to examine her failings or admit she'd been arrogant and had lost concentration when she was singing in the cockpit. "Yes, but the wind direction was different from what I'd calculated, and I didn't see the airfield, so I overshot it by a few miles."

"I always plan to fly to the right of the airfield I'm looking for, so I'll see it on my left, with my good eye." He crossed himself again.

Beryl's face had probably turned the colour of beetroot now. How could she have been so insensitive? She couldn't see the airfield with two good eyes, how much harder must it be with just one? Her admiration for Piotr went up threefold. "That makes perfect sense and shows what a brilliant pilot you are."

He nodded and looked pleased. "How many hours have you flown now?"

She tried to do the calculations, but her mind was too tired. "About two hundred and eighty, I think."

Piotr nodded. "Every pilot seems to do that. Around three hundred hours, they believe they know it all. That's when they make mistakes." He pointed to his scarred face. "You can never be too careful in an aeroplane. I know."

Not knowing what to say without being insensitive, she whispered, "Yes."

He pushed the throttle forward to increase the speed and trimmed the tailplane, so he wouldn't have to constantly adjust the controls. "We're starting to lose the light," he said.

What he wasn't saying was that he had waited longer than he should have and was breaking the rules for her by flying faster than the ATA maximum speed to get back before nightfall.

"Thank you for waiting for me."

He shrugged, but a slight smile played on his lips.

As they flew along, she checked her map against the very few features: a church tower with a winding river here, a larger town with barrage balloons there. Finally, they approached Hatfield.

Piotr cleared his throat. "If you're not doing anything this evening, do you want to come with me to the Old Boar's Head? It's not too far from where you live, is it?"

Her heart sped up even faster than when she was lost earlier today. Was he asking her as a date? Surely not. Why would he go for her when he could have the pick of women? How could she say she was into women, one woman in particular? She couldn't. For a start, he was very religious, and her desires were against regulations. There had been a rumour that two women from another ferry pool had been dismissed in disgrace when they were caught together. "I..." She needed to put him off but didn't want to upset him. His mouth became a thin line as she failed to find words that would explain without revealing the truth.

"Is it because of my face?" he asked.

She stared at him, horrified. "No, of course not. I really like you, but..."

"You like someone else. It's that RAF officer. The one who hangs around with Maisie and her boyfriend."

His whole demeanour was so deflated, she wanted to comfort him, but that might be misinterpreted. "Mike." It wasn't exactly a lie to say that she liked Mike, it just wasn't in the way Piotr thought. She hated to lie to him, but she could never tell him the truth. There are some truths that cannot be forgotten or forgiven.

"If it doesn't work with him, maybe I can take you to the cinema or the pub?"

She smiled, hoping to break the tension. "Maybe. Or we could all go together?"

"No." He turned his face away from her, whether to genuinely check his approach and instruments or because he wanted to signify the end of the conversation, Beryl wasn't sure.

This day could not become more bizarre, and she was struggling to parse her tumbling emotions. She closed her eyes and forced her shoulders to relax. A noisy cockpit wasn't a relaxing environment, but she tried to shed the tension and slow the conflicting emotions. Now she had to deal with having hurt Piotr. Nothing she could say would make it better, so they sat in awkward silence, as silent as it could be in a noisy, draughty cockpit.

She'd never been so glad to see flares giving them permission to land. Anything to get out of this awkwardness. "Thank you again for waiting for me," she said as he started his final checks after landing. He nodded but didn't look at her.

Beryl scrambled out of the cockpit as fast as she could and rushed to Ops to check in for the night. She was out to her bicycle before Piotr had come in from the plane. Perhaps he'd been waiting for her to leave.

She hoped things wouldn't be awkward between them. Although, as more women were signed off to carry passengers, more of the experienced women pilots were also doing taxi pilot duties. She'd always hoped Odette would do that one day, but now she was down in Hamble, she wouldn't see her and had no excuse to fly down there. *Odette.* Every time Beryl thought about her, the yearning to see her became physical and was accompanied with a tumbling in her stomach and a clenching around her heart.

Cycling back in the dark was tricky with her blacked-out bike lamps, but she was particularly reckless pushing down hard on the pedals, praying that she wouldn't meet anyone on the virtually empty roads back to the lodgings she shared with Maisie.

The house was dark when she arrived there. There was a scribbled note on the kitchen table. "I'm meeting Rob and Mike at The Old Boar's Head. Come and join us. M."

Perhaps it was as well she'd turned Piotr down. It would have been awkward if they'd all been there. Beryl slumped onto the chair as though all the air had been released from her. The last thing she wanted to do was go out again. At least Maisie had stoked up the range to warm the place up. They'd been left some eggs, so she could rustle herself up an omelette if she could find the energy to cook. First of all, she'd need a cuppa and some time to unwind.

By the kettle were two letters. Her heart skipped in delight when she recognised Odette's spiky handwriting. She traced her finger over the numbers and marvelled at the way Odette made her one with a leading stroke so it resembled the number seven in a serif font. Fortunately, the post man knew where she lived so posted them through the door anyway.

While she waited for the kettle to boil, she carefully sliced open the letter. Odette had touched this paper, had licked down the envelope. That thought always made her smile. She sniffed it before unfolding it. It was probably her imagination, but she thought she caught a whiff of Odette's perfume.

Dear B,

How are you doing? I hear via Maisie and Joyce you've been signed off on class 3 twin-engine planes. Congratulations. That is great news, but I'm not surprised you did it so quickly.
A couple of women here have been transferred to Cosford to be near their husbands, and we're looking for some more pilots to join the all-women's ferry pool here. I recommended you and Maisie, although I know she hasn't been signed off yet. I hope you can come. If you do, you can share the lodgings with Joyce and me. Joyce's father owns the cottage, so we don't have to put up with a

landlady breathing down our neck. Please say you'll come.
Hopefully I'll see you soon.

Yours, Odette

Beryl clutched the letter to her chest and skipped around the old kitchen table. Odette wanted her to go to Hamble. All the tension and anxiety of the day dropped away as she sang aloud and danced with an unexpected jolt of energy. She would see Odette every day if they lived in the same place. And she would fly Spitfires. It was like all her dreams wrapped up in one happy bundle. She prayed it would come true but didn't dare believe. First thing tomorrow, she would ask at Ops and make a request for a transfer.

How typical that Odette already knew she'd been signed off on twin-engine planes. It had only been two days ago. The kettle boiled, and she poured the water into the pot. She let the tea steep for a few minutes and opened the second, more formal-looking letter. It was from her head of the ferry pool, saying she would be transferred to Hamble now that she'd been signed off on more complicated aeroplanes. If she could do a backflip, she would have. Waving both of the letters in the air, Beryl danced around the kitchen again. "I'm going to Hamble," she shouted, although she was most excited about going to stay with Odette. Life had a strange way of playing out, and she couldn't keep the grin off her face.

An hour later, she'd written a short reply to both her station commander and Odette, accepting both the transfer and the offer of lodgings. She sat back and reread Odette's letter for a third time, not quite believing how her life was changing. She heard the key turn in the lock, and the kitchen door opened. Maisie entered, and she shook her coat off and hung it on the back of a chair beside the Aga.

"You didn't come to the pub," Maisie said, sounding a little peeved. "We missed you, especially Mike. He was so upset, he went home early."

Beryl's high spirits faltered a little and the tendrils of guilt poked her conscience. "Sorry, I got back late and had letters I had to reply to. I've been transferred to Hamble. When you get signed off, you probably will too."

"What? I don't want to go. Rob is based near here. Why would you want to go down south when Mike is here?"

Maisie looked hurt and baffled, as though she couldn't consider anything less desirable, and the last thing Beryl wanted was to hurt her. She cracked her knuckles. She would need to be careful how she responded to this. "Oh. I assumed you'd want to come too. We'll get to fly Spitfires regularly."

They had never been so misaligned before. Maisie shook her head as if trying to fix the news in her brain.

"Seriously? You'd rather fly Spitfires than be with Mike?"

Beryl snatched up her teacup and saucer and took them to the sink to wash up. She couldn't witness the hurt in Maisie's face. "I like Mike an' all, but it's been my dream to fly a Spitfire since I first saw one, and Hamble's so close to the factories, there will probably be lots of opportunities to fly them."

"But what about Mike? I thought we'd have a double wedding."

Beryl wiped the saucer with a tea towel, wishing she could erase this conversation. "What? No. We've never even been on a date—"

"We've been on lots of double dates. He's a braw man. Do you no' want to marry him?"

Maisie stood beside her, and turned to look Beryl straight in the eyes, her gaze boring into her. She didn't want to lie to her best friend, but she couldn't tell her the truth. "No. I don't. I like him but not in that way. Are you sure they can't get a transfer to near Southampton too? I'll really miss you if you don't come."

Maisie stared at Beryl as if she'd never seen her before. "Och, I'm going to bed. I can't have this conversation now. I was hoping you'd be excited about my news that I'm going to marry Rob, but you seem insistent on transferring to the other side of the country. Good night." She swung around and marched upstairs.

"You're marrying Rob? That's wonderful. Congratulations. Good night," Beryl called out, but Maisie didn't respond.

That she could never explain to Maisie became obvious, another consequence of having to hide who she was. She hoped the cost of happiness and being close to Odette wasn't the loss of her friendship. Maisie had been her friend for years, and she had smoothed Beryl's path to acceptance at the ATA. She had always been there for Beryl and encouraged her to mingle, even when she hadn't wanted to. Beryl would miss her and hate it if they parted in bad blood, but she had to take this opportunity. Moving to Hamble was the right thing to do, for her. She turned down the Aga and switched off the light, hoping she wasn't closing down a great friendship.

Chapter Eleven

THE HOUSE WAS IN darkness when Odette wheeled her bicycle around the side alleyway of the cottage she, Edna, and Joyce shared on the river Hamble. She stored the bike in the rack and hurried to get inside out of the deluge. Shivering, she shook off her sodden coat and draped it on a chair to dry. Joyce and Edna were already in the kitchen, a picture of cosiness and warmth.

"That smells nice," Odette said as the smell of cooking hit her. She nodded at Edna, who looked up from her letter writing and smiled.

Joyce was stirring a stew made with their meat rations for the week. They'd agreed it would be a nice welcome for Beryl. She was the picture of domesticity, complete with a homemade pinafore. "Thank you."

"No new lodger yet?" Odette tried to keep the excitement from her tone, but she had to tamp down the flutter of anticipation in her stomach.

"No. I still don't understand why Beryl wanted to transfer here," Joyce said. "I thought she would have wanted to stay near Mike. She seemed quite sweet on him, and he's definitely sweet on her. But Maisie said Beryl cares more about flying Spitfires."

Odette set the cutlery on the linen tablecloth. Nothing but the finest for Joyce, of course. "They *are* beautiful machines."

Joyce shook her head.

"What? Have you never felt the thrill of a fantastic flight?" Odette asked.

She looked at Odette as if she was mad. "Not really. You and Beryl are like peas in a pod. I just want this war to be over so

Tommy and I can settle down to proper married life."

A knot twisted in Odette's stomach. "All I want to do is fly." That wasn't really true, but she would never get what she wanted. No amount of yearning was going to change anything.

She opened the blackout curtains a crack to peer into the darkness. The rain hurled at the windowpanes.

"Don't let the wardens catch you," Edna said, looking up.

She spent most of her free time writing letters to all her friends and family back in Canada, they joked she was keeping Royal Mail in business.

"No one would be stupid enough to try a bombing raid on such an awful night," Odette said but closed the curtains anyway and stepped back to the sofa. "I thought the taxi would be here by now."

Edna put down her pen. "Maybe she couldn't get one. It's only a small station."

Joyce stopped stirring and added a pinch of salt to the pot. "I do feel guilty I couldn't pick her up by car, but I've already used my petrol coupons this month."

"It was for a good cause. I'm sure Tommy was grateful to see you again," Edna said.

Before he was sent overseas hung between them, unspoken.

Joyce nodded but said nothing. Odette glanced at her to gauge how she was doing. Longing and worry were Joyce's constant companion now, and her mouth was set in a grim line. In the last few weeks Joyce tried to join in, but she was never quite present emotionally, as though her heart was split in two. She was the very embodiment of keep calm and carry on. As if she knew what Odette was thinking she cast a wan smile.

"She'll be drenched if she walks in this weather. I'll go and put the hot water on," Joyce said and left the kitchen.

When she'd gone, Odette turned to Edna. "How is Dorrie settling in at Cosford?" A look of pain crossed Edna's face before she forced a smile that didn't reach her eyes. "Okay. Her mom is pleased she's staying at home, although how she can help on the farm as well as do a full day's flying, I've no idea."

Odette frowned. "Don't they have any land girls?"

Edna shook her head, sadly. "Yes, but her mom thinks they're all townies who don't do it properly."

Seeing the same look of longing in Edna's expression as she'd seen in Joyce's raised Odette's suspicions. "Maybe you can get a transfer to Cosford soon too."

Edna's wide eyes and round mouth were as much a confession as she needed. Odette winked. If only they could be open and acknowledge who they were, what they were doing, and with whom. "Tea?"

Edna blinked a couple of times. "Please. I'm just going upstairs to get my stamps." She left with such haste, she probably needed to calm her nerves.

Odette filled the kettle and chuckled to herself. She suspected there were more people similar to them hidden away, living their lives. She would broach the subject when she knew Edna a bit better. Maybe they could talk about the attitudes in Canada and their experiences. She'd only moved in the previous week, and their schedules hadn't synchronised yet.

Odette heard the tell-tale clicking of bicycle wheels above the sound of the battering rain, so she opened the back door. There, wheeling an old bike was Beryl. Water dripped from her nose, her heavy coat, and a large duffel bag. With her hair slicked back with the rain, she looked more masculine, and Odette could just imagine her fitting in at Le Monocle club. Odette's heart jolted. This might be harder than she imagined. Could she really remain impartial and uninvolved? "Leave your bike around the back and come in. Pass me your bag."

Beryl handed over the rough canvas bag and grinned. "Thanks."

She disappeared down the alleyway and through to the tiny back yard where she'd find the bike rack in the coal shed. Odette poured the boiling water into the teapot and stirred it vigorously. She needed to be careful. It would be so tempting to take Beryl to bed—she was sure Beryl wouldn't say no—but they couldn't risk getting caught.

Beryl knocked on the door again and entered. Delight danced over her face as if she couldn't control her features, and despite what her head instructed, Odette softened and smiled. She kissed Beryl on both cheeks and caught the faint scent of her soap. Beryl's face was wet and cold, and she wanted to envelop her in a welcoming embrace, but she pulled back.

Their gazes met and held, and for an instant, the truth of life from the beginning of time was written on Beryl's expression. Desire, in all its glorious, intoxicating life-altering beauty was there in the depth of her gaze. How could Odette know this and shuffle back as if nothing had changed? If Edna and Dorrie were an open secret, and they were careful, Odette couldn't risk being discovered. They couldn't do anything, or act on it, or share it to the world. They could never stand up and declare their attraction. It would always be hidden, unacknowledged until it withered away from lack of nurturing. How could something exist if it couldn't be expressed, if it couldn't grow or develop into a full blossom of beautiful petals and heady scent? She shook her head to clear her thoughts. The proximity, the knowledge of how she felt would need to be enough, and she would have to keep Beryl at arm's length.

Yet she wanted to warm herself in Beryl's admiration, and she leaned towards her. "Welcome," she murmured in Beryl's ear, and Beryl shivered. *Why can't I control myself?* "You must be cold. Take off your coat and hang it by the range to dry off. There's a cupboard for coats and shoes by the front door."

Beryl's smile was so wide, her jaw must have ached. "Thanks. I'm glad to be here."

"Come and have tea, then I'll take you on the tour."

The kitchen door burst open, and Edna and Joyce rushed in.

Edna flung her arms around Beryl. "It's so good to see you. You must be drenched. Why didn't you get a taxi?"

Beryl laughed at the barrage of questions, clearly delighted to see her friend. "They wouldn't bring the bike by taxi, but there weren't any taxis to be had, otherwise I might have left the bike at the station to collect tomorrow. It wasn't raining when I started off."

Joyce helped Beryl out of her coat. "Come into the sitting room and get yourself comfortable."

The energy of the newcomer invigorated them all out of their torpor, and they chatted inconsequentially while they sipped their tea and tucked into the stew Joyce had prepared. It helped that whenever Joyce went back to her Surrey home, she was sent back with a parcel of vegetables from their market garden that stretched out their meagre rations.

"If you've finished, I'll show you your room. It's tiny and up in the attic, I'm afraid. Probably the old servants' quarters," Joyce said and looked slightly embarrassed as though she wasn't being the perfect hostess, or it wasn't the standard she would normally have provided to a house guest.

"I'm very grateful for a room. It's going to be fun with the four of us."

Knowing Beryl, she meant just that and already, the dynamic had changed, and the atmosphere was lighter with her presence.

"I'll take her up," Odette said and led Beryl upstairs. She pointed to the three different doors on the first floor. "That's Joyce's room, and mine, and the bathroom. The line painted in the bath is the regulation four inches."

Beryl stared around the rooms. "Wow, when Joyce said it was a cottage, I imagined something tiny. It's really a townhouse."

Odette turned. "Yes, but I guess if you're used to a place in Mayfair and an ancient estate in Surrey, it's probably quite small."

"True."

Odette tried to look anywhere but at Beryl. She didn't trust herself not to give in to her weakness, fold her in her arms and kiss her passionately. The only way she could survive intact was to pull back.

Odette took one pace back, and Beryl held onto her arm. "Why are you avoiding me?" Beryl whispered.

"I'm not."

Beryl snorted. "You seem uncomfortable. Why did you invite me if you don't want me to stay here?"

She looked so hurt, Odette had to physically hold her hands down so she wouldn't trail them over Beryl's slicked-down hair and comfort her. Now it was drying, a cowlick was beginning to form on one side, begging to be smoothed down. "I feel conflicted. I enjoy your company. I want you here, but we can't start anything because it can't go anywhere."

Beryl's expression shifted from hope to one of disappointment, and she frowned. "I know you're petrified of being thrown out of the ATA. I don't think Edna would say anything, but I don't know about Joyce. I don't really know her."

If Odette's suspicions were correct about Edna, that would be the case. Her fear forced her to speak. "But we can't be sure. Beryl, I've already lost everything because of who I am."

She inhaled deeply, wondering how much to reveal. She had always vowed to hold Simone's identity a secret, but Beryl needed to understand why this was all too much. "You asked once why I left France. I left because my life fell to pieces. I was in love with a woman. When she died, I escaped by joining the flying circus in England. Now even that is gone, and I can't lose what I've built again. I'm sorry." She knew she'd need to reveal more to convince Beryl, but she couldn't tell her whole inglorious truth. It was too hard.

Beryl's expression changed from confusion to sorrow and her frown deepened. "I'm so sorry. That must have been terrible."

Odette nodded. The briefest of acknowledgements to the most life-gouging despair.

Beryl cracked her knuckles. "Okay. I understand you don't want to do anything, but I'm sure we could be careful." She let out a huff of air. "I might have my bath now, so I'll turn the tap on. If you wish, you're welcome to join me."

Why couldn't Beryl see? Why was she being so blasé? "The risk is too high for me," Odette said.

Beryl looked hurt. "I disagree, but if that's how you feel, I won't push you. Now, are you going to show me my room, please, so I can take this bath?"

The anger and disappointment pulsed in every word and Odette tried not to flinch. Beryl may be inexperienced, but she was brave. Odette admired that but couldn't emulate it. Or could she? It was torture seeing Beryl look so hurt. She wanted to pull her in to warm herself against her and kiss her until she smiled again. Her heart screamed at her to take a chance, to break the loneliness and yield to her desire. It had been too long, and she yearned for Beryl with every cell of her being. But her head counselled against it. She had a feeling this could be the biggest mistake in her life. But she didn't know which was the mistake and which she'd regret the most: being with Beryl, or not being with her.

Torn between being safe and sensible and risking everything, Odette asked, "Shall I bring you a towel?" It was an innocuous question that could have been the start of something or nothing.

Beryl clearly knew the significance given the gleam in her eyes. "Yes, please. Will you bring it in?"

There was no ambiguity there. She would have to be quiet. She could hear Joyce and Edna washing up downstairs. She would volunteer tomorrow, although her culinary flair was limited with the number of foods on ration. But she'd think of something.

Odette went to the airing cupboard and picked out the fluffiest towel. Beryl deserved it. As she tapped on the bathroom door and entered, her heart fluttered and her legs were sluggish. She seemed to be stepping into a place of no return and staring down at the start of an aerobatic spin. If she thought about it too long, or even at all, she would leave the towel just inside and close the door without peeping.

Beryl was just stepping into the bath, all lithe legs, trim body, and faded tan from where she had worked outside on cars and engines. She had broader shoulders and slimmer hips than Odette had imagined, and she had imagined them a *lot*. When Beryl turned around, Odette swallowed and couldn't stop ogling even if she'd tried.

Beryl had perfect pink nipples surrounded by pale skin. "Ravissant," she whispered as much to herself as Beryl.

Beryl's cheeks blushed pink. "Thank you, I think. But why are you smirking?" She settled down in the water.

Now it was Odette's turn to blush. "Your nipples are like cherries against your pale skin. It reminds me of those luscious almond buns you English loved before the war. Your mother gave me some." It wasn't romantic, but she thought honesty was best. "Cookwell?"

Beryl laughed and flicked water at her. "Bakewell tarts, you mean."

"Ah, yes, how could I forget? Bakewell tarts. Now I will always remember."

Beryl flicked some more water at Odette, but she sidestepped the cascade of drops.

"Careful. You want some water left to lie in." Odette knelt by the side of the bath, and Beryl gripped her arm.

"I love that the tables are turned, and you're watching me in my bath."

With her other hand, Odette cupped Beryl's face. "So am I, although I'm also petrified."

"Is everything okay up there?" Joyce called from below.

Odette started and jumped back as if she'd just been scalded, her heart thumping hard. She held her finger to her mouth. "Fine. I just found Beryl a towel, and she's going to take her bath now."

"Super. Care for a cuppa?"

"I'll get one when I come down, thanks." Odette lowered her head and placed her hand over her chest, trying to slow her heartbeat. That was a close call.

Beryl's eyes were as wide as hers felt. So she didn't want to get caught either. Good. At least they agreed on that.

Odette stood and blew a kiss at Beryl.

"Let's talk later," Beryl whispered.

Odette nodded and made a big show of shutting the door, so it could be heard on the floor below. As she sauntered downstairs, she heard Beryl getting up and back into the bath.

"Is everything okay?" Joyce asked as Odette entered the room.

"Everything's fine, thank you." *As long as we don't get caught.*

Chapter Twelve

Despite the heat of the water, Beryl had goosebumps all down her arms. That was too close for comfort and her head buzzed and her heart skipped. Perhaps they could explore a little more if ever they were alone together. Would Odette really allow them to take things further? The look on her face had been one of fear, and Beryl wasn't sure she could cope with another rejection. It was too much. Each one crumbled her certainty a little more and cut a little deeper.

She rubbed herself down and dressed in her thick pyjamas and dressing gown and pulled on her slippers. It wasn't attractive, but it was comfortable. Should she go downstairs again or just hide in her room? Too unsettled by their near miss, she didn't want to mix with the others just now. She needed to unpack, and this was the ideal time, so she plodded up the stairs to where she'd left her bag by the door in a dripping mess.

A few minutes later, there was a knock on the open doorframe. She spun around, hoping it would be Odette, and tried not to let her face fall when she saw it was Edna.

"How are you settling in?" Edna asked.

Beryl pulled the cord on her robe tighter. "Good, thanks. I'm just unpacking my bag, although it won't take long. I rarely wear anything but uniform now."

"Me too. Sorry that you got the smallest room. Mine's slightly bigger, and I've got a view over the river."

Beryl peered out of the dormer window and could make out trees and sky. It was still preferable to looking out on the garage yard with its half-dismantled cars back home. "It's not a problem.

I'm guessing we won't be in the room much."

Edna shrugged. "Perhaps not. Did Odette tell you the rules of the house? Whoever gets in first has to crank the range up to heat the water and oven, and then start to prepare food. Officially, we take it in turns to cook and wash up, and we pool all our rations."

"That's great. I'm happy to contribute my rations too, although I'm not really a cook. I was always too busy helping at my dad's garage to learn properly, much to my mum's despair. Perhaps I can do any repairs and maintenance that are needed? Is there anything I shouldn't do?"

"Not really. But maybe you could mend the door to the coal shed that seems to stick whatever we do. Honestly, I hate going in there. It's always full of spiders, and they creep me out."

"I thought you came from Canada?"

"I do. From Toronto. We don't get as many spiders or midges in the city."

"Do you want me to bring in the coal from the coal shed for you as well?"

"In exchange for cooking? You're on."

Edna stretched her hand out for Beryl to shake. If she didn't have to cook she was happy. "Anyway, we have an early start tomorrow, so I'm going to head to bed. It's not far to cycle to the airfield. If you're ready to leave at seven thirty, I can show you the way."

Beryl breathed out in relief, grateful that Edna was making her so welcome. "Thanks."

She smiled, but Edna seemed as flat as Joyce was. Gone was the bubbly Canadian who tried to mediate between everyone and had a witty remark at the ready. "Are you okay?" Beryl asked.

"Sure. Why?"

"You seem to be more homesick now than you were when we were training."

Edna blinked and opened her mouth as if she was about to speak, then shut it again. She smiled, but it didn't reach the creases around her eyes. "I'm fine. Are you looking forward to starting at Hamble tomorrow?"

"I am. Thank you for making me so welcome."

"Anytime. Good night." Edna waved and went to her room.

Beryl walked back to her single bed. There wasn't much space, just enough for a chest of drawers, and behind the door were hooks from which three coat hangers waited, ready for her uniform and the one dress she'd packed. Now they were allowed to wear uniform trousers when they flew, she would only need the skirt for best. She took her uniforms and blue blouses out of her bag and hung them up, hoping the creases would fall out by the morning. She didn't have an iron, having always borrowed Maisie's. Her stomach dropped a little at the thought of her friend. Beryl hoped they would make it up when Maisie got over her requesting the transfer. Was the upset worth it, given Odette had blown cold again?

Would Odette come up, or would she hide? Beryl decided she would give her fifteen minutes and then go downstairs under the guise of going to the bathroom. In theory, she could use the chamber pot, but she much preferred to use the modern facilities. It made her feel sophisticated. Not that she'd ever say that with Joyce or Maisie around. They'd probably laugh at her, and she'd hate that, if Maisie ever spoke to her again. She would write to her in a few weeks' time, after she'd written to Mike, like she'd promised.

Twenty minutes later, she went downstairs to brush her teeth and use the bathroom. As she came out, Odette peeped out of her bedroom and waved Beryl across.

Beryl entered the much larger room with its double bed, wardrobe, and chest of drawers. "Ooh, you've got a wardrobe," she said before she caught herself.

"Feel free to share. It's not as if any of us can go and buy clothes at the moment."

Beryl cinched in her bathrobe as if trying to cover her feelings.

Just being close to Odette had her heart picking up pace, but whether that was excitement or anxiety, she couldn't say.

Odette patted the bed for Beryl to sit. She obeyed, sitting ramrod straight and leaving a huge gap between them. Odette picked up Beryl's hand and intertwined their fingers, encouraging Beryl to look at her.

"It might be easier if we talk in your room, so Joyce can't hear. I'll follow you up in a couple of minutes."

Five minutes later, Odette sat on Beryl's bed facing her. She caught both her hands in hers.

"Beryl, I really like you, and in another place and another time, I would have taken you off to Le Monocle club in Paris, and we would have danced the night away, or sat around and played cards and been ourselves, and kissed and no one would care. And afterwards, we would have gone home and made love in a tiny apartment. But that isn't how we live or where we live. That was a different land. The past. With every concession and acceptance won, we took it all for granted, but with a change of regime and a different set of rules, all that liberty, equality, and fraternity has gone. Now it's about survival. Not just in the institution of the ATA but in the critical culture of the church and society. We are doing what we can for freedom, and hopefully we will win liberty, but we will not get equality or sisterhood any time soon."

It was as if Odette had rehearsed the speech, which didn't help. She understood that this was not pre-war Paris, but still... Beryl dropped Odette's hands. "I don't agree. If we get liberty, and if we can persuade the Americans to come and help, we have a much better chance of that. We can work towards the other." She stretched out her arms and cracked her knuckles. It always helped to reset herself. "No one ever thought women would get the vote, but we did. Society has been changing, slowly, but it has. I know we'd have to keep us a secret, but I wonder how many women living together are really more than they seem. You're too pessimistic. We seem to have stopped an imminent invasion for now, and we're doing our bit."

"Maybe I am pessimistic, but my country is split in two, and each part is run by a regime that will not tolerate who I am and what we are. I don't know what happened to my friends and may never know. So forgive me if I'm scared to start anything, however beautiful and engaging you are. You're the first person I've even contemplated anything with since...before. You're the first I've even thought about in any way but friendship. You're the first person who has stirred me and challenged me and who I'd love to get to know better, beyond the superficial. But all I can offer you is friendship."

As Odette continued her speech, Beryl's heart sank and settled like ballast in her stomach. To be so close she could almost grasp the promise and to have it snatched away was almost too much to bear. "I don't agree. If we're careful we can do more but—"

"Please, Beryl, you're making this so hard. I don't want you to risk getting caught. I don't know how many times and how many different ways you need me to say it before you really hear me."

"Yet it's you who risks the most each day when you're flying."

"That's a different thing altogether. I volunteered. I have nothing to live for. No one who would mourn for me."

Hope drained away, and the joy and anticipation she'd had on coming here was replaced by fear at Odette's indifference about her life and safety.

Odette must have caught sight of the tears which now fell silently onto Beryl's cheeks because she added, "Until now. Please don't cry, Beryl." Odette thumbed Beryl's tears away and leaned forward to kiss her on the forehead. "Maybe in some future time, we can be together. Now we need some rest. Good night, beautiful. Sleep well."

Odette pulled away and slipped out of the room, padding softly on the bare floorboards and downstairs. Beryl wanted to scream, and rage, and shout at Odette that they could do this, but it wouldn't make any difference. Odette had decided for them both. The echoes of the sounds were the only sense that Odette had ever been there, and Beryl was bereft with nothing but the loneliness of her silence.

Chapter Thirteen

A FEW WEEKS LATER, a dense fog had settled on the ground, making it impossible to fly. The Station Commander, Josephine, had sent the rest of the women home, keeping only the four who didn't need organised transport: Joyce, Edna, Beryl, and Odette. They lounged around in the Ops room playing bridge and hoping for the weather to clear.

As dummy, Odette leaned back to watch Beryl finesse her way to twelve tricks, confounding both the bridge experts of Edna and Joyce, who stared open-mouthed.

"Are you sure you've never played bridge before? I feel we've just been taken for a ride." Edna grinned.

Beryl returned the grin. "No, never. I've no idea how to call or score."

"But you can play cards," Joyce said with more vinegar in her tone.

"I played cards with my dad and brother when it was quiet at the garage. Bridge is just a complicated version of whist, really."

Odette disguised her smile with a cough. Beryl was playing with fire. Joyce hated being outsmarted.

"It's a good job we're only playing for chores, not pennies." Edna picked up the cards and began to shuffle. "And Beryl not cooking will be a blessing for us all."

"Hey, I only burned supper once."

"All our meat rations in one meal."

Beryl's flushing and mock pouting was adorable, but Odette couldn't say that. It was harder than she'd imagined trying to keep friendly but professional when all she really wanted to do was run her fingers through Beryl's hair, kiss her with a passion that burned deep and hidden, and take her to bed. She needed to pull herself together. She rose. "Anyone for tea?"

"Thanks."

At least Edna was taking it in good spirit. Joyce looked genuinely miffed. Before Odette crossed the room, the door opened, and Josephine walked in looking harassed, though that seemed to be her perpetual way of being.

"The latest Met reports say this fog is set in for most of the day. Edna and Joyce, you may as well go back home. If by some miracle, the weather lifts, I'll call you back in. Odette and Beryl, please stay behind. If anyone can get out later, it will be you two."

Odette glanced at Beryl, who flushed pink at the compliment. She always seemed surprised when she was acknowledged as an excellent pilot. Beryl deserved all the praise she could get, and it warmed Odette to her soul that Josephine acknowledged that.

As Josephine exited to go back to her logistics, Joyce riffled through the cards and slapped them hard on the desk to straighten them. It would have niggled Joyce that Beryl was praised for her flying skills, even though it was true.

Joyce inserted the cards into the wooden box. "We'll leave the two favourites then and get on home. Toad in the hole this evening?"

Odette shook her head. She'd never get used to the bizarre names the English had for their food. Sausage in batter was nothing like its description. In France, the description of their food was entirely accurate.

Odette handed the second pack to Joyce. "Thank you. I look forward to eating the toad."

Joyce put the second deck of cards in with the first and closed the inlaid lid. "One of these days, I may surprise you and put a real one in."

"And I might surprise you even more by eating it." They all

laughed, and the tension eased.

Joyce grabbed her coat and handed Edna hers. "We'll have to scratch that game of bridge."

Odette could sense Beryl bristling, preparing to respond, so she cut in. "No. You two doing the laundry for the next week will work fine."

"I've never done laundry in my life," Joyce said, as though that would be the epitome of shame. Then she smiled. "You're teasing me. You know I take it home."

Odette returned the smile and raised her hands in a "you got me" gesture.

Beryl cracked her knuckles. "I'm not very good at the laundry either. When I was a kid, my dad and I invented an electric mangle for my mum. I'm not sure we'd patent it though. Every time the water dropped on the electrics, it would spark."

"Sounds lethal. Are you sure you're an engineer?" Edna asked and leaned over to kiss Beryl then Odette on the cheek before following Joyce to get their bicycles.

If only Odette could kiss Beryl on the cheek without her heart beating so fast. For weeks now and months, Beryl had been in her thoughts and dreams, inveigling her way into her heart. Odette was confused and uncertain, two things she hadn't been for a long time. The physical response to Beryl was both startling and unbidden. She'd never felt constant arousal around someone for a long time. And the physical attraction had been supplemented by the deeper appeal of her whole being: her kindness, intelligence, and courage.

The door clicked shut, and they were on their own in a room that normally buzzed with activity as people picked up their chits, mapped out their routes, and checked their pilot's notes, or filled the time when the weather was bad.

Now it seemed full of dangerous potential. This attraction was growing between them, blossoming and entwining them together, and if they acted on it, they could be exposed at any moment by Josephine or any of the other ATA staff blundering in. Odette rose to stop herself from reaching out. It would be so simple.

Beryl cracked her knuckles again. "I don't think Joyce likes me very much, and I can't work out if it's the class thing or if it's more than that."

Odette looked up from retrieving the backgammon board. "She's jealous because you're a better pilot than her. And you're better at cards and very clever at fixing things."

Beryl replaced the box holding the bridge cards onto the desk by the telephone. "All things I shouldn't be able to do because I come from a humble background, no doubt."

Odette shook her head. "No, I don't think that's it. Tommy isn't from a wealthy family, is he?"

"He may not be old money, but he still went to a good university and his father's a doctor. She doesn't approve of me or something."

Wishing she hadn't started this conversation, Odette chose her words carefully. "She thinks you should try and fit in more-"

"Why? Wearing a skirt and lipstick and painting my nails won't make me a better pilot."

She should have known better than to wander towards territory that Beryl was easily incensed about. "It doesn't. And you're beautiful as you are. However, the ATA wants us to look glamorous for the press—"

Beryl slammed her fist on the desk, causing the box and telephone to rattle. "I know all that, but why should Joyce care what I do?" She pivoted on the spot. "I'm going to make tea."

"Don't let's argue. I'm not agreeing with her, just trying to explain. Let's have a game of backgammon."

Beryl's shoulders dropped a little. "Okay. Cuppa?"

"Thanks."

The corridor was dark and cool as Beryl strode into the galley. Anger burned in her chest, and her hands shook as she filled the kettle with water. She was so fed up with being judged. That Odette seemed to agree, or at least was pushing Joyce's opinion made her seethe even more. She slammed the kettle on the hob and tried to calm herself as she waited for the water to boil.

Why was she so sensitive about her looks and how she was expected to dress? Because she hated not being herself, hiding who she was. Surely the key matter was whether she could fly a plane safely and efficiently from a to b, not that she'd had to wear grey stockings because her black stockings had been laddered scrambling out of the aeroplane. She would never be glamorous like her friends; the press would never clamour for her photo. Of course, she didn't want to be a pin-up girl for the forces, but she hated being thought of as less than or different.

Perhaps Joyce was ashamed of her because she didn't conform, but she'd never got that feeling from Odette or Edna. She would have to prove herself over and over. All her life, she'd been an oddity, but when she flew, nothing else mattered. Not their petty rules or their judgements. What she hated was Odette's judgment. Though it wasn't judgment, it was kind advice, and Beryl should take it in the spirit in which it was intended. She exhaled loudly and picked up the mugs to carefully carry them back to the Ops room.

Odette looked up. "That's the first time we've argued. Sorry."

Beryl set down the tea. "It doesn't matter. It doesn't mean anything." Beryl sat down opposite Odette and picked up her mug.

"You want to know what does mean something? You. You mean something to me."

Beryl shrugged, but she hid her smile behind the cup. A tingle of excitement grew, and the smallest shoot of hope bloomed in her chest. She placed her mug on the table and waited, hoping Odette would continue.

"It's just I've protected myself for so long. I have walls surrounding my walls."

"That must be a heavy load to carry around." Beryl grinned and asked, "Do you have to make adjustments to your weight and balance calculations?"

Odette laughed. "Only you would make a silly flying joke like that."

Odette's smile was so genuine, it warmed Beryl to her toes. "I'd say sorry, but it worked. You laughed."

"I did."

Beryl set out the counters for the backgammon board. "Red or white?"

"Red," Odette said and picked up her tiles to place in the starting position.

Beryl neatly arranged her white counters, giving her hands something to do while she decided whether to ask her question or not. "I noticed the scarf you always wear is red."

"It's my lucky scarf. It belonged to Simone. She wore it every day except when she died. It's the only thing I have of hers to remind me of her."

"How awful. Is that the woman you were in love with? Why you left France?"

Odette bit her bottom lip as if she was unsure whether to say more. Beryl was certain very few people knew Odette's story. She was the master of deflection. Beryl held Odette's gaze, willing her to trust her with her truth.

Odette stretched her hands out and placed down some counters. She seemed distant now as if she was in another room. "Simone died before the war. I watched her plane crash. There was nothing anyone could do. We just watched as the aircraft spun—you could see there was something wrong with the controls. She hadn't taken her lucky scarf that morning. We'd had an argument, and I'll never forgive myself."

Beryl felt as if her lungs were collapsing. She couldn't imagine how Odette must have felt, how she could have survived and continued to fly after that. "Is that why you always wear the scarf below your uniform?"

Odette put her long, elegant index finger to her lips as if to shush her. "Yes. You're not supposed to see it, but it's so bright."

"Pillar box red," Beryl murmured. "I'm so sorry about Simone." Connections clicked in her head, and Beryl's heart skipped. "Wait, do you mean Simone Bouvier, the brilliant record-breaking pilot?"

She had newspaper clippings of the exploits of Simone Bouvier on her bedroom wall at home. She had no idea Simone loved women or had lived with Odette and had another life. If she did, and she was so famous, maybe they could too?

But one glance at Odette showed she was close to tears—the first time Beryl had seen such emotion from her. She laid her hand on Odette's. "I'm so sorry. You lost everything."

"Exactemente. My love, my lifestyle, my country. My family disowned me when I went to Paris with Simone, officially as her co-pilot. I flew a spotter plane, and we shared lodgings. Every fortnight or so we'd go to Le Monocle club where we could be ourselves amongst people like us."

Beryl stroked the knuckles of Odette's hand with her thumb, expecting Odette to pull away. Her heart ached when she didn't. "Thank you for telling me," she said. "I can't begin to understand how you must feel."

"So do you see how I can't go through that again? It's too much."

Beryl tried to imagine having to move to a different country and starting all over again, and her heart went out to the younger Odette. "But hasn't the worst already happened?"

"Which is why I volunteer for the riskiest flights. I've nothing left to lose."

"You make it sound as if you've nothing to live for either."

Odette didn't say anything. She pulled her hand from Beryl's and picked up her last two counters.

Beryl so wanted to tell Odette that she could live for her. "I'd be devastated if anything happened to you," she whispered.

Odette paused in placing her piece and caught Beryl's gaze. Her expression was a mask of rueful sadness. "All the more reason to not take things further. I wouldn't wish what happened to me on my enemy. And you are too wonderful for that. I care for you. You're my dear friend."

Beryl's shoulders sagged. *Friend.* She wanted to be so much more than a friend.

"I'm sorry if that isn't what you want to hear, but I can't give you anything more."

Beryl looked up at the ceiling to avoid letting the tears slip over her bottom lid. She blinked and cleared her throat.

Now it was Odette's turn to grasp her hands and weave her fingers in Beryl's. Despite trying to will her body not to react, her nerve ends tingled under the skin where Odette caressed her. This was so unfair. She had fallen for Odette even though she tried not to, and she was heading for a crash-landing. It would never be reciprocated.

She would have to settle for friendship then. She cleared her throat and sniffed. "Come on, then, let me thrash you at backgammon."

And she did. Though she wasn't sure if Odette deliberately threw the game. Understanding Odette's position didn't make it any easier to accept, especially as the attraction seemed mutual. She had been so sure they could make a go of it, but now she had to chalk it up to experience and carry on regardless.

Chapter Fourteen

DAYS TURNED TO WEEKS, and Britain held on to freedom by a thread. They even had a glimmer of real hope now that America had joined the war. Even with the additional pilots coming across, they needed more women to be signed off on more complex planes to fulfil the demand. Odette had been selected to attend the advanced twin-engine bomber conversion course at White Waltham. She'd been away for a few weeks. It was better she had time away from Beryl. They hadn't spoken about anything real since Odette had opened up about her past and tiptoeing around each other was becoming unbearable. Part of her considered asking for a transfer, but the prospect filled her with dread. She'd hate not to see Beryl regularly; she had missed her while simultaneously needing time to think. She was a mess and needed to concentrate on today and the verdict on her flight test.

She drummed her fingers on the wooden arms of the armchair. The book *Le Comte de Monte Cristo* splayed open in her lap, unread. To find a book in French was a thrill, like sipping her favourite champagne, familiar and decadent, yet even Alexandre Dumas could not hold her attention. She felt an affinity to Dumas who was also in the shadows but still got to achieve his dreams like she had.

Why were they taking so long?

The door swished open, and Joyce entered. On spying Odette, she smiled and crossed the room to join her. "Any news yet?"

"No."

Joyce picked up the book then replaced it on Odette's lap.

"Missing the home country?"

"Sometimes."

Joyce dropped into the chair opposite Odette and retrieved the well-thumbed morning paper. Her affected casualness, so different from her usual prim self, seemed an invitation for conversation.

"How's your conversion course going?" Odette asked.

Joyce pulled a slight face. "I'm not sure I'll ever get used to the complexity of the class two A planes."

"You'll get it. The system really works."

"I know. But I never seem to have time to read all the detailed handling notes. Unlike Beryl, who seems to have memorised them all."

Odette smiled affectionately, her breath catching a little at the mention of Beryl's name. "True. She probably knows all the engineering notes too."

Joyce laughed. The door swished open again, and they both looked up, but it was just a couple of sprogs who joined their rather raucous colleagues awaiting their flying tests.

"Did you hear that Edna has asked to replace Elspeth Muston in Cosford?" Joyce asked.

"Oh?" Odette had heard but was sure no one else had understood why Edna had asked for the transfer.

Joyce ran her fingers to smooth down the newspaper, but it was beyond saving. "I thought she enjoyed being in Hamble and our little band of four in the house. I'll miss her parcels from Canada. I'm surprised you two haven't spoken more French together."

There seemed to be a slight accusatory tone to her voice, as if it was Odette's fault Edna would be moving out, and that more conversations in French would have made Edna feel more welcome.

Odette shrugged. "She's not French Canadian. She comes from Toronto and only speaks English."

Joyce laughed. "Ah." She leaned forward so the newbies in the corner couldn't hear. "Is it true she asked to be transferred because Dorrie is in Cosford?" She shook her head. "I can't see it myself."

So Joyce *had* put two and two together. Odette schooled her expression and affected nonchalance. "Who knows?"

"I always wondered if Beryl was, you know..." Joyce wiggled her eyebrows.

Odette prayed Joyce couldn't hear her heart thumping in her chest. "Beryl's passion is flying. I thought she was seeing Mike?"

Joyce leaned close enough for Odette to feel her breath on her cheek.

"Well, that's the strangest thing," Joyce said. "Maisie said Beryl didn't even consider staying around for Mike when she was offered the transfer."

Odette clamped her jaws together so they wouldn't chatter and settled herself. It didn't mean Joyce knew anything.

"Perhaps she thought they would be stationed abroad soon anyway? She made no secret she wanted to fly Spitfires, so it was logical to move closer to the Spitfire factory. Also they want the best pilots in Hamble, and Beryl is the best of her intake." It was a carefully constructed reason they had concocted for why Beryl wanted to transfer, and as with the best of lies, it held a kernel of truth.

She shouldn't have encouraged Beryl quite so much. For her own selfish reasons, she wanted her nearby. The push-pull drove her to distraction; she wanted Beryl near but was scared to get too close. Maybe she was being unfair, expecting her to stay around when Odette would offer her no more than friendship, but she couldn't let her go. Letting Beryl go would be as hard as giving up flying.

"Maybe." Joyce didn't sound convinced.

Odette was about to say something else when Joyce clapped her hands as if something had just occurred to her.

"We need to celebrate your advanced twin rating this evening. I'll call Maisie and see if she's free. Usual pub?"

"Wait until we know. They seem to be taking forever. Maybe I've failed."

"Nonsense."

As if on cue, the door opened again, and Claude Whitehead, the new commanding officer of the training school in White Waltham, approached them. Although the ATA was a civilian organisation and there was no need to salute, Odette sat up straight in her chair and made a conscious effort not to fidget.

He shook her hand and gave her a set of broad stripes to accompany the narrow stripes on her uniform. "Congratulations, Odette. You got top marks in the flying test. They'll be very grateful you can fly more complex bombers at Hamble so they can release some of the men."

She bowed her head. "Thank you." And she should have felt delighted. *Top marks.* Simone would have been thrilled. Her skills and the complexity of the planes she was now signed off to fly was so much more than Simone had ever done just ten years ago. Would she have been proud of Odette or wished she'd had the chance to fly such complex machines? Probably a bit of both. But instead of elation, she was hollow inside, and she wasn't sure why.

He nodded and exited.

"Well, he doesn't stand on ceremony, does he?" Joyce asked, staring after him.

"It's all in a day's work for him."

"Yes, but top marks! I bet some of the men hate that. Shall we go out this evening?" Joyce sat up straight and bounced on her seat.

Odette didn't want to celebrate, but since Joyce was so excited, she couldn't say no. She thought of calling Beryl; she'd be delighted on Odette's behalf. And maybe some of her enthusiasm would rub off, allowing Odette to bask in it.

Later that evening, she sat in the dark, smoke-filled bar and accepted the toast from Joyce.

"Strange of Maisie not to show," Joyce said.

"Maybe Rob's got some leave?" Odette took a sip of her gin and tonic, which still seemed easy to acquire, and looked around the pub. It was odd to be here and not see people they knew. She half-expected Beryl to come sauntering over to play darts with Mike, or Charlie to be his usual bombastic self, but the pub was packed with unknown faces. New, fresh faces of people who had just joined the ATA.

"What's the difference between an engine and a sprog?" Odette nodded toward the newbies, who were very rowdy and looked to be playing some drinking game.

Joyce frowned. "I don't know."

"You can switch off the noise of an engine."

It wasn't very funny, and she didn't usually make jokes at the expense of others, but she felt unsettled.

"What's got into you today?"

Odette shrugged. "I'm not sure. I guess I thought getting signed off on class four aeroplanes would be a really big thing, as if my skills are acknowledged and special. But it won't be long before everyone will be doing the same—even the sprogs over there. How does that make us different or better?"

Joyce tapped the coaster with her long fingernails. Odette could never work out how she could fly with such long talons.

"Do we have to be better?"

"Most of my flying career, I've been the best pilot. The one who could land on a sixpence, who could do all the aerobatic manoeuvres when no one else was doing them. Now, pilots are everywhere." She knew she sounded arrogant, but she couldn't really explain her disenchantment. If and when this awful war was over, there would be many more pilots than jobs. She had no other skills, unlike Beryl, who could take over her father's business. She had no one and belonged nowhere. The last thing she wanted was to crawl back to her family in Reims and ask for forgiveness, and to be married off like some prize heifer to the highest bidder. She shook her head, attempting to clear her melancholy.

"And you'll always be the best pilot. No one can take that away from you. But comparing yourself or your skills won't help. Growing up to privilege, I've realised people will always compare themselves against others, and it doesn't make any difference if they're kind people or not. It's why I'm so glad I met Tommy. He's ordinary and my parents still don't approve, and we would never have met but for the war, but he's a kind man and a respectful husband. I can't wait for him to come home, so we can have a family. What you need to feel special is a man. What about Charlie?"

Odette shuddered. "No. He's too full of himself. Anyway, flying is who I am, who I'm meant to be."

"And you're a magnificent pilot." Joyce patted Odette's arm. Then, as if she was bored with Odette's poor mood, she asked, "Why don't we ask Maisie to transfer to Hamble now Rob and Mike are away with their squadron? I know how lonely it is when your man's away fighting. It would be super to have us friends together."

Odette pulled herself out of her maudlin self-pity and took a sip of her drink. "Isn't she still cross with Beryl?"

"Oh, no, I'm sure that's just a silly misunderstanding. It's a splendid idea. If she hurries up and comes, we can discuss it this evening."

So Edna had been dispatched and moved out already. Should she warn Edna to be a bit careful about the rumours about her and Dorrie? But what could she do differently? Odette didn't think Joyce would say anything, but she did have a strong sense of duty and liked to adhere to the rules. Which was probably what made her such a cautious pilot. Odette grinned to herself, recalling the ATA regulations. "Have you ever flown above three thousand feet or flown in cloud?"

Joyce blinked as though she'd missed half the conversation. "Not willingly. Only in that snowstorm when you talked me down. Why?"

"Just curious. And I think inviting Maisie is a great idea."

Joyce clapped her hands together. "I'm so glad you agree. Let's do it."

A few minutes later the bar door opened, and Maisie came across looking flustered, and her makeup wasn't perfect.

"Sorry I'm late. The air taxi had to wait, and you know how meticulous Piotr is; he won't start the engines until he's checked every dial and said fifteen Hail Marys. I thought I wouldn't get here in time. I couldn't wait to tell you the great news. Rob's squadron are coming back to England."

Odette shared in her joy and settled into the easy conversation of friends, letting it wash over her. They seemed to be as at ease as they were before the war, but they were simply keeping calm and pretending all was well in their world. There were shortages of food, and fuel, and everything that made life easier, and the news was bleak. Yet, in their own little bubble, life was hard, and life was perfect. Their days were long and sometimes frightening, but every day she got to fly, to see her friends and admire Beryl from a distance.

Chapter Fifteen

January 1945

WEEKS TURNED TO MONTHS, and months to years in the same routine of flying and friendship. Now the Allies were making advances in Europe, and it was only a question of time before victory.

With the end of the war in sight the mood in Hamble shifted to one of expectation; what next? Excitement at peace and of picking up the life they left in limbo. For Odette it was how she could cling on to the satisfaction and achievement over the past four years. And how to stay flying and still see Beryl.

Odette had arrived home first and had put the cassoulet on to cook, although with the rationing, it was more gravy than cut-up sausages and beans. Of course, Beryl would call it a sausage stew, but Odette would pretend it was the finest French cuisine. She cut up a sprig of the rosemary they'd grown in an old barrel in the back yard and added it to the pot. The aroma of the freshly cut herb caused her to pause, close her eyes, and salivate. What she would give for a fully stocked kitchen and a range of foods, especially a little garlic to enhance the taste. She could almost imagine a ripe camembert or silky brie and some of her family's champagne to finish off the meal.

The telephone ringing in the hall disturbed her drooling. She wiped her hands on a tea towel, hurried to the hall, and picked up the receiver.

"I have a call for Miss Mairead Stewart," the operator said without even waiting for Odette to speak.

"She's not home yet. Can I take a message?" Odette grabbed the pad with a pencil attached by string that they kept near the phone. Maybe it was Rob to say he was home already. His squadron had been abroad again and were due back in England any day. If Maisie needed to take some time off, she was happy to do extra shifts. Beryl probably would as well.

The operator put through the call, but it wasn't Rob.

"Maisie, it's Mike."

His voice sounded choked as he struggled to speak, and she could hardly hear because of his sobs. "It's Odette, Mike. Are you okay? Maisie's not home yet."

"Rob's dead. They won't inform her because she's not family, but I thought she'd want to know as soon as possible."

Time slowed. Odette slumped onto the floor and leaned against the wall. "Mike, I'm so sorry. What happened?"

"Engine failure on take-off. I was behind him. He didn't have a chance. Anyone but Rob. Not Rob. He's a brilliant pilot and-and my friend."

Mike could hardly get the words out with his weeping. So much for the stiff upper lip. Immediately she was thrown back to 1933, watching in horror as Simone's plane plummeted to the ground, knowing there was nothing anyone could do. Her life had been gouged out and crashed along with the plane. The depth of his despair was so much more than the appalling horror of watching a plane crash, terrible though that was. And the truth came to her with a clarity she knew and understood so well. Mike loved Rob. She had wondered before, but now it was so obvious. Not that she could say anything on the phone. Now Mike was facing the same fate she had. It was illegal for men and could get him thrown in prison. "I'm really sorry for your loss. It must be really hard for you now, especially as you've just come home."

"I don't know how I'm going to live..."

Even in his grief, he was wary about revealing anything over an unsecured line, but that was confirmation, and she admired his fortitude.

"I was going to say something. Today."

That would have been risky and dangerous if Rob hadn't felt the same. "You were going to tell him?" Odette asked. How did he know she was a safe person to talk to? Had she given herself away too?

Mike grunted in what seemed like agreement.

"Perhaps we can meet up sometime and talk about it?"

Maisie, Joyce, and Beryl burst through the front door chatting and laughing. Odette frantically waved at Maisie. "It's for you. Mike's on the phone. It's about Rob."

All three women stopped and stared at her.

Maisie swallowed hard, her face turning ashen as she took the receiver. "Mike?" she whispered, anticipating what he was going to say.

The others followed Odette out of the hall to give Maisie some privacy, and Odette explained what had happened. The glass bubble of their happy existence cracked and fell about them as the war came howling in and shattered their equilibrium. Dead. So much pain in such a small word.

Maisie ran upstairs to her room.

"I'll go and sit with her. Do eat. Leave some for us, and we'll grab some later," Joyce said and followed her up.

Odette and Beryl sat in the kitchen, though Odette's appetite had gone. They hardly spoke, beyond explaining what had happened. She wiped up the gravy with a piece of thin white bread, debating how much to reveal. "Mike loved Rob," she said. Beryl's head shot up. "Did you know?" Odette asked.

Beryl shook her head vehemently. "You mean, he's like us?"

Odette nodded.

Beryl cleared her throat. "Does Maisie know?"

"No. I don't think so."

Beryl's eyes went wide. "Did Rob feel the same about Mike?"

"I don't know. I'll write to him and see if he wants to meet up at some time and talk about it."

Beryl nodded as understanding seemed to slip into her consciousness. "You know how he feels because you've been there. Did it bring up feelings for you?"

And there she was: the empathetic, kind Beryl who put others before herself. Beryl said she was never enough, yet she stayed and clearly loved Odette from afar. Never touching, never being inappropriate, and Odette had given her nothing. Beryl deserved more, and Odette needed a soul to cry with. She needed to curl up and be comforted in her grief, for Simone, for Rob, for her life that was gone. Unbidden, the first blooming of tears came. She hadn't cried for years. The barest of nods passed for consent, and Beryl put her hand on Odette's and caressed the back of her hand with her thumb.

"I'm sorry. Sorry for you, for Mike, and for Maisie. I had no idea. We shouldn't ever tell Maisie about Mike. But we should do what we can to support him. He'll have no one, and he'll have to pretend he's just getting on with life. It would be a kindness to talk to him, if you can bear it."

Odette blinked back tears and squeezed Beryl's hand, acknowledging her thoughtfulness. "Yes. I will."

They sat there for a while, accompanied by the ticking of the grandfather clock. Odette leaned forward so she was almost touching Beryl's shoulder. Beryl licked her lips, and Odette mirrored the action, staring, mesmerised. It would be so easy to move in just a little closer and brush those soft full lips.

The grandfather clock chimed the hour, and Beryl blinked like she'd been awoken from a trance.

"I'll go up and see if Maisie and Joyce want anything to eat."

Beryl extracted her hand, and it felt cold where she had been. She stood and exited abruptly.

They had been about to kiss, yet Beryl had pulled back. Perhaps she wasn't interested anymore. But the look in her eyes said otherwise. Her pupils had been wide and filled with desire.

Desire that stirred emotions in Odette she had buried for many years.

Needing to distract herself, Odette walked outside to collect more coal. She stopped on her way back to look out into the night. In the pitch-black sky, the moon rose and cast silver on the ripples on Hamble river. It was all fenced off for use by the admiralty. So close and yet unreachable. Like Beryl.

If she peered into her soul, she could see herself falling for Beryl. If Rob's death and Mike's distress demonstrated anything, it was the fragility of existence.

Odette placed the coal skuttle by the range and washed her hands before starting on the dishes. The grief once buried bubbled to the surface. She had lost but loved. Now there was an opportunity for love again, and she had denied it for so long, pretending it was just friendship. And for what?

The grip of loneliness tightened around her heart. She had feelings for Beryl, feelings she didn't want to name, because that might mean she had to declare them and act upon them. They were feelings that ran deep and hidden like submerged mines in the Hamble river. Could she cause ripples? Should she? Was it really love if she was so afraid? Love was the opposite of fear. Fear, the crushing, heart-stopping stifler of dreams. Was she really going to be controlled by her fear?

She needed to talk to Beryl to explore what they might have together. Her hands trembled, and she almost dropped the plate she was drying. Then she stiffened, murmuring to herself as she did in a plane in a difficult situation. She needed to be brave. She owed it to Beryl.

When Beryl's footsteps sounded down the hall, Odette's mouth went dry.

"They said to leave the stew on the range. They might have some later, or they'll reheat it tomorrow." Beryl stopped and frowned at Odette. "Are you okay?"

"Yes. No. Not really." She was so conflicted, and her mixed

emotions swirled around her head, making it difficult to articulate anything. "I was thinking about Mike. He said he had planned to tell Rob how he felt today. And as I washed up I couldn't help wondering what if I didn't tell you how *I* feel."

Beryl tilted her head to one side like she did when she was trying to solve a mechanical puzzle. "How *you* feel?"

Odette breathed in deeply to give herself courage. "I like you. I enjoy spending time with you. I look forward to coming home to hear how you've got on during the day and which planes you've flown. But more than that, I'm attracted to you. I don't just mean your body, but to who you are as a person. I find myself smiling when I hear you at the weather office or the Ops room. Hearing you laugh fills me with joy. I wonder about you all the time, and it's frustrating and appealing in equal measure."

"Oh."

But Beryl wasn't smiling, nor were her eyes gleaming as Odette had expected. Had she misjudged, or had she pushed Beryl away so much that she'd finally turned away from her? Yet that didn't match with their almost kiss just a few minutes ago. This was too hard. How much easier it was to hide away and never talk about deep feelings or risk anything. She was being ridiculous. The high emotions of the evening had probably brought this on.

Beryl picked up the dried plates and put them back into the cupboard. She closed the door, echoing closing the door on Odette, just when Odette was ready to open her heart.

Beryl turned slowly. "I don't know what to say. I'm not sure what you're telling me. Do I just say thank you, and we continue as we are, or what?"

If Beryl was being brave, so should she. Odette cleared her throat.

But before she could speak, Beryl held out her hands and stood. "We're both raw from today, and honestly, the only thing I need now is comfort. Why don't we just have a hug and talk about this when we're both less emotional?"

Odette stepped into Beryl's open arms and put her arms around her waist. The sinking feeling in her stomach sagged into a heavy weight. The rejection stung more than she thought possible. Though it wasn't a complete rejection, it wasn't a whole-hearted yes either, which is what Odette had expected. Perhaps Beryl was now being the sensible one.

She stroked Beryl's back. The hug was comforting, and she tried to ignore the tell-tale flick of arousal as Beryl's hard nipples pressed against her own. *Keep calm and have no carry on.*

Chapter Sixteen

Later that evening, Maisie went to bed with a hot water bottle and extra blanket, even though it wasn't a cold night. They'd all said if she needed to talk, she could wake them up, but she'd said, "No, you all need to fly tomorrow. I'd never forgive myself if anything happened because you were too tired to concentrate."

Beryl slipped under the bed covers and clicked off the light. She stared up at the ceiling, the total blackness surrounding her as deep as her thoughts. Poor Rob. He wouldn't have had a chance. It could happen to any of them, just a twist of fate. They knew that every time they took off.

Odette's revelation that she was attracted to her gave her a fizz of delight underneath her skin, and despite schooling herself to be wary, she couldn't help but grin. *Odette likes me.* She had wanted to fling her arms around her, but it was too unexpected, too much, and she needed to think. A tiny bubble of hope grew in her chest, then popped. Odette was so petrified of the consequences if it all went wrong. No, not wrong—if they were discovered. Could she trust this, trust Odette to follow through? Her head screamed at her to be careful, not to do anything rash, but the pull was almost too much to bear. She had wanted this, wanted Odette for so long.

A few minutes later there was a gentle knock on the door.

"Beryl, are you awake?" Odette asked.

Daft question. She was tempted to say no, but she sensed Odette might need a bit of care and attention. "Come in," she whispered and sat up in bed, clicking on the bedside light. She blinked against the brightness as Odette entered. One look at

Odette squashed any excitement she would have had for her entering her bedroom in the middle of the night. She'd never seen Odette look so nervous or shrunken. She patted the bed covers for Odette to sit down. "Are you okay? Do you need anything?"

The mattress tilted as Odette rested on the bed. "I—I don't know."

Where was the confident, brilliant pilot? The younger, lonely, haunted woman had made an entrance instead.

"Can you just hold me?"

Beryl's shoulders sagged, slightly disappointed Odette had not come to explore things further. "Of course. Do you want to come in?" She lifted the bedclothes, and Odette climbed in. She lay down but didn't touch Beryl at all. Hardly being held. Maybe now she was too scared.

Odette's breaths were shallow and uneven indicating she was wrestling with emotions.

"Thank you. I keep thinking, what if Mike had told Rob, what would Rob have done? I can't imagine he would have called off his engagement with Maisie. Then I thought about how I'd feel if you got involved with a man—"

"That's not going to happen." A flicker of irritation made her sit up. Was Odette never going to give up on this? The flare of annoyance faded, and she settled into the more familiar longing and disappointment.

"I'd be so jealous if you had a lavender marriage to Mike—"

"A what?"

"You know, like they have in Hollywood to hide that one party is homosexual."

She snuggled down again and faced Odette. Her heart did a little skip although she tried hard to control it. "Really, I've never heard of that."

Odette smiled and stroked Beryl's cheek. Did she have any idea what that was doing to her? Heat coursed through her body, and she crossed her legs to stop the throbbing. Odette needed comfort, nothing more. She'd been very clear. This was so unlike her. Normally, she did not flip-flop between emotions, but Odette unsettled her and not always in a good way.

Odette shuffled towards Beryl, so close she could feel the warmth of her breath on her cheeks. "May I hold you?"

No, this isn't safe or sensible. Beryl nodded. Odette wrapped trembling arms around her and caressed her back. Her legs brushed against Odette's and burned at the touch. This was delicious torture and very unfair if she wanted to keep it platonic. Her breathing matched the shallow fast pace of Odette's. Heat rushed through her body as though screaming at her to wake up, to come alive.

"It's hard not to kiss you right now."

Was Odette trying to kill her with that comment? "It's hard for me too. I want to comfort you, but my body is craving for more."

"Mine too."

Beryl pulled her bottom lip with her teeth as Odette leaned towards her, and she willed herself to keep still. Odette traced her finger across Beryl's lips. *Oh, lord.* She wasn't sure how long she'd be able to maintain this position without giving in to her urges.

"You really are beautiful, with your full lips and naturally long eyelashes," Odette whispered. "May I kiss you?"

"I thought you wanted comfort?" What was she doing? Her body screamed at her to say yes, but her head said no, you'll get hurt.

Odette raised an eyebrow, looking amused. She knew Beryl would cave; she was just waiting.

"Yes, I'd love to kiss you," Beryl said, her voice thick with desire.

"Mm," Odette murmured before pressing her soft lips against hers.

Beryl responded and the kiss swiftly changed from gentle to needing, an outpouring of years of longing and yearning. It was a kiss to open her world. She was cracked open, full of pent-up lust and desire, and she wanted more. Their breaths came hard and fast, and when Odette slipped her cool fingers underneath Beryl's pyjama top, she thought she would pass out. She stifled a groan, conscious of Joyce and Maisie on the floor below.

Odette's fingertips pattered down her back, activating vibrations that tingled through her whole body, awakening it. So much for holding back and being careful. Every nerve in her body jangled with glorious energy. And the kissing became much deeper and more ardent.

Odette was everything she imagined; experienced, passionate, and a magical kisser. How else to explain how her body responded, silencing her brain that squealed at her to stop, to take it slow. But the slow thumping of her heart sped to a fast staccato. She shivered.

"Are you cold?" Odette whispered as she kissed below her ears and chin and to the side of her neck.

Beryl gasped. "No, please don't stop."

As Odette kissed her way down to the hollow of her neck, Beryl unfurled like a blossom in the sun. She squirmed beneath Odette's kisses, trying to encourage her to move down to her aching nipples.

Odette kissed across her collarbone and slipped down to the crease between her breasts. She looked up and raised her eyebrow. "Are you okay?"

She was melting into a puddle, and her brain had gone AWOL. Her body had been possessed by some spirit she didn't know existed. No, she was not okay. She was a beast straining at the leash. "Honestly, I'm fine. Please..." She wasn't too proud to beg.

Odette reached up to unfasten the buttons of her pyjama top, too slowly. Beryl tugged at the rest to lay her breasts bare.

Odette raised up on her elbows. "Luscious," she whispered. "You have such perfect pink nipples."

Beryl moaned and arched her back, willing Odette to touch them. Finally, she complied, kissing and licking until she took one erect nipple into her mouth and sucked hard. The sensation zipped from Beryl's nipple to her core, and she bit her lip to stop from crying out. She looked down at all her secret dreams coming true. Odette kissed, and sucked, and gently bit her way down her body, then blew on her skin to soothe the spot.

Odette traced a line of fire down her sides to her pyjama bottoms. Odette looked up, but she didn't need to ask. Beryl was already shrugging off the impediment as quickly as she could.

Beryl shut her eyes so she could focus on Odette's lips and fingertips that trailed everywhere, over her stomach and to the ticklish spot below her belly button. Slowly, Odette caressed her way down between her thighs and her slick folds. The thick aroma of arousal stung her nostrils.

"Don't stop," she gasped and opened her eyes to meet Odette's soft gaze. She smiled in a way Beryl had never seen before: a soft smile just for her, a vision she hoped she would always remember.

"Are you sure?" Odette asked.

Beryl nodded. "Please." And she was rewarded with that smile again warming her to her toes. Odette kissed one nipple and then the other. The sensation was almost too much, then when she thought she could get no higher, Odette's fingertip parted her folds and then she couldn't focus on anything else. She was so wet, Odette's finger slipped in easily, and her hips raised to meet Odette's hand. She huffed out a breath to still the buzzing in her ears. Odette set up a gentle rhythm, then went faster and the bed springs squeaked in syncopation. Somewhere in the back of her mind, she was conscious they needed to be quiet. But she couldn't stop even if she tried, and she really didn't want to try. This was so right, so gloriously, ridiculously right.

Odette flicked Beryl's nub with her thumb, and Beryl bit hard on her lip to stop from crying out in delight.

"Look at me," Odette said.

Beryl opened her eyes as they thrashed and writhed. Odette curled her finger, and she triggered an explosion in Beryl's brain. Her toes curled, and lights flashed in the inside of her lids, and her body seemed to float in the air as if it no longer belonged to her.

She had never felt euphoria before, and she couldn't help but giggle. "Oh, my God. Thank you." Her brain was so befuddled, she couldn't manage anything else.

Odette smiled at her with warmth in her eyes. "My pleasure, believe me. Thank you for letting me be the first."

The one and only, Beryl hoped but didn't say that as she snuggled closer. "Give me a few moments, and I'll return the favour."

Odette shook her head. "We need to be quiet. This has to be the noisiest bed ever. Do you think they heard?"

"If they were paying attention, yes." Beryl was struck with a sudden guilt that she'd lost her virginity on the day Rob died. Shouldn't they cling onto this and celebrate life?

Still quaking from the aftershocks of climax and the seismic shift in visceral understanding, Beryl turned to Odette to smile. But Odette was lying on her back, blinking rapidly.

Beryl immediately rose to lean onto her elbow and stretched to stroke Odette's cheek. "What's wrong? Are you upset about Rob?"

"No. Yes, I am, but that's not why I'm upset." Odette turned to fully face Beryl, and the tears trickled down her face. "It was wonderful to make love with you. To share your body in intimate knowledge, but you know we cannot risk this again. Tomorrow we must go back to being just friends."

No, no, no. Beryl plummeted from elation to dejection in a heartbeat. This was everything she wanted, everything she dreamed of. How dare Odette use her like this? She inhaled deeply over the trembling still coursing through her body.

Arguing now wouldn't help and seeing Odette crying was softening her anger. "But why, if we are discreet? Don't you want to be with me?"

Odette tugged Beryl's hand to her lips and traced kisses over her knuckles. "Of course I do. Nothing would give me greater pleasure than to make love with you every night and use you as my hot water bottle, but, ma cherie, we cannot have the others hearing us, or seeing us, or reporting us to the authorities. There is too much to lose."

The joy that buoyed her just seconds before sunk with the weight in her stomach, and Beryl swallowed hard. Why would she say that unless... "Wasn't I very good? Did I do it wrong?"

Odette pulled her close. "No, you are perfect as a lover. I'm crying because you did it so right. You make love as you fly, by instinct, and being entirely focused on what you are doing. Please don't ever think that. You are perfect."

The words slapped at her, but she didn't absorb them. How could this glorious sensation be within her grasp only to have it stopped again? "What about when they are not here? If they're not at home?"

Odette cupped Beryl's jaw and used her thumb to wipe away the tears that now tumbled from Beryl's eyes. "Oh, Beryl, when you look at me like that, you'll give us both away. Every drop of longing is written in your eyes. If we are lovers, I will want to touch you, hold you, stand behind you at the sink and circle my arms around your waist and kiss your neck when you wash the dishes. At the airfield, I will want to reach over and wipe an oil smear from your face and kiss away the frown you get when you concentrate on mapping your route, and share the gleam in your eye when you are offered a Spitfire or a new plane to fly."

Beryl nibbled her bottom lip. "I didn't know you watched me so closely."

Odette smiled. "I watch you all the time. You bite your bottom lip when you are thinking."

Beryl stopped biting and forced her lips into a wry smile. "But why can't we just be careful?"

"Because you radiate your feelings like a Very flare: hot, red, and intense. I love it, but it attracts attention. I want this as much as you do, but it cannot be after tonight. So maybe instead of being sad, we should not waste another minute. We should make love till dawn, so we have something we can remember as we pleasure ourselves."

A blush burned up Beryl's cheeks. "How do you know?"

Odette smiled. "Because I do it too. Come."

She shouldn't be drawn in again. She knew that, but it was so hard. Almost without thought, she leaned towards Odette. Their lips sealed in a kiss, gently at first but then as desire kicked in again, more frantically, searing it into her memory, knowing this could be the last time.

"Thank you," Odette said. "I'll treasure this memory forever." She huffed out a long breath. "Just hold me. That's what I need."

That was it? Odette was happy to stuff that into one brief moment. Beryl wanted to scream that no, they needed more and often, whenever they were alone in the house. This couldn't be the end; it was just the beginning. She squashed down the disappointment, but she couldn't push Odette. They kissed chastely.

"Good night," Odette whispered and opened her arms for Beryl to lie on top of her.

She loved the comfort of laying her head on Odette's chest. The smell of sex and sweat filled the air, and vaguely Beryl thought she would need to leave the window open to freshen the room up. She switched off the bedside lamp and snuggled back into Odette. "Good night," she said. She could stay here forever, warm against the fabric of Odette's nightie and listening as Odette's heart beat slowed to a gentle thud and her breathing slowed to somnolent puffs of air.

She couldn't sleep. Her mind was rotating faster than a supercharged Merlin engine. She wanted to skip and sing—and she was terrible at singing—but clearly Odette didn't feel the same. For Odette, the benefits didn't outweigh the risks. Beryl wiped her eyes with the back of her hand, careful not to wake Odette. She wasn't crying, she was just tired. That was it.

The very act of reliving their time had her heart racing and parts of her body reacting as they'd never done before. Logically, she understood Odette's viewpoint, but that didn't help her body and her heart that wanted to repeat this tomorrow and every night after that. What could be more perfect than flying by day and loving by night?

Not that Odette had ever said love. That was just Beryl's imagination, which she needed to rein in. She inhaled the scent of Odette: a mixture of sweat, and arousal, and a hint of her expensive French perfume. If only she could bottle it to absorb when she needed. She could get used to this, being pillowed by the rise and fall of Odette's chest. Rise and fall. It was so obvious she was falling for Odette and being friends would never be enough. But Odette had said it wouldn't work.

Beryl awoke with a start. The sweat on her back had cooled, and the bed was empty beside her. Odette had gone. She wasn't surprised, although it would have been glorious to wake up with her. If it wasn't for the faint scent of sex in the air and a slight soreness between her legs, she could almost believe she had dreamt it. But Odette looking up at her with that soft smile was recorded in her mental logbook she could flip through and enjoy later. A thrill ran through her. The stunning, self-contained gorgeous Odette had taken her; it was all too exciting.

Then her heart sank. It wouldn't ever happen again. Maybe they were both just raw, and emotional, and seeking comfort in their upset.

But now Beryl had tasted the forbidden fruit, she was stirred up and desperate for more. Odette had enjoyed it as much as she had. She couldn't just walk away from Odette, from last night and say never again. This war was already stuffed with can't have and can't do, don't speak out of turn, or say what you saw. It was all too much. She would speak to Odette when she was calmer. Surely, if they were careful, they could do this again.

Chapter Seventeen

ODETTE WAS TRYING TO get Maisie to eat porridge, her favourite breakfast as it reminded her of home. But Maisie sat in her silk dressing gown, staring at the half-eaten, lukewarm cereal, her eyes hollowed and empty.

Maisie didn't seek conversation, so Odette scrubbed the dirty saucepan with wire wool and recalled the events of the previous night. The memory of Beryl letting go and tumbling over the edge was one she would treasure forever. She had been so passionate and present, it had been a revelation. It was both wonderful and disturbing.

Beryl had shaken Odette's belief about herself and everything that made her safe. She had made a promise to herself when she came to England that she wouldn't let anything or anyone interfere with her flying. To date, she had succeeded in that completely.

She scrubbed harder, and there was a satisfying scraping as she cleaned the congealed slop from the pan. Who knew what it was doing to Maisie's insides. She glanced back at Maisie, who stared into space, her breakfast virtually untouched.

Odette had been right to speak to Beryl last night, and she warmed at the remembrance of their lovemaking. So why was she so reluctant to take it further, despite wanting it so much? Fear wore the face of reason: they were too busy, they could lose their jobs, it was too difficult when they shared a home with others. At its crux, Odette was clinging to the life she had after Simone. Simple, secure, and safe.

She inhaled sharply. She was scared. Having sex could easily fall into something deeper, something she didn't want to name. No. It was there already, puttering at the edges of her consciousness, poking at her to express it. Her feelings had already developed into more than friendship. She looked forward to coming home and discussing their days, their flights, the vagaries of different planes, and sharing food preparation—with Beryl as sous chef— then backgammon and the simplicity of domesticity.

For a few brief seconds, she thought about going to Josephine and confessing how she felt about Beryl, then maybe they could both be discharged and do what? War work in an armature winding factory? They would go insane to know they could be flying but weren't allowed. And the discharge would be dishonourable, so they would never work in flying or the forces again. No, she had to be firm.

Beryl came into the room and hugged Maisie. "How are you?"

Maisie shrugged.

Odette took the opportunity to observe Beryl as she spoke to Maisie. Her eyes were red-rimmed, but her face was glowing. Was she upset following their conversation afterwards or basking in their lovemaking?

The memory of last night as Beryl climaxed came flooding back, and she couldn't stop the smile from forming. They couldn't have sex again in the house; the noisy bedsprings were testament to that, and they couldn't do it anywhere else either. And she wanted more with Beryl, more than sex, but she couldn't see how they could make it work. It was impossible. Not with sharing their space with two others. Her nose stung and her throat thickened, but no tears fell. She felt numb.

Beryl was avoiding eye contact, and she sat opposite Maisie. "Do you want me to phone and say you can't come in?"

Maisie rubbed her face with her hands, scrubbing away her memories. "No. I'm going in. I can't cope with being here all on my own," she said.

"I'm on taxi ferry duty today," Odette said and placed the

pan upside down to drain. She wiped her hands on a towel and replaced it by the Aga, which put her in Maisie's sightline. "How about you come with me in the Anson and wind the undercarriage up and down."

Beryl nodded. "That's a great idea."

"Perhaps. I'd better get myself ready then." Maisie pushed down hard on the table to lever herself up. She seemed to have aged thirty years overnight.

Beryl picked up the dirty bowl and whisked it over to the sink. "Leave your cup. I'll wash it up."

Maisie muttered a thanks before she plodded upstairs to her room.

When the door closed, Beryl swung around and flung her arms around Odette. "Thank you. Thank you so much for last night. I can't tell you how happy you made me."

Odette couldn't look Beryl in the eye and stood rigid in Beryl's embrace. How she wanted to sink into her arms and kiss her, but she needed to be strong for both of their sakes.

"It was wonderful, and I was honoured to share that with you. But as I said last night, we can't do it again."

Beryl stepped away, and the guilt rose into Odette's throat, making it difficult to speak.

Beryl scowled. "What do you mean? We'll be careful. Anyway, I doubt Joyce or Maisie would say anything."

"It's not just that."

Beryl washed the saucer vigorously. "Why? What else?"

Odette snatched at the tea towel and picked up the cup from the draining board. If she kept busy she didn't need to face Beryl. "I've been going over and over how we can make this work. I really enjoyed last night, and I'd love to continue—"

Beryl clattered the saucer on the draining board with more force than necessary. "But you came to me. You said you wanted to tell me how you feel. I feel used and spat out."

"I know. I'm sorry."

"Are you saying you don't feel anything?" Beryl plunged her hands into the washing up bowl. "You're like Aladdin's genie; you grant one wish, then puff, you disappear."

Odette almost smiled at Beryl's analogy.

"Or wasn't I good enough?"

Odette's smile dropped, and she dried the saucer. "You know that's not true. I've already told you. What we had was wonderful, and if I thought we could keep it a secret, I would. But secrets seep out. And I can't do it again."

Beryl had stopped washing and was watching her, listening, absorbing every word as if she was going to file them away and re-examine them all later. Odette would have to reveal all her insecurities if she had any chance of keeping something with Beryl.

"Everything changed when Simone died. I couldn't bear to be at the same airfield, seeing the scar where her plane had crashed into the ground. Even after they'd removed the wreckage, the plants echoed the damage by twisting as they grew. Nor could I visit the club without sharing it with a ghost. The sponsors wanted the planes and the apartment back. I thought they were hers, but they were on loan while she was the chief test pilot. Her family claimed all her money. When the advert for trained pilots for the flying circus in England was pasted to the notice board, I applied. I'd learned English at school, and we had an American at the airfield who I'd talk to."

Beryl reached out as if to comfort Odette, then dropped her hand, unsure whether she was allowed to touch her. "Oh. That's terrible. I can't imagine how you must have felt to lose it all."

Odette continued drying the crockery. "It was. It'll never come again. We were just one lost generation who had a modicum of freedom. And it's all gone with a change of regime. So do you see why I can't promise anything? I'm too jaded and hurt and angry. You need someone light and—"

"Don't tell me what I need. I know what warms my soul—or

rather who does. You may be jaded, but you still have time to mentor people and to be kind and thoughtful. You're hurt, but I'll do everything I can to soothe that hurt and ease your burdens. It won't be the same, but we can take what contentment we can and make the most of what we have."

Odette put down the tea towel and brought Beryl's hands to her mouth to kiss her knuckles. "You're such a good soul. I would just bring you down."

Beryl shook off Odette's hands. "You won't bring me down, and you can't hide who you are forever."

Odette shook her head. It seemed nothing she said made any difference to what Beryl thought. Beryl was determined to believe they could have a future together, but it was futile and would lead to more heartache. She had to squash this vain hope, for both their sakes. "I have to. Last night was wonderful. Beryl, please trust me. If we lived in a different time, I'd be proud to be seen with you, and I'd make love to you every night. But we can only live in the reality we have."

Beryl picked up the dried cups to stash them in the cupboard with a rattle, avoiding Odette's gaze. "All the more reason to take that moment and snatch our happiness. We get on so well together. Even when we're fighting, we're working side by side. We fit." She took the saucers Odette proffered and put them on the bottom shelf beside the cups.

"If there was only us, and the world didn't intrude, I would be there working beside you, openly and with joy. But it's impossible!"

Beryl slammed the cupboard door shut. "And how many times have you flown the impossible, when you've threaded your way through the high ground and the low cloud in a plane that shouldn't fly?"

"That's different."

"For someone so brave who faces death every day, you're spineless when it comes to emotions. Surely you know of women who share houses, and share their lives? We can be that."

"I can't be trapped in some claustrophobic English village. I need to fly. If I die flying, de rien. Flying is only playing with my life. Loving is playing with my heart, and my heart is too scarred to be open and vulnerable. When I fly, I forget everything else. There's just the focus to keep alive. If I do something wrong, I'll kill myself. But when I get it right, there's a rush of achievement. You know what that's like. Up in the sky there are no societal rules, no judgments, no misogyny. I'm just absorbed in the activity of staying alive. I'm only truly alive when I fly."

Beryl vigorously wiped down the sink. "Not alive, even when we had sex? Or are you going to say sex is just sex, like you said a kiss was just a kiss?" Beryl wrung out the dishcloth, twisting it tighter and tighter. "What about companionship and joy and love? No, don't answer that. It's very clear where your priorities are. You'll die a lonely old woman. I thought you were brave. I never took you for a coward."

"Merde! I'm not a coward. It's all right for you to be condescending. If everything goes wrong, you can go back to your family and work in your family business. I have nothing: no home to go to, no life to go to, no family and no country."

"There's no reasoning with you." Beryl spun on her heels and banged the door on her exit.

"Beryl, come back," Odette said. But she'd gone and her footsteps clumped up the stairs to the top floor. She took the stairs two at a time and knocked on Beryl's door. "Can we talk?"

"There's nothing to talk about. I'm getting ready for work, and don't want to be late. I'll see you later."

Beryl's voice sounded so choked Odette wanted to put her arms around Beryl and comfort her. She had done that to Beryl. She was responsible for Beryl's tears. Odette's teeth began to chatter. She couldn't lose Beryl as a friend, she meant too much to her. Odette put her face up to Beryl's bedroom door, but no sound came from within. "I'm sorry. Let's talk about it later. Maybe we can work something out," Odette said.

"Perhaps."

Beryl didn't sound convinced, and Odette wasn't sure either. Defeated, she went into her room and closed the door.

Everything had just gone wrong. She should have known Beryl wouldn't understand. Could they do something? Could they be together when the others were out? Not that that happened very often.

What a mess she'd made. The last thing she wanted to do was hurt Beryl. She tucked her scarf inside her uniform. Beryl's door creaked open and the sound of her rapid footsteps disappeared downstairs before the back door slammed shut. Within seconds, Odette heard the crunching of the bicycle wheels on the gravel. She was gone. Perhaps it was better if they calmed down and talked together tonight to see if they could come to a compromise.

Odette's hand shook as she applied her lipstick and inhaled deeply to calm her nerves, before facing the others. She checked her watch and couldn't delay any longer, and padded downstairs, where Joyce and Maisie waited so they could cycle together.

Joyce looked almost as tired as Odette felt. "Couldn't you sleep either?" she asked. "We heard you tossing and turning after you went to bed."

Odette dropped to the floor and hurriedly retied her shoelaces to hide the burning in her cheeks. So they *had* heard the bed springs. She cleared her throat. "No. We're all upset."

"True. Beryl seemed annoyed and in a hurry this morning. I've never heard her raise her voice before."

Joyce seemed to be fishing for more information. She wouldn't get any from Odette. She shrugged as though it was nothing, and her heart wasn't racing at the prospect of being discovered. "She's upset too. Okay. Let's go. I hope your arm muscles are ready for a day of turning, Maisie."

Maisie gave her a wan smile and followed behind her. It was safer if she didn't fly today. They didn't need any more accidents to add to the tally.

Later that evening, after Odette had ferried many pilots to and from airfields, she returned to the Hamble Ops Room. There were a few women sorting out their paperwork, but no Beryl.

Joyce looked up from writing her pilot logbook. "Hello, Odette. Good day? How was Maisie?"

"She managed really well. She's gone home now to start cooking; she said she needed to do something useful today."

She didn't say that Maisie sobbed nonstop for almost an hour and had completely exhausted herself. Odette suspected not much of the food would be prepared by the time they got home, but it didn't matter. She'd do what she could to help. She picked up her papers and recorded the flight details in her logbook. Another six flights completed today in the trusty Anson.

The telephone rang on the table beside her, and Josephine, their commander, picked up the receiver. "Hello, Beryl."

Odette's head shot up, and her pulse quickened. Logically, if Beryl was on the end of the phone, everything was fine, and she'd just been delayed. She breathed out slowly to calm her racing heart.

"Sure, of course. See you tomorrow." Josephine replaced the receiver in the cradle and turned to Odette and Joyce. She smiled, presumably to put them at ease.

"Beryl was delayed getting to Cosford, so she didn't have enough time to get back before nightfall. She said she'd stay with Edna tonight and see you both tomorrow." Josephine retreated to her office to reschedule her planning because of the failed delivery from Cosford to Hamble. Hers was a never-ending task.

Odette held back a snort. Beryl always made her way back home if she could. She didn't believe she was delayed. Beryl was efficient and had a huge sense of duty to deliver what she had been requested. Clearly, Beryl was avoiding talking to her.

"Are you okay?" Joyce asked.

Odette turned and managed a smile. "Yes, why?"

"You're crumpling your papers."

She tried a laugh, but it sounded false. "I'm just a bit jittery."

"Understandable. I'm about done. Shall I see you back at the cottage?"

She nodded. "D'accord. I'll be there shortly."

Was Beryl avoiding her because she was angry, upset, or needed some space to recalibrate herself? Probably all three. She never intended to upset Beryl, but sometimes the truth hurts. To use Beryl's analogy, was it too late to put the genie back in the lamp?

Sometimes love is about what you are prepared to risk. If you risk and lose, love is picking up the pieces and putting them together. Beryl had picked up Odette's pieces and slotted them back, and now Odette had shattered them. Tomorrow she would do what she could to put those pieces back together.

Chapter Eighteen

SIMONE WAS INSIDE A *burning plane, but she wasn't trying to escape.*

"Get out, get out," Odette cried as she frantically extinguished the flames enough to get to the plane and take the cockpit cover off. But it blistered her skin, and there'd been a sharp pain as she tried to touch it. And it had been a Spitfire cockpit. Simone had never flown a Spitfire.

"You should have your cockpit canopy open for take-off and landing, Beryl." And then it had been Beryl in the plane, but she wasn't speaking anymore. She turned her head away from Odette seemingly not bothered to listen to her as she screamed at Beryl to get out, to save herself.

She awoke with the bed clothes wound around her legs, making it difficult to move. Sweat started to chill on her back and neck, and she stretched, looking to see the time. Two thirty-four am. Odette groaned. It would be a long day; Josephine had told her to expect a series of longer flights and to take an overnight bag in case she had to stay out.

The dream disturbed her. It wasn't difficult to parse that she may have lost Beryl as she'd lost Simone, this time because of her actions. How could she be so heartless? Beryl was not the kind to go off in a huff. She was normally so even-tempered, so she must be angry and upset and needing space from Odette. She'd hurt Beryl by her cowardice, and that thought weighed like a heavy stone in her stomach.

"I'll make it up to you. Perhaps we could sound out Joyce and Maisie or just go for different lodgings, even though we're so lucky being where we are. How would we tell them we're moving out? Maisie in particular would feel bereft having just lost Rob," she said into the dark room. It was strange how fear provided so many reasons for not doing something even if desire pulled the other way. If desire won, guilt followed quickly behind. So there was never a clean or clear positive emotion that roared up with the passion.

She spent all the spare time in her flights trying to find an acceptable solution that minimised the risk. By the time she had delivered a plane to RAF Valley in Anglesey, later that day, the weather had closed in, and there was thick fog. If it was only around the coast, she could fly above it, and it might be clear beyond. Although it was a mere twenty-minute flight to her next pick-up, the commanding officer invited her to stay at the airfield.

"This is set in for the rest of the day. It's up to you, but you're welcome to join us in the Officer's Mess, and there's reasonable accommodation for the women on site." He stole an appreciative glance then smiled. "If it helps you decide, we have coffee and tinned peaches."

The thought of coffee made her mouth water, and she could almost catch the whiff of roasted beans. "In that case, I can't refuse. Thank you, that's kind. I'll just phone base to let them know."

Men were so uncomplicated, and they wore their admiration so openly. She enjoyed flirting and being flirted with, knowing it was harmless fun.

"I hear you've caught the short straw and are taking the beast off the base tomorrow," Andy, one of the officers said as they sipped coffee.

She turned in her seat to face him. "Anything I should know about it?"

The commanding officer glared at Andy. "It's being worked on overnight and will be flyable tomorrow."

"Just check your parachute is all I'm saying," Andy said with a shrug.

Being teased about taking the old bomber off their airfield tomorrow was easy to respond to and deflect. And it was a welcome distraction from the hurt of loving Beryl and having argued with her. She could admit it now, when it may be too late, that she loved her. She was aware of Beryl in the background constantly, her pulse quickened when she saw her, and she deliberately unravelled interactions so they could spend more time together. Yes, she was smitten with her.

The following morning when the ground crew showed her the plane, she almost did a double take. She had rarely seen such an old dog. The cockpit windscreen was cracked, making forward visibility difficult, and judging by the new pool on the ground, it was losing oil too. "Has she been signed off?"

"For one flight only." Bob, the ground chief, fidgeted as if they wanted to get rid of their problem child.

Odette checked the aircraft thoroughly. It didn't help that the weather forecast suggested a lowering cloud base and precipitation later. Fortunately, it was a short flight to take her to pick up the next plane of the day down south.

She carefully plotted her route from RAF Valley on Anglesey to Hawarden, near Chester, avoiding flying over water and to the north of the Snowdon range of mountains. If she had an engine-out she didn't want to do an Amy Johnson and ditch in the cold sea. It meant flying close to the hills, but if she followed the River Dee, she would be fine. She agreed to take the plane and was rewarded with a look of relief on the ground crew's faces.

"We've had two pilots refuse to take her," one of the guys said.

His look seemed to imply she was stupid or gullible whereas the others hadn't been. What they didn't know was she lived for these moments.

About five minutes after she'd taken off, the compass started to flicker wildly. *Merde.* She tapped it hard, and the needle seemed to settle, which was encouraging. The cloud base hadn't lowered, so she decided to press on. She could divert to another airfield en route, but she didn't want to have to fly this old crock more than once or get stuck trying to get home from North Wales to the south coast, which would be a long train journey. She double-checked the ground to her map. There was the River Dee, although it was getting hazier as a sea mist rolled in. Looking down, she could still see the river, even if it was murky straight ahead.

Her dream from the other night had disturbed her, but she shook it off. She was still annoyed and upset that Beryl had avoided her. *Focus.* As she looked down again, there was a carpet of cloud. No features at all. She swallowed. The compass was showing she was flying in an easterly direction and seemed to be stable. She decided to continue on this heading for another ten minutes and then reassess her position. To her right, she could make out mountain tops shrouded in cloud. As long as she kept them to her right, she was fine. She couldn't fly further north though because of the barrage balloons stretching across from Liverpool.

"Stay on this heading," she said and scanned the instruments. The starboard engine temperature was running hot. She lowered the throttle, increasing the power of the port engine, and pushed her foot hard on the rudder to stop the plane from flipping over. She trimmed the plane so it was stable, even if it was crabbing along. She glanced around the crack in the windscreen. On her left was a mountain that shouldn't be there. She swallowed hard. There were mountains to the right too. She was flying up a valley with the tops covered in thick cloud. The rocky snow-covered outcrops were too close, and it was too narrow to turn around. Ahead, the mountain was higher than her current position and covered in cloud. Her only option was to climb above the mountains which, at three thousand feet, were higher than the ATA's official flight ceiling, but she didn't have a choice.

"Okay, let's be logical here. If in doubt, fly higher and give yourself time to think. If the local terrain is three thousand feet, climb to at least four thousand feet on the same heading. Hopefully, there'll be a hole in the cloud later I can come down in. If not, I'll climb again and bail out. Better to lose a plane than a pilot."

Decision made, she increased the throttle in both engines to climb. The starboard engine temperature climbed too. If she was going to abandon the plane anyway, conserving the engine wouldn't matter.

The roar of the engine became deafening. A pungent smell of burning enveloped her, and she coughed as it invaded her nostrils. She glanced out of the cockpit to see flames licking up the starboard engine, being fanned by the draught of the airstream. Sweat trickled down her temples. "Come on, come on, take me higher, so I can safely bail out." She peered ahead through the thickening clouds. Instead of a valley, she was hurtling directly at the mountain wall. *Merde.* She pulled up to increase the angle of attack to stall into the ground rather than smash into it. Ahead, she could just see the snow on the top of the mountain, and she lifted her buttocks off the seat urging the aeroplane to climb with just one useful engine. If she just had an extra few ounces of power to lift her above it and clear, then she could try an emergency landing. The engine fire was hotter, searing her cheeks, and for a second, the vision of Piotr's damaged face flashed across her mind. The smell in the cockpit became acrid, a mix of burning oil and hot metal, and she started to cough. The starboard engine failed completely, and she cut off its fuel supply. She could just see the top of the mountain as it passed below her, and time stretched. White completely covered the windscreen, and she must have pulled back on the stick to level off the plane, but she was too close to the outcrop on the port side. The wing clipped the rock, jerking the plane and throwing her shoulder against the hard cockpit frame. She yelled in pain as the side concertinaed and crumpled with a screeching of metal. She pushed her feet frantically on the rudder, somehow still flying the lump of metal.

But it was useless. The ground below her tore at the underside with a cacophony of shrieks and judders. Then the cockpit dropped suddenly, slamming her forward into the instrument panel. *I never told Beryl how I feel about her*. It was the last thing that went through her mind before she blacked out.

Chapter Nineteen

B<small>ERYL SCRUBBED HER FACE</small> as she waited for her ferry taxi home. A hard couple of days' flying hadn't been helped by little sleep, but at least there was just one short flight today, and with any luck, she would be home by mid-afternoon. Edna had been lovely, even giving up her bed and sharing with Dorrie, so she could take the spare room. Of course, she couldn't tell them why she was so upset. She couldn't tell them about her and Odette, or about the elation at the wonderful intimacy, and the upset of their argument, and how she had run out. Who was the coward now? She had promised to talk but what was there to talk about? Odette had rejected her. Again. Could she go back to being just friends? She'd said some harsh things. How could she have called her a coward when she was the bravest woman she knew? Maybe she should ask for a transfer like Edna had done.

No. She couldn't cope with not seeing Odette, not hearing her wonderful accent that sent a thrill down her spine. Not to revel in the domestic routine of preparing meals and discussing the news, or playing backgammon and bridge while they waited for the weather to clear. She loved spending time with her, wanted to spend even longer with her and to explore the physical side now that door had been opened. Odette had laid her bare, and it had been as wonderful as she thought it might be.

It had been less than two days, but Beryl missed her with an ache that was almost painful. She could no more give up being around Odette than a drunk could stop slugging sherry at Christmas. Beryl stretched out her legs and rubbed her arms to warm up. The cockpit cover of the Typhoon she'd just flown had been broken, and she'd had to fly with her goggles on, wrapped up against the cold. She must be getting soft; flying in an open cockpit had once been the norm, and it hadn't bothered her at all.

The sound of an aircraft taxiing to dispersal had her staring out of the window: the ATA Anson and her ride home. As the propeller spooled down, three pilots clambered out of the cockpit, no doubt glad to be back at their home base. They came into the Ops room, nodded a greeting to her, and completed their paperwork. The pilot in command was still in the cockpit. Beryl had a little bet with herself. He was taking so long it must be Piotr, going through his instrument tapping, finishing in a flourish with the sign of a cross and clutching his St Christopher medal he always wore around his neck. At the unmistakable limp as the pilot walked across the apron, she grinned. Bet won.

Great. They could recommence their discussion about the relative merits of the Spitfire and Hurricane. Given he had been so badly burned in a Spitfire, it wasn't really surprising he preferred the Hurricane.

They always had the same friendly debate, like they were discussing rival football teams, and they both loved it.

Piotr smiled when he entered the room. "Well, well. They didn't tell me I'd have trouble on the way back down south. If I'd known, I might have done a detour."

He shook her hand, which always struck Beryl as very formal. She knew his preference would be to kiss her on the cheek, but he was always so polite. It must be his good Catholic upbringing. The rumour was that he had built an altar in the back of one of the hangars, which had proved surprisingly popular even amongst those who weren't religious. One day, she would go and look at the pictures of all the people who had died, and honour them, but she didn't need that grisly reminder when she took to the skies daily. "Ha. You wish. You enjoy me being your crew because I can unwind the undercarriage faster than most."

He lowered his chin slightly. "I'll just report in, then we can get on our way."

He picked up the phone and asked to be put through to ATA control. She was glad there would only be the two of them flying back so they could have an uninterrupted discussion. He didn't speak much when other pilots were in the taxi plane.

He glanced at Beryl and sagged onto the seat. She frowned at him, but the sparkle had gone, and his face drained of colour.

"No, she's not here. Are they sending a search party? Okay. We'll just refuel and make our way home. I'll tell her."

Beryl's stomach dropped. A search party was only needed if a plane had gone down. Her hand shot to her mouth to stifle a cry. She knew what he was going to say before he spoke.

Piotr replaced the receiver in the cradle and turned to Beryl. He took her hands in his.

"Odette?" she asked, wanting to know before he could work out how best to tell her. Piotr nodded and squeezed her fingers. Nausea rose up her throat, and she tried hard to tamp it down. "No," she whispered, as though that could stop it from being true. It couldn't be Odette. She was the best pilot she'd ever known. But even the best pilots could fly into bad weather or have an engine problem. Trembling started in her legs and crept up her torso until her whole body shook.

"She was on a twenty-minute flight from RAF Valley to the maintenance unit at Hawarden airfield. She didn't report in at Hawarden, so they're sending out a search party along the course of the Dee."

"She won't fly over water if she can help it. Not since Amy Johnson. And she says the gunners onboard the ships in the river are too trigger happy; they don't check to identify a plane before shooting it down. We have to go and search." She had never been so certain of anything in her life and doing something was so much better than waiting for news.

Piotr shook his head. "It's miles out of our way."

Surely he saw they had to try and find the plane? "So what? The search plane will look in the wrong place. We have to go, in case there's any chance she's still alive."

He frowned.

"Please, Piotr. I've never asked anything of you before, and I'll never ask anything again. How would you feel if someone hadn't managed to drag you from your burning Spit? This is really important. I know it."

It was underhand to use his own accident, but she would ask for forgiveness another time.

His chest heaved up and down. "I suppose we could make one pass and fly down the west coast of Wales."

"Thank you. Okay, let's get going."

But Piotr wasn't to be hurried. It seemed to take ages to refuel and line up to do their pre-take-off checks. He tapped each instrument as normal and then touched his St Christopher medallion before replacing it under his uniform. "Come on, Piotr. Every minute counts."

He paused to glare at her. "I don't intend to have another accident, thank you."

He was right, of course, but it was so frustrating. She wanted to snatch up the control column and fly it herself. She placed her hands on her knees to stop her legs from jiggling up and down. "I've plotted a route I think she would have taken, but it means flying higher than the mountains and above the official ATA ceiling. At least the weather is clearing."

He grunted. "We'll start from the north-east corner and work our way from there in a series of parallel lines..."

She allowed herself a brief upturn of her lips. He clearly intended to do more than one pass. "Thank you."

The speed of the Avro Anson was less than half that of the Wellington bomber, so it took many leg-twitching minutes before they passed overhead Hawarden Airfield to start their search. Beryl cleared her throat and gave Piotr the bearing to follow.

"That takes us over the mountains," he said, more in clarification than judgment.

"Yes," she said. "We should start there. The search party will probably come down to this point here."

"I'll bank the plane a little to your side, so you can search the ground."

As she'd calculated, it took about forty minutes to arrive overhead RAF Valley on the island of Anglesey, and the knot in her stomach tightened. There was no sign of a downed aeroplane. Surely Odette wouldn't have forgotten to check in? The ATA controllers would have phoned the destination airfield to see if she'd arrived. "Please let her be okay," she muttered to herself.

Piotr turned the plane and flew the reciprocal bearing, parallel to the first pass. They climbed over the Snowdon mountain range. Odette had no chance if she'd come down here. The sides were too steep. With the increased altitude, it was even colder, and she was glad for the furs Piotr kept under the seat. The engines seemed noisier too, with more vibration from the air currents coming over the mountains. She scanned the ground and could see nothing on her side. They crested the saddle of the all-white mountain, which made it difficult to judge features. Beryl's hope began to fade.

Then she saw it. In the spread of white was the carcass of something manmade. Her heart in her mouth, not wanting it to be true, she pointed at the debris.

"Piotr, circle over there," she said, her voice reedy and weak. She didn't want to believe what she saw, but fear drew her eyes towards the scene.

Piotr slowed the plane right down, just above the stall speed and circled. Now they were closer, she could see the fuselage snapped in half and facing upwards like two sticks in the ground, and the characteristic geodetic airframe of the wing, broken and charred black by the starboard engine. There must have been an engine fire, but it seemed to be out now. The nose was crunched up, and the remains of the cockpit was misshapen. How could anyone land there at all? Or get out alive?

A sound, primordial and in pain echoed around the Anson, and it took Beryl a few seconds to realise she was making it.

Piotr glanced across at her. "Beryl, please."

She couldn't reply. The contents of her stomach seemed determined to make an appearance. She grabbed the paper bag Piotr handed over just in time and vomited into it. Coughing, she wiped her mouth with the back of her hand. Her nose and eyes were running, but she didn't care.

"If she managed to escape and decided to walk down, she would probably head for the tree line over there," he said. "I'll go slowly. Keep your eyes out."

Beryl sniffed and wiped her eyes. Of course. He was right; she needed to be rational. She peered out of the window into the white of the snow. There seemed to be nothing. But what was that flash of colour? *Red*. There was nothing *red* that belonged in this landscape. "Circle around again. I think there's something there."

Piotr circled and as they flew even lower, she could see a lonely figure staggering down the mountainside. "Oh, my God. I think it's her."

He circled around and dipped his wings to indicate he had seen her.

"Can you find this spot again?" she said and pencilled it onto her map with an arrow indicating the direction in which she was travelling.

"Sure. I wish we had a radio now," Piotr said.

So do I. For the first time since Piotr had taken the call, Beryl breathed out a long breath and allowed herself the glimmer of hope.

"Where's the nearest place to land?" he asked.

"According to the map, probably RAF Llandwrog. They

should have a vehicle that can drive towards the mountainside where she came down." But it wouldn't go all the way, and the terrain was inhospitable, and Odette was probably hurt. Beryl hoped that seeing the plane would give her courage and spur her on.

"Hold on, Odette. We're coming." She prayed they would get there in time.

Chapter Twenty

COLD STUNG THE HAIRS in Odette's nostrils, and she coughed. Her lip was sore where she must have bitten it. The wind whistled through metal with the same clanging sound as the rigging on the masts on the boats in Hamble. Something must be loose. She couldn't be in bed. Her eyes flew open and immediately, her teeth started to chatter. Metal had crumpled in front of her to form esoteric art works. The acrid smell of burning oil and molten metal wafted to her senses. *The starboard engine!* She twisted her head to see it blackened but steaming. The snow must have put it out when she crash-landed. She exhaled loudly. Crash-landed. It wasn't just her teeth that chattered now: her whole body quaked. Okay, she was alive, and the plane wasn't on fire. That was something to be grateful for. And although there were tell-tale clouds of smoke caught like webs in the corners of the cockpit, it was no worse than a noisy pub. "Good."

Odette tried to check her watch and screamed with the pain in her left arm. Now she was aware of it, more pain rushed in and raged through her body. She dry-heaved, and perspiration formed on her forehead as she fought not to pass out. Everything ached, but her arm burned with such an intense pain she wanted to yell.

"It's probably broken and needs support," she said, hoping that hearing a voice would calm her. But she didn't have a sling. It was so hard to focus beyond the blast of pain. Through habit, she touched her lucky scarf. That would have to do. She plucked at the cloth, but it snagged on something, and she couldn't tug it free. Sweat or blood stung her eyes, and she wiped at them before tugging at the scarf again. Exasperated, she pulled her right glove off with her teeth and forced her frozen fingers to untie the scarf. When it slipped from her neck, the biting cold seeped in beneath her flying suit. Now was not the time to die of hypothermia. She pulled the neck flaps closed as best she could to keep her precious body temperature in, but a draught set off extra tremors throughout her body that would not stop.

Protocol dictated to stay close to a downed plane. She'd never had an accident before, but at least she'd got over the lip of the mountain before she'd pancaked on the other side. The undercarriage must have clipped the ridge. But she was alive, so lucky to be alive. It must have been Simone's lucky scarf. What if she hadn't managed to get enough power to clear the top of the mountain, or if the snow hadn't put out the engine fire? It wasn't the time to think about that. She'd come back to it later, so she stuffed all that into the forgetting box.

Reluctantly, she forced her brain to consider her current predicament and the best course of action. If they set up a search party, they were sure to look in the wrong place, and she would freeze to death up in this cold, biting wind. If she could walk, it would be better to walk down to the tree line where it would be warmer and hopefully, she would find a farm. Did anyone see her go in? That would be doubtful, since the cloud was too low, and there was no one around to hear. She had to support her arm, but she couldn't get her flying suit off, so she needed to wrap the scarf on top. Why was thinking so difficult? She seemed to be standing outside her broken body, watching herself and judging her lack of logic.

After a few attempts, she still couldn't tie the scarf around her neck as one end or the other kept dropping down. A tear trickled down her cheek and stung as it reached her cut lip. "Salt and open wound don't go, Odette. Je peux le faire. Think logically." This was supposed to be her forte, being calm in a crisis. But it was tricky with the shock, cold, and pain all fighting for dominance.

She inhaled to clear her mind. *One thing at a time.* By holding one end of the scarf between her knees, she managed to fasten a loose knot in it but still struggled to get it over her head. "Come on, Odette. This is not the time to give up. Push your head through the loop. Good. Now for the painful bit." She gritted her teeth and forced her broken arm in the crude sling, trying to ignore the pain. She was now sweating and panting hard. *Bien. Breathe.*

In the fog of her mind, a checklist popped up, and she followed it. She turned off the fuel, and the switches were in the correct position. What was she doing? There was no post-flight check on a crashed plane. What was it they said, any landing you walk away from is a good one? Well, she would walk out.

She unclamped her harness, which was difficult as it had become twisted by the crumpled side panel. How was she going to leave the plane when the access hatch was crushed below her?

She carefully looked around, trying not to jostle her arm. There should be an axe at the rear, but she wouldn't be able to get to it. The fuselage was severed in two, and she could see grey clouds where there should be ceiling. The floor of the plane was sloped at forty-five degrees and just looking at it made her sweat. She would have to scramble up the fuselage to where it was broken then drop down onto the ground.

Once she left, there would be no return, so she scanned the plane for what she needed. Her tatty maps had been with her since the beginning, and she didn't want to lose them, so she grabbed them and stuffed them in her overnight bag. It was unwieldy with one hand, and she grunted with pain as she hoisted her bag onto her shoulder. She also dragged the forty pounds of parachute from below her. Bizarrely, she checked she had her chit, though the plane would never be delivered. It did its one flight but would never reach its destination. What would the investigation say? Pilot error? Could she have done anything else? She took in a deep breath and stuffed down her panic. Right now, she needed all of her functioning brain cells to take her to safety.

It took a few torturous minutes to drag herself and her parachute bag up the fuselage to the jagged edge where it had snapped in two. She shivered and it wouldn't stop. It was too cold to stay here exposed to the elements. At least it had stopped snowing.

With a grunt she pushed the parachute out of the hole onto the snow beneath, to check the impact. Good. It looked soft, which should help dampen her fall. She dangled her legs, leaning on her good arm. Shards of metal had formed a rough edge, it was like grasping a knife, but she had no option. Gritting her teeth, she slowly levered herself over the serrated metal until she was holding on with her fingertips. Her grip gave way before she was ready, and she dropped to the ground. She rolled instinctively, jolting her arm. The pain flayed a path through her body, and she had to take in a few gulps of air to push enough oxygen into her lungs. Curses left her mouth in a torrent as she tried to readjust the sling. At least the snow wasn't too deep—enough to break her fall but not so deep she wouldn't be able to walk in it.

A few minutes later, after concentrating on breathing in and out, the pain had subsided enough for her to stagger to her feet. There was no way she could carry her parachute as well as her bag. Maybe if she used it to indicate which direction she was going it would help. She tried making it point downhill, but the wind kept blowing the chute around.

"Stop wasting energy, you need all of your reserves to get out of this." After one more attempt to point it downhill, she took her first steps in the deep snow in the direction indicated. This was going to be a slog, and the tree line seemed a long way away.

Even in her flying boots, her toes were numb, but she had to put one foot in front of the other. After consulting her map, she decided to head for a track in the dip between the mountains and follow it downhill until she came across a settlement—hopefully. She lumbered towards the distant dip, and hunger made itself known. Trudging in knee-deep snow was exhausting. Perhaps she'd made the wrong decision to hike out.

Then she remembered she had a chocolate bar in her bag for emergencies. It wasn't her favourite dark Belgian chocolate, but when she broke off a piece of the Cadbury's, sweet, creamy chocolate filled her nostrils, and nothing had ever smelled so appetising. She let it melt on her tongue. Pure heaven. The first rush of sugar coated her mouth, sweet and seductive like the taste of a woman. She didn't care if it was more milk than chocolate: it was a lifesaver. A few minutes passed as she savoured the sensation until the cold seeped into her again, and the wind stirred the fallen snow, reminding her to keep moving.

Tempting though it was to scoff it all, she returned the remaining half to her bag and hauled it back onto her right shoulder. The bag seemed heavier than when she stopped, which couldn't be right, but she supposed she must be getting fatigued. Every part of her body ached as if she'd been run over by a tank.

Gingerly, she pulled back the sleeve on her broken arm and checked her watch. It had stopped. That was the final straw. There was no obvious shelter marked on her map, and she didn't know the time to calculate how long it would take. She looked back at the debris of the plane, which seemed only a few hundred yards away, despite taking so long to get to where she was. Judging by the light, it was already mid-afternoon, and she needed to find shelter out of the incessant wind before nightfall, or she would perish. What bad luck if she survived the crash and died in the mountains. She trudged on, lifting one foot then another, wondering what she'd achieved by clinging on so hard to flying.

Somewhere along the way she'd lost her raison d'etre. Who was she kidding that it was just about flying? She was gripping on to the comfort and familiarity of fear, not having to expand her boundaries and known world in the mistaken belief it would keep her safe. But she wasn't safe. She hadn't been safe since Beryl entered her life again and began to challenge her at every level, physically, emotionally, and practically. Beryl had pulled her in and melted her defences with her delight and enthusiasm. However Odette had tried to push back and deny it, she'd fallen for her, and now the last thing they'd done was argued. It pained her to her soul that they might not get to reconcile, and she might never be able to apologise. Again.

She would get through this. Odette picked up her feet again, but the dip seemed as far away as ever. Tonight would be bitterly cold, but she would walk until she dropped to get back.

Was this to be her legacy, her life? She'd given herself to flying and for what? Beryl's words came flinging back at her. *"You'll die a lonely old woman. I thought you were brave. I never took you for a coward."*

"I am a coward," she said through her tears to the wind. She wasn't even sure if the tears were because of the cutting cold or because she had reached the end. No, this couldn't be the end. She'd get through this. Perhaps if she put on her goggles, it would be easier to withstand the wind blasting in her eyes, whipping up the snow into a frozen meringue. She pulled down one side and then the other with her undamaged hand and immediately she experienced a different world. Her world of flying. She picked up her feet to wade through the snow, and the snow seemed less deep here. Somehow, the water had trickled into the non-rubberised part of her boots, and her feet weren't just wet, they were now frozen.

Damn it, she wasn't going to lose her feet to frostbite. Maybe she would die a lonely woman, but if she hurried on a pace, it wouldn't be today. She rolled the word around her head. She *was* lonely, and the last few days without Beryl had been torture. She missed her easy smile and the way she was constantly doing little jobs around the home, as though that was her way of being of service, and how she demonstrated her love for Odette. Like how Beryl had a cup of tea brewing for when she woke, or on one glorious occasion, real coffee that Joyce had managed to acquire from some source or another. Beryl was always the one to check if there was a problem. Well, there was a problem now, and how she wished Beryl was here to help her with it.

Every time Beryl entered a room, a tingle shot up Odette's spine. And their lovemaking had played on repeat in her head like a Pathé newsreel. For the first time since Simone, Odette could imagine being with someone. And why had she pushed back and pushed back when she should have been bringing her closer?

If she had to imagine the perfect scenario, she and Beryl would be out flying together all day, then they'd come home to make love and make dinner in whatever order felt good.

And damn if Beryl wasn't a natural pilot. Yet Beryl was prepared to give it all up for them to have a chance. They'd never be able to go on official dates, but they could still go to the cinema or a meal even if it had to be in the company of others. If she would have her.

The last two days had showed Odette how often she thought and dreamt about her, how much she loved her. Love. That was not a word she thought she would utter again. But it was true. And now she'd completely blown it by pushing Beryl to the limit. She felt she had lived an entire lonely life in those hours apart, a life with no meaning. Now, she was clearer than ever that Beryl gave meaning to what she did, and she needed to apologise and beg her to try again.

Joyce was right. She'd never heard Beryl raise her voice before. And Odette had deserved the anger. She'd been unkind and dishonest, as well as selfishly trying to protect herself. To protect what? So she could fly again. But it might be months before she could fly now depending on how bad her injury was. So where did that leave her? Broken, bereft, and desolate. She needed to make it down the mountain to seek out Beryl and make amends. More than that, she had to ask forgiveness and tell her how she felt.

Above the noise of the wind came the sound of an engine. Odette turned to see a plane circling low over the crash site. Her heart leapt into her throat and beat wildly as she jumped up and down, trying to attract their attention.

"Over here, over here," she called and waved with her good arm.

But it wasn't the RAF search and rescue planes. An Anson was flying really low. As it circled again, she could just make out the marking N9946 on the fuselage. Curiously, it was tipping to the right, not the left, so the pilot could check the ground. That could mean Piotr was flying it. What was it doing here? She didn't dare hope they were looking for her. Had they seen her? Now it was circling, and she could see the plane waggling both wings to show they'd seen her. Her knees buckled, and she stumbled. Beryl had come to find her. They would get into terrible trouble, but Beryl could be very persuasive when she wanted to be. As the plane left, tears streamed down her face, and she picked up her pace to chase after it. "Don't go. Don't go." But they had no radio, so they had no choice. When they arrived at an airfield, they would notify the authorities and send the RAF search team to her position. It could be hours.

The snow no longer seemed to hold her back, and she was definitely getting closer to the tree line. Maybe, just maybe, she would live through this day. It certainly looked a whole lot brighter now Beryl was looking for her. The snow was shallower, and she moved along faster. It had to be Beryl. No one else would risk getting a reprimand by flying so far out of their way.

Beryl gave her life and hope. Beryl was not hearts and flowery language; she was sensible, stable, passionate, her true north. She was her home base, around whom Odette circled and flew home to. Why had she never seen it before? Never admitted it to herself or to Beryl. Now was the time to put the fear in the forgetting place and stride towards her future. Resolve quickened her pace and as the weak sun slowly dropped towards the horizon, she plodded with purpose.

Later, she didn't know how long, she thought she heard the sound of a vehicle in the distance. A tractor, maybe? She shifted her direction slightly to head towards the sound, hoping it wasn't reflected off a mountain or was the auditory equivalent of a mirage. She kept her eyes trained on the horizon wishing it, willing it, to be so. Then a vertical shape emerged, clear against the outline of the hill. She laughed aloud and waved. "I'm here! I'm here!"

Where before, every step had been an act of will, a fight over exhaustion and pain, now she seemed to glide across the ground. The tractor made its way slowly over the terrain, and as it got closer, she could see it pulled a trailer with four people on the back, clinging to the upright boarding. And then it stopped, like a dragon being yanked on a chain. Odette squinted. Between them was a gulley, not too wide but too deep for the tractor to traverse.

The four figures scrambled off the trailer bed. Two seemed to be collecting something, the other two approached. One was quite a bit smaller than the other. Was she dreaming this? Elation called her to whoop, although it came out more as a wail. They were coming for her. She was sure the smaller figure was Beryl, her saviour, coming to rescue her in more ways than one.

She clutched her hand to her chest to calm her racing heart, and she no longer felt the pain in her arm or the ache of cold. She wanted to laugh, and cry, and dance as her heart expanded. Odette ran, in so much as she could call it running. It probably resembled the limping gait of the Hunchback of Notre Dame as she held her broken arm in place. Then Beryl was in her arms, kissing her cheeks, her nose, her mouth. Her mind screamed at her to stop. There were witnesses. But Odette's shoulders sagged as she relaxed into the kiss. A kiss on a Welsh mountainside ankle deep in snow, the wind howling about them. A kiss of relief and joy, to reconnect, to express the raw emotion, to signify potential. She'd been merely existing, but from today, she would live life in all its glorious ups and downs.

Chapter Twenty-One

A COUGH FROM BEHIND bought Beryl back to her senses from kissing and whispering, "I'm so glad you're alive." Oh my, Piotr, the most religious person she knew, had a front row seat to that passionate kiss. She'd forgotten all about him in the joy at seeing Odette was alive.

A shudder swept through her entire body, and it wasn't the cold. How could she have been so reckless? Everything they had been so careful of, had denied themselves for years, could be exploded in an instant because she had responded with her heart not her head.

What would he say? Would he talk to the ATA to report her unbecoming behaviour? Beryl flashed a strained smile at Odette, trying to convey her sorrow if they were going to get into trouble. But Odette just shrugged as though it didn't matter to her. That was probably still the shock at having survived a nasty accident. She saw that Odette had fashioned a sling from Simone's scarf. "Are you okay?"

"I think I've broken my arm. And I might have a number of other scrapes and dents."

"It's good to see you. The rescuers are bringing a stretcher," Piotr said.

Odette shook her head. "I'll walk."

"It might be quicker if you accept their help," Beryl said. "Let me take your bag."

The rescuers joined them. "Hello. Odette? I'm George. Let us help you from here."

After a few scowls and grumbles, Odette sat on the stretcher.

"Lie down," George said. "We'll get you looked at faster if you let us do our job."

Odette lay down, and they ran back to the tractor and trailer. George and his buddy Alfred efficiently strapped the stretcher to the trailer, and Beryl sat with Odette on the bumpy ride back. Tears trickled from the edges of Odette's eyes, and Beryl wished she could brush them away. For someone who prided herself on never having an accident, she was probably mortified. The accident investigation would go through everything in fine detail, but Beryl was convinced anyone else would have died in the crash. If Odette hadn't cleared the ridge of the mountain, she almost certainly would have done. When they'd flown overhead, Beryl had noticed it was a sheer vertical wall on the other side.

The trailer jostled and jerked its way towards the road and Odette winced at the motion. Beryl leaned forward to whisper in her ear so the men couldn't hear, "You did brilliantly."

Odette turned to face Beryl and opened her eyes. The look of anguish made Beryl's heart ache. "We'll get you flying again in no time, if, you know, nothing is said..." Beryl flicked her eyes to Piotr who was staring down the rugged path towards the waiting ambulance, which had parked at the edge of the road. She just wanted to take Odette in her arms again and hold her and make all the pain go away.

The next few minutes brought a flurry of activity as they transferred Odette to the ambulance, and Beryl didn't have an opportunity for any further words as she handed over her overnight bag. Their gaze held as Odette was carried away on the stretcher, and Beryl was so close to mouthing the words that bubbled in her throat, but fear held her back. Fear that they wouldn't be reciprocated. Besides, Piotr was watching her intensely.

He remained silent for the transfer back to the airport. Surely he wouldn't say anything as he reported back to ATA control. She tamped down the panic rising in her throat.

In a whirlwind of organisation, George took Odette off to hospital and dropped them off at the airfield. Beryl picked up the telephone receiver and tried to call, but her hands were shaking too much.

"I'll speak to them," Piotr said and spoke into the phone.

Beryl was partially listening as he explained what happened, and he told Josephine that Odette was safe and had been taken to the local hospital to have a medical check-up and for her arm to be set. Beryl could almost hear Josephine's sigh at the other end of the line.

Feeling stronger, Beryl stood and held out her hand. "Can I talk to her?" Beryl asked, and Piotr handed over the receiver. "Josephine, I'm sorry we've put your schedule out, but the air search and rescue team were looking in the wrong place, and Odette wouldn't have survived if she'd been out all night."

Now Josephine did sigh. "I'm really glad Odette is fine, but it's not your job to subvert the system and demand that detours are made. I know it was you. Piotr would never dream of doing such a thing. Beryl, this has to be the last time, or we'll need to send you a written warning."

"Of course, I understand. Thank you, and I'm happy to cover extra shifts to make up for it."

"We'll see. It's too late to fly out this evening. Go and get yourselves a hotel and a meal, and maybe you can bring Odette back to Hamble with you. I'll see if we can borrow another air taxi for tomorrow. You might need to pick up some other pilots en route too."

"That's not a problem at all. Sorry again for putting out your schedule. Goodbye." Beryl put down the receiver and bit her lip. "I don't think they're going to reprimand us." She hoped that was true. She caught Piotr's gaze, but he just stared at her, causing her cheeks to heat up. She may be too hasty. "About that, anyway. Shall we go and find a hotel? I'll treat you to a meal. Then we can check on Odette at the hospital."

"Okay."

His face was stony, but she had to believe that she could bring him around. Beryl grinned and squeezed his fingers. "Do you think George will give us a lift into town?" She rushed out to check they hadn't left already.

Not only did George give them a lift into town, but he also arranged hotel rooms for them. He then drove them to the hospital so they could wait for Odette after she'd been seen by a doctor.

It needed two emergency phone calls to the ATA admin offices to get authorisation for payment, but then like magic, the hospital couldn't do enough. As they waited for Odette, Beryl gazed around her and put her hand over her nose to reduce the stench of harsh disinfectant assaulting her senses.

The whole hospital looked tired, not unlike the patients. A child with a fever and fractious siblings, whose mother seemed too exhausted to keep them under control, took up one end of the room. There was an old man coughing, and a young man who looked as though he'd come straight from a farm who appeared to have damaged his leg. They seemed to have been there a while, so Beryl and Piotr settled themselves on uncomfortable metal chairs to wait.

George, who had been an absolute godsend, came back from his telephone call. "Okay. I've phoned the hotel. They'll keep some sandwiches back if you're going to be late." He glanced around at the waiting room and flushed. "With the war and everything, the hospital is understaffed, and there's only the inexperienced or the very old around. I hope Odette doesn't get Dr Thomas. He was born in the last century, and he thinks people are making a lot of fuss. I wouldn't be surprised if he uses leeches." He must have seen the look of horror on Beryl's face, as he added quickly, "but I'm sure she'll get to see Dr Evans. Now she's a bright young thing and very popular with the men."

"Let's hope it's Dr Evans then." Yet another example of how

the war had provided opportunities to women who probably wouldn't otherwise be given them. Beryl flashed a glance at Piotr, but his eyes were closed, and he was muttering as he touched his rosary beads. He hadn't said a word since they had arrived in the hospital, and it was making Beryl more anxious by the minute. Was he deciding how to rat on them? Seeking absolution for their souls? Was he regretting risking being reprimanded by diverting the flight?

If Piotr said anything to the ATA authorities when they returned, their flying careers would be over.

Odette would never forgive her if that happened, nor would she forgive herself. Bile rose in her throat at the thought of not flying again, and she swallowed hard. She should have been more discreet, but she'd been so happy to see Odette she'd forgotten there were witnesses. And Odette had kissed her back.

Her fingers touched her lips, and she couldn't help a slight smile at the thought. George was still hovering. "George, you don't need to stay. I'm sure Odette will be fine from here. I can't thank you enough for everything you've all done."

"Well, if you're sure. I told the missus I'd be late, but I know she picked up some pork chops for tea this evening. I'll ask my brother-in-law to pick you up when you're done. He runs a taxi service. Here's his number." He scribbled a number in his notebook with a stub of a pencil and carefully tore off the corner. "There you go. Odette is extremely lucky or a brilliant pilot. I've never known anyone to walk away from a plane crash in the mountains before, normally they just fly straight into the face of the mountain. It must have taken extreme skill to get over the lip."

The comment was a punch in the gut. Of course they saw death all the time. Odette had almost died. A chill travelled down her spine. The realisation began to break, and it froze her to her marrow. She managed a wan smile. "She's a brilliant pilot."

Piotr shot his head up and looked around. He stood and shook George's hand. Beryl hugged George. Protocol be damned; he'd gone out of his way to help rescue Odette so quickly. "Thanks again. Go and enjoy your tea."

After George left, Beryl reclaimed her seat beside Piotr, not wanting to ask him what he planned to do, but also needing to know. In that limbo of uncertainty either possibility could still occur, and she took a couple of deep breaths to steady herself. She didn't want her flying career, or Odette's, to finish now because she had forgotten herself and where she was in the relief of seeing Odette. She needed to know Piotr's intentions and whether his religious beliefs would take precedence. With her heart in her boots, Beryl cleared her throat. "Please, can we talk about earlier?"

He canted his head and finally nodded. "Let's go to the corridor."

It was chilly, and fortunately, no other patients or staff were loitering there. The corridor was rather dreary with dark green wainscot panels at the lower part of the wall and yellow above the wainscot. To try and make it less institutional, a few sepia photographs of the surrounding area had been hung on the walls. Piotr seemed to be absorbed by one photo in particular. It was of a mountain that resembled where Odette had crashed earlier.

"She was very lucky," he said, still staring at the photo.

Beryl came to stand beside him. That he couldn't look at her didn't bode well. Gone was the easy banter they normally shared. She hoped they hadn't lost their friendship too.

"I understand why you turned me down now," he said, his voice cracking a little.

Her stomach knotted and reknotted itself. "Piotr, I'm sorry. No one was supposed to find out, ever. Please don't say anything. I know because you're very religious you won't approve, but—"

He held up his hand. "No. I don't know what to think about that. I always hoped you'd see me in that way."

Beryl shut her eyes. Had he nursed feelings for her almost

as long as she had been in love with Odette? If so, she was even more sorry for hurting him. He was a great friend and an even better soul and deserved some kindness and good fortune, but she couldn't be the one to give him that.

Perhaps he was disappointed rather than disapproving. Sorrow for him and the spark of hope for her warred within her, and she had to compose herself before continuing with the conversation. She opened her eyes to find him watching her. "I'm sorry you're hurt. I never meant to do that to you. You are my favourite pilot to fly with, and I really enjoy our time together."

Piotr hugged his arms to his chest, and Beryl was tempted to comfort him.

"But you don't want me. Are you and Odette together?"

"Kind of, yes. No…I don't know. We had a big row two days ago, and I hid away in Cosford, then I freaked out when you said she was missing. Seeing the broken aeroplane made me realise what's important. But I don't know if she wants anything to go forward. To be honest, I'm just so glad she's alive. I couldn't help myself when I saw her, I was so relieved. Please don't say anything to anyone." Her voice cracked as she spoke.

"I won't."

She flung her arms around him, and he stiffened. Eventually he sank into her embrace. "Thank you. I've been petrified you wouldn't approve and think it your duty to say something to the authorities."

He shook his head. "Beryl, you're my friend. That matters most to me. I wish it were more, but I understand. I've probably broken a dozen ATA rules today anyway, so I'm not going to be a hypocrite and tell on you for breaking another."

"Thank you. I can't tell you how relieved I am."

They were still hugging when the door opened and an elderly nurse entered from the far end, followed by Odette in an arm cast. She had a bit more colour in her cheeks, and her lips were adorned with her trademark, bright red lipstick.

She raised her manicured eyebrow on seeing Beryl hugging Piotr. "Is there something you want to tell me?"

Yes. I want to tell you I love you, but I can't. I don't know how you feel, and this isn't the time or place. "I was thanking Piotr for making the detour to find you, and for not worrying about the rules we've broken." It seemed the best way to indicate that he wasn't going to tell the ATA about them.

Odette gave her brilliant, full-dazzle smile. "Thank you, Piotr. You saved my life. I would probably have still been out there if you hadn't bent a few rules, and I don't think I would have survived the night." Her smile faltered as the truth probably hit home.

He nodded. "You saved yourself first by flying over the ridge of the mountain."

The nurse perked up at that. "Are you all pilots then? My Jimmy's in the RAF, abroad somewhere."

Piotr turned away to hide his disfigured face. A mother didn't need to see how her son could end up. Beryl squeezed his hand and addressed the nurse. "Well, let's hope this war's over soon, and he can come home safely."

"Amen to that. Thank you for what you're doing. You're all so brave. You should have everything you need, Miss de Lavigne. I hope you'll be able to go back to France soon. And don't forget to take your painkillers."

Odette made a little bow. "Thank you."

The nurse handed Odette's bag to Beryl. "I've tucked your scarf in there."

"Thanks. That's my lucky scarf."

Beryl stroked it and was surprised how soft it was. It must be silk. "It is. That's how I saw you."

Odette looked surprised. "You didn't see the parachute then?"

"No."

They made their way to a pay phone at the entrance of the hospital, to call George's brother-in-law. Beryl should be elated, and she was, but a little niggle played in her mind. The nurse talked about Odette returning to France. Is that what Odette really wanted when the war was over? Would she leave Beryl behind? She wasn't having that. She'd follow her to the ends of the earth if she had to. And she'd make it a little easier by learning French.

When they finally made it to the hotel, they were greeted by the landlady, Mrs Jones. She was probably only in her forties, but she wore her life experiences in the lines on her face, the stoop of her shoulders, and the furrows between her eyes.

"Supper's finished, but I can rustle up some spam and lettuce sandwiches and homemade cake."

For three hungry souls, it was a feast, and Beryl smiled broadly. "Yes, please, that's very kind of you. We're famished."

The three of them sat in the rather dreary empty lounge to wait for their sandwiches. Beryl was grateful there were no other guests in there, and they could relax and talk freely. Except they didn't. Instead, they sat in silence, a clock ticking on the mantelpiece the only sound. Exhaustion and the turmoil of the day hung heavy, and Odette's head nodded a couple of times as she fought off sleep and the sulfa drugs. Beryl so wanted to touch and comfort her, to hold her in her arms and smooth the pain and trauma away, but she couldn't.

Mrs Jones entered with the food. "I'll just stoke up the fire for you."

She'd probably been trying to save coal and had let it die down, but Beryl was grateful for the extra warmth. When Mrs Jones left them, they ate hungrily. Beryl hadn't eaten since breakfast.

"This is a bit different from last night," Odette said. "I was given peaches and coffee at the RAF station I bunked down in.

That was delicious, but I'm enjoying this so much more, because I wasn't sure I would be eating tonight. Or ever again. Thank you for bending all the rules to search for me, for finding me, for rescuing me." Her voice caught on the last sentence as though the realisation of what could have happened had finally engulfed her.

Piotr stopped with his half-eaten sandwich to his mouth. "It was Beryl. She's very insistent."

"He normally calls me bossy," Beryl said, because if she didn't joke, she would cry with both relief and fear at what might have happened. Even so, her tears bubbled close to the surface.

He grinned. "That's because you are."

Odette put her plate with her half-finished sandwich to the side and leaned forward. "Thank you. I can't tell you what it means to me."

It was all too much, and tears slid down Beryl's cheeks. She sniffed and roughly wiped her eyes with the back of her hand. Piotr squeezed her shoulder, and Odette grabbed Beryl's hand with her good one.

"Don't mind me. It's silly. You're safe, and you're okay. Or you will be. How embarrassing," Beryl said through her tears.

"It's not silly or embarrassing. You care," Odette said, stroking the back of her hand.

I do more than care. Both Piotr and Odette were holding her, comforting her, and she felt loved. Perhaps for the first time ever she was loved by someone, two someones outside her family, and it warmed her soul, but she couldn't say it, as her tears might not stop. She cleared her throat. "Come on, our sandwiches will be getting cold."

Piotr frowned. "I'll never understand the British humour."

Odette smiled. "It's strange, isn't it?"

She didn't want the two non-Brits to gang up against her, even though it was all in good humour. "You both understand it very well. Now, eat. I'm sure poor Mrs Jones wants to wash up the plates and go to bed."

She hid her smile at the sleeping arrangements. A thrill went through her. There had only been a couple of rooms left. Piotr had taken the tiny attic room like the gentleman he was, which meant Odette and Beryl would have to share. She'd already decided she would sleep on the floor so Odette could get some rest.

Piotr indicated at Beryl and addressed Odette. "You see what I mean? Bossy."

Odette smiled. "I see."

Piotr stood to poke the fire, and it crackled into life.

Mrs Jones entered again, nursing a bottle in her hands. "Good Welsh coal, see. Soon warms up the place."

Beryl smiled, hoping her face wasn't a mess from the tears she'd shed. "Yes, thank you. We're very grateful."

"I know you're not allowed to say what happened, but George said there was a plane crash up in the mountains today, so I thought you might want something stronger than tea." She took the tea towel down from her shoulder and wiped the dust from the bottle. "It was my Fred's, but he won't be drinking it anymore. He died in France before Dunkirk."

They gave their condolences. The war had touched everyone's lives. Those who had losses mostly hid their grief and kept going in memory of their loved ones and to provide a future for their children.

"Ah, I'm sure he would've liked it to be enjoyed by people from all over the world doing their bit for our freedom."

"That's very kind," Piotr said. "Do you want to join us?"

Mrs Jones extracted three crystal tumblers from the sideboard and gave them a quick polish with the tea towel. "No, thanks. I'm not really a drinker. If you don't mind, I'll go to bed. Just leave the tumblers and bottle on the sideboard. And make sure you put the guard in front of the fire before you retire. Goodnight."

They wished her goodnight, and she left.

Piotr examined the bottle and sniffed it after taking off the top. "This is a nice whisky. Would you like a glass?"

"Just a drop for me," Beryl said. She was exhausted after the day they'd had, and alcohol would probably send her to sleep.

"I shouldn't, given that I'm taking pain killers, but I need to celebrate that I'm alive," Odette said and indicated a tiny amount between her forefinger and thumb.

Piotr poured them all a small tot then raised his glass. "To Odette, for flying the impossible."

Odette raised her glass. "To life and great friends."

They toasted again and drained their glasses. *Friends.* Is that all she was to Odette, even after that kiss? The warm fire and the alcohol dulled Beryl's senses. "We ought to go to bed. We've got an early start in the morning."

"You go up. I might just have another small glass." Piotr went to the sideboard and fixed himself another drink.

Odette approached and kissed his cheek. "I know you underplayed it but thank you for rescuing me. Goodnight."

Beryl mirrored Odette's sentiments and whispered into Piotr's ear, "Thank you for everything. I owe you."

Piotr grinned. "Big time. I haven't decided your penalty yet. But I will." He raised the bottle in salute. "Goodnight."

Beryl followed Odette as she shuffled upstairs, not sure if it was the exhaustion, pain, or drink that was causing her to stumble. "If you use the bathroom first, do you want me to help you get undressed?"

"Please."

Odette's voice was hardly more than a whisper, at the very edge of sleep. Perhaps alcohol and pain killers were not a good combination.

"Use the WC first, then I'll help you get undressed."

"Not sexy," Odette slurred.

As if Beryl cared. Placing a hand on her back, she opened the bathroom door and tried to guide Odette in. "Okay. Do you need a hand in the bathroom, or can you manage?"

Odette shook her head. "I'll be fine."

"Don't lock the door in case I need to come in."

Odette shrugged, and Beryl was unsure whether that was assent or dismissal. Sometimes she could be infuriating with her pride, her need to be in control and not appear weak. Odette was anything but weak. A tendril of guilt crept over Beryl... When she'd said that Odette was cowardly, it must have really cut deep. "I'm sorry I called you a coward," she whispered. Odette raised her good arm as she stepped into the cold, tiled bathroom, indicating what? She'd heard her, or she'd accepted the apology? They needed to have a proper talk but now wasn't the right time. Beryl's sense of timing was terrible, and she never seemed to learn.

Beryl pulled the door to and stood guard in case anyone else wanted to use the bathroom. She heard the chain being pulled. A few seconds later, Odette asked, "Beryl? Can you help?"

Beryl knocked and entered. Odette was struggling to pull up her uniform trousers. Her flying suit pooled around her ankles. She couldn't look Beryl in the eye. Odette had never been so vulnerable-or trusting. "Here. Let me help. Do you want me to run a bath if the water's hot?"

"I'd like to, but I have to keep the cast dry, and I'm not sure how I'll get in or out. I'm sure you'll help, but I don't really want you to see all the bruises."

A few bruises couldn't mar Odette's beauty. "How about I run the water, and you just see if you can put your feet in. I'll try not to look, but I'll be here."

"I'm not at my best. I feel broken—"

Beryl turned on the taps and mercifully, hot water poured into the bath. "No, your arm is broken. You've probably got bruises, but you're miraculously okay because of your brilliant piloting skills." How could she convince Odette that she didn't care? And she was just so grateful Odette was even alive. "Let me just help take off your uniform." This shouldn't be sexy, but despite everything, Beryl felt the heat between her thighs as she unknotted Odette's tie and carefully slipped off her pale blue shirt.

"It's broken in two places," Odette said as if she was discussing the weather.

Though she probably spent more attention to the weather given it dictated how and when they flew. But she wouldn't be flying for a while. The same thought may have just occurred to her, as Odette took in a sharp breath and blinked hard.

"Are you okay? I'm not hurting you, am I?"

Odette shook her head but didn't speak. Beryl flicked her gaze away from Odette's shiny eyes and onto her lacy bra. Of course Odette would have on a sexy bra, and Beryl was so tempted to trace the delicate lace over the swell of her breasts and the nipples that had risen to peaks. *Stop it.*

Odette leaned forward and said huskily, "You're turning me on, Beryl, by your eyes undressing me as well as your fingers, but I can't do anything about it. Yet." She smiled sheepishly.

"Good. You're turning me on too. It's very hard to not caress you. I want to make love to you."

Odette shook her head. "I'm too bruised and sore, and I want to enjoy it when we do. Besides, I shall be asleep in a few minutes. You need to be quicker, or you'll be dragging me to bed."

"Sorry." Beryl carefully undressed her and couldn't help but notice the savage blue bruise blooming on her legs and side. Years of living on rations had taken away the fullness of her curves, but she was still beautiful.

Odette gripped Beryl's shoulder and lowered her feet into the shallow bathwater. She winced and pulled her foot up before returning it.

"Fortunately, they said I don't have frostbite, but it's still painful to put my feet in the bath. They've been so numb, and now they're all tingly." She squatted down and slowly lowered herself into the water, still holding onto Beryl for dear life.

Beryl removed her uniform jacket and rolled up her shirt sleeves, then picked up the face flannel Mrs Jones had provided with the towel. "Shall I wash you down?"

"Please."

She gently washed her face and neck and tried not to stare at Odette's nipples hardening.

Odette leaned backward and held her cast arm in the air. "Now you can do more than my back." She smiled at the memory. "That seems like such a long time ago."

"It is a long time ago."

Their eyes met, and Beryl juddered to a halt in stroking the flannel over Odette's chest. The softness in her eyes and her wide, dark pupils showed that Odette was as affected as Beryl was. "But we need to get you sorted before you fall asleep."

Odette grinned. "I don't seem that sleepy anymore."

Beryl grazed the flannel over Odette's nipples. "I noticed."

Odette pulled at Beryl's tie and pulled her closer. "You're trouble. If you continue to taunt me, I will have to take you in hand."

Beryl attempted an eyebrow raise but didn't achieve the arch look she was going for. Odette laughed and pulled Beryl closer so their lips almost met. Suddenly she withdrew, dropping her good arm to touch her lip tenderly.

"I forgot I cut my lip."

"I'm so sorry. I'll behave." And she did, but her heart pounded, and her eyes feasted on Odette's body, giving her images that she would store to delight her in her darkened room alone. Somehow, seeing Odette's bruised and vulnerable body made Beryl love her more. And she did love her. The truth was as clear and pure as the whisky they'd drunk and just as intoxicating.

"I'd better do the rest of me," Odette said and swiped the flannel from Beryl's hands.

She paid particular attention between her legs and chuckled softly at Beryl's reaction. Beryl wasn't about to complain because her throat had become dry.

"I'll get your nightie," she said to give herself a distraction. "Will you be okay for a moment?"

"I'll manage."

"Please don't drown." Beryl ran from the room and rummaged through Odette's overnight bag. She hurried back with the silky garment. The material was soft under her fingers. How typical of Odette to have beautiful clothes, so different from her own cotton pyjamas. When she knocked on the door and peeped inside, Odette's eyes were closed. "Don't go to sleep yet. Maybe it's time for you to come out before you get cold."

"I'm not asleep," Odette said and then immediately yawned.

"Come on." Beryl grabbed the towel and placed it on the raffia chair beside the bath. She leaned forward to wrap her arm under Odette's shoulders.

"You'll get wet," Odette said.

Ignoring the fact her body was already wet, she continued to get a hold. "It doesn't matter. Come on. That's it."

Odette rose and wobbled, and they reversed the procedure from before so that Beryl could wrap her in the towel. Very gently, she dried Odette and slipped the nightie over her head and one arm. The material bunched up above the cast, but there was little she could do about it.

She also put a dab of toothpaste on Odette's brush and handed it to her. "If you do your teeth, I'll just get ready so I can have a bath too. Mrs Jones has given us a hot water bottle, so I've put it in the bed, but if you need it for any part of your body, please take it. I'll bring all your clothes through."

"Thanks." Odette meekly took the toothbrush but was clearly struggling to stay awake.

Beryl returned to the bathroom a few minutes later to help Odette back to their room. Odette leaned against her heavily and collapsed onto the bed. Beryl picked up Odette's hairbrush, but Odette held out her hand to take it.

Odette shuffled back on the bed so she could see herself in the long mirror on the wardrobe door and started to drag her brush through her hair. "I can brush my hair if you want to have a bath while it's still warm." She looked up at Beryl. "And please share the bed, even if I've fallen asleep by the time you get out."

Odette probably wouldn't last more than a few minutes before passing out, but she seemed to need to brush her hair to show she wasn't completely helpless. Beryl nodded. It wasn't hard to agree to something she wanted so badly anyway.

By the time Beryl returned from the bathroom, having washed herself and cleaned the bath after her, Odette was sprawled back on the bed. Her legs were still on the floor, and she still had the hairbrush in her hand. Beryl gently extricated the brush and manoeuvred Odette into bed as best she could, careful to leave her cast outside the blankets so it didn't get caught up. She kissed her lightly on her forehead then climbed in the other side.

In the gloom, Beryl stared at Odette's profile as she slept soundly. They were still as uncertain as they had been before. The kiss had given her hope, but as the evening had worn on, the doubts crept back in. Odette had referred to her as a friend. She tried unsuccessfully to squash her disappointment, instead letting the relief of Odette being okay and breathing beside her wash over her. It would be so hard if they never made love again or couldn't be open, but Beryl would bear it if she could be close to her. Odette had suggested there could be more, and that would warm her for now.

Beryl gently pushed back a strand of hair that had fallen over Odette's face and inhaled the scent of lavender from the soap. She feathered the lightest of kisses on Odette's temple before laying back on the pillow to observe her. Their breathing matched, but sleep wouldn't come. She wanted to watch over Odette, protect her and keep her safe. She wasn't just falling in love with Odette. She had well and truly plunged into love, was swimming in the depths, and there was no way up.

Chapter Twenty-Two

THE FOLLOWING MORNING, JOSEPHINE gave Piotr instructions to drop off Beryl at Ringway and bring Odette back to Hamble.

Beryl picked up the ancient Fairey Swordfish biplane that could have come from the Great War as it was all string, metal, and open cockpit. At least she would have a direct flight to the Royal Naval Air Station at Worthy Down, near the South Coast. As she pulled her goggles over her eyes, she wondered if Josephine was punishing her for mucking up yesterday's schedule. This would be a slow, cold, and arduous flight, with no break for refuelling. Beryl rolled her shoulders. If that was what she had to do for the rest of her ATA career, she wouldn't complain. It was a small price to pay for persuading Piotr to divert the Anson to search for Odette. She was safe and would be back home this evening, when hopefully they would have a conversation about what they wanted and where they were going.

As she flew along, taking the less frequented eastern route around Birmingham, where the weather was better, the turn markers were clearly visible ahead. That gave her thinking time.

The strength of her fear when she thought Piotr was going to shop them had surprised her. So much for her not minding. Her heart seemed to have ceased beating, and the consequences of her lack of thought had washed over her. Odette was right. They did need to be careful. Neither of them wanted to stop flying now. That would come soon enough when the ATA was disbanded. The war was moving on apace, and it seemed only a question of time. For most people it couldn't come fast enough, but Beryl wanted to continue flying as long as possible. Even if she set up her own business, she would never fly as much as she did now and get paid for it. The ATA was the perfect job.

She understood now what Odette had been trying to explain. That didn't mean she loved Odette less, because she did love her. She yearned for her, wanted to come home to her every night as she did now, to talk about their days and prepare food together, then go to bed together. She longed to be able to wrap herself around Odette while she cooked at the stove, to grasp her hand and entwine their fingers when they went for a walk in the evening, to sit behind her and fly together. In some ways, she had the perfect life already, and she didn't want it to stop. The domesticity and companionship were wonderful, but she wanted so much more, needed so much more. And with every passing week, it was becoming more difficult to maintain her self-discipline. Yesterday, it had broken when her relief and joy had overwhelmed her.

She checked her time and bearing and then had to double-check her location. The Swordfish was almost one-third of the speed of a Spitfire, and with the constant noise and buffeting, it was probably twice as tiring. But it was undoubtedly flying at its most basic, and she never wanted to be where she couldn't fly, like Odette must be feeling now.

The spectre of Odette returning to France had never occurred to her before the nurse mentioned it last night. Beryl shivered at the thought. She paused her musings to double-check where she was going and reset her watch, noting the time above her turn point on her map in pencil. Her map was so tattered now, it was being held together at the back by yellowing sellotape, but she didn't want another one.

She had naïvely assumed Odette would stay in England after the war, but of course she'd want to go back. Everybody was changed because of the war, and Odette would probably long to return. What she would give to be able to fly over with her and see Paris. Beryl yearned to go abroad, and although the ATA were now doing delivery flights to northern Europe, they were reserved for the men, because it was supposedly too dangerous for the women if they came down in enemy territory. In other words, the boys arranged it so they had all the fun.

Every woman pilot knew their flying time was limited. Some had asked to transfer to train for their commercial pilot's licence. Odette had already applied, but because of her new injury she probably wouldn't get to do it—for now, anyway. Her fears looped back to whether Odette would return to France, and however the knot in her stomach tightened at the thought, she needed clarification. Tonight, they would have a conversation that would determine both their futures. She was more uncomfortable about that prospect than facing a crosswind landing in the Swordfish.

Later, back at the cottage after supper, Maisie said, "I need to get out to the pub. Who's coming?"

Joyce snapped her book shut, eager for something else to do. "I'll come."

Odette shook her head. "I'm feeling fatigued. I think I'll have an early night."

Maisie looked up. "Aye, that's fair enough. How about you Beryl? Are you coming for a wee dram?"

Beryl picked up the plates, pretending to be nonchalant. "Not tonight. I need to write some letters to my parents; I haven't been around for the past few nights. Leave the dishes. I'll wash them."

"Do you mind? You are a darling. Thank you." Joyce blew Beryl a kiss and rushed upstairs, followed by Maisie, and within minutes, they came downstairs again, and the outside door clicked shut behind them.

As easy as that, they had finessed themselves some time to speak. Beryl took the kettle from the range. "Tea?"

Odette stood and put her hand out for the kettle. "I'll make it. I feel useless."

Odette stood close while Beryl turned on the tap for her. She needed to build up to have the conversation about them. *Now who was being cowardly?* This conversation could make her soar or stumble.

Beryl picked up the dirty dishes then plunged them into the hot water. "How was your day?" She mentally kicked herself for being so banal.

Odette stood behind her, and she could feel her breath on the back of her neck. "I can't sit here for six weeks before they take my cast off. I'll go crazy. I said I'd walk up to the airfield and help Josephine with the despatch and organisation. I'll give you all the interesting planes."

She grazed her lips over the back of Beryl's neck, causing a shiver all down her spine. Beryl half turned, and Odette placed soft kisses below her ear, across her temples and down her nose. Beryl extracted her hands from the hot water and turned fully to return the kiss.

Odette moved her broken arm out of the way and placed a gentle kiss on Beryl's lips. "I've been thinking of this all day."

Beryl's heart hammered in her chest. "You have? Me too."

Odette licked Beryl's bottom lip, requesting entrance, and their tongues met with a passion that did more talking than a hundred words. Any doubts Beryl had were eradicated by the kiss. It lasted only a few minutes but hinted at more to come.

Odette pulled back, and Beryl couldn't help but smile when she saw Odette's lipstick was smudged. But her lips were swollen and perfect.

"Joyce told me you received your second broad stripe today. I'm so proud of you, First Officer Jenkinson."

Beryl affected indifference but was delighted she was now signed off on all the planes the ATA flew. She hadn't mentioned it, because she didn't want to rub salt in Odette's wounds, but she couldn't keep the grin off her face at the prospect of flying in the mammoth four-engine Lancaster bombers. "I don't mind what I fly."

Odette turned away to pour out the tea using the Spitfire

tea strainer Beryl had bought her for Christmas. "It's properly stewed now."

"You mean brewed," Beryl said.

Odette shook her head at Beryl's teasing. "Well, hurry up, then we can go upstairs, and I'll show you how proud I am of you, and what I feel for you."

Oh. Had she just said that? Beryl rapidly finished the rest of the washing up before Odette stopped talking. They needed to talk but if Odette was promising what she seemed to be, a conversation could wait. A fluttering started in her belly that she needed to quell. She took another tea towel from the drawer and hurriedly picked up a stack of plates to dry them. "What if Maisie and Joyce come back?"

"They'll be gone ages. Besides, they need to finish their education."

Beryl paused wiping the plate as she stared at Odette. "What do you mean?"

"What we have, what I'd like to have, with you is not illegal, just against the ATA regulations. At this stage, I don't care. The war may be finished before I fly again anyway. We're all going to be demobbed soon. A few, too few, women will find flying jobs elsewhere, but it'll be similar to before the war, a woman pilot will be a novelty not the norm. If you still want it of course." She shrugged.

Beryl put away the last of the plates and hung up the tea towel to dry by the range. "But I need Maisie after the war, if my idea comes about. I don't want to talk about it yet, but I'd love you to be involved if you want."

Odette laughed as she placed the cups and saucers on a tray. "We seem to have reversed roles. It was always me who was scared before."

The fluttering churned faster. "You're right. Getting Maisie is the icing on the cake, not the cake itself."

"What are you talking about? Will you carry this tray upstairs to my room, please."

Beryl mock-saluted and picked up the tray. "Yes, ma'am." With each step to Odette's room, Beryl's heart picked up pace, and her chest heaved in shallow breaths. They had been together before, but this felt more open, more committed. As she followed Odette to her room, she pushed aside her doubts and fears for the future. The more immediate concerns about whether Odette would still find her attractive peeped in unbidden. She inhaled sharply and laid the tray down on the dressing table.

Odette's room was bigger than hers and overlooked the river, now empty of the landing craft that had moored from bank to bank before the invasion of Europe the previous year. Apart from the admiralty boats cruising up and down occasionally and the barbed wire prohibiting access, it could easily be a river during peace time. "I'm feeling a bit anxious."

Odette sat on the bed and patted beside her. "No need to be nervous. We'll only do what you feel comfortable with. Come and drink your tea first."

Beryl handed Odette her tea in an enamel mug to make it easier to drink than with a cup and saucer. She sat beside her and tried to stop her own saucer clattering, advertising that her hands were trembling.

"Let's just talk for now," Odette said. "This has to be mutual. What do you want from this? Where do you want it to go?"

Discomfort clogged Beryl's throat so she couldn't speak. The words she wanted to say, that she'd practised, just wouldn't push past. She took a sip of tea to steady her nerves. "Are you going back to France when the war is over?" she asked, not able to keep the hurt and confusion from her voice.

Odette held her gaze, searching Beryl's expression, sifting through what was behind the question. Beryl could have kicked herself for being so needy, just an unsophisticated hanger-on.

Odette put down her mug and stilled Beryl's hand. "I want to see France again," she said carefully. "But my previous life doesn't exist anymore. I want to explore what our future will be. If you'll have me, with my broken arm and limited prospects."

Beryl heard the words but couldn't believe the sentiment behind them. After all this time, Odette was saying she really did want her. "Are you sure it's not your near miss talking? You talked to the nurse about going back to France?" She was just digging herself in further, but she didn't seem to be able to stop. She had loved Odette for so long and had always been rejected; she couldn't trust this apparent change of heart.

Odette responded with a raised eyebrow. "What if my near miss gave me some perspective about what's important? You. Us." She broke into a smile. "To answer your second question, I do want to visit France. I want us to fly our own aeroplane over Calais and Normandy to Reims so you can see where I grew up. Where we can eat some real cheese and taste proper champagne—my family's champagne, if it hasn't all been drunk." She sighed. "I doubt my family will want to see me though. Then we'll fly on to Paris Le Bourget. So, yes, I want to go back to France, but only to visit with you, to show you, so you understand."

She cupped Beryl's cheek, which burned at the touch. "Thank you," Beryl whispered. "And I'd love to explore our future too, but you've always been so against it before."

"Not against it. I was scared. I'm *still* scared, but my near miss showed me flying is no longer my most important passion. I can live without flying—" She raised her broken arm in its cast. "And will have to live without flying for a while at least, but I can't live without you. I tried so hard not to be weak, not to give in to temptation with you, but I'm drawn to you, and I've loved living with you for the last few years. It's like we've been married without the physical intimacy, and now, if you want, we could explore that too."

Beryl's heart hammered hard, and Odette's chest seemed to be heaving as much as her own. She put down her half-finished tea. There were more important things to do with her hands, like tracing them all over Odette's body, but first she needed to accept the invitation in the best way she knew.

She wrapped her hands behind Odette's neck and enjoyed the sensation of her silky hair cascading over her knuckles. Odette's lips had a slight uptick to them, as though she was amused by Beryl taking control. Within a second though, the smile dropped, and her pupils dilated as her intense gaze focused on Beryl's lips. Then their lips met, colliding and opening, welcoming each other in. A thrill shimmered down her spine, and her desire unleashed as their passion increased. Their breaths came in sync, shallow and fast. She lost herself in the now, in the moment, and slipped out a groan. "May I?" she asked and indicated Odette's uniform.

Odette nodded. "Please."

Beryl unfastened the buttons slowly with her trembling fingers and slipped the jacket off Odette's shoulders. This was really going to happen. She calmed her excitement enough to unknot her tie and unbutton her blouse until she reached the last button, just above the waistline of Odette's skirt. Keeping eye contact, Odette rose, allowing Beryl to gently peel off her blouse.

Beryl swallowed at the sight of Odette's smooth skin and heaving breasts, the swell of which were visible above Odette's lacy black bra. It was such delicious torture.

"Like what you see?" Odette asked, her tone more raspy and deeper than normal.

"You're stunning," Beryl said, raising her gaze from Odette's torso to meet her eyes, "all over."

Odette smiled. "Thank you."

She was so much better at accepting compliments, probably because she had received so many more than Beryl had ever been given. Odette was even on the front of *Picture Post*, for heaven's sake. If that wasn't the very definition of being a pin-up girl, she didn't know what was. And Odette was about to go to bed with Beryl. The thought made her glow inside.

"Take those off for me, slowly," Odette said.

Rather than try and speak, as her vocal cords probably weren't functioning, Beryl unknotted her tie and unbuttoned her jacket and blouse. She folded them, then unfastened her trousers and placed them on the bedroom chair.

Her own bra and knickers were plain cotton, not sexy like Odette's, yet Odette was staring hard. "Please take those off."

Beryl obliged, hoping her face had not become pink as she was burning up with the admiration and lust.

"Nice," Odette said. "Now, please help me with mine."

"How did you manage this morning?"

Odette shrugged as though it was no big deal. "With difficulty. I had to clip it together loosely in front of me, then shimmy it around."

"I never thought. I'm sorry. Let me help dress you in future."

Odette canted her head to one side. "I'm more interested in you undressing me right now."

The words caused Beryl's body to throb. She leaned forward, basking in the heat radiating from Odette's body. Somewhere along the way, she'd fallen so deeply in love with Odette, and her head was in a whirl. Yet part of her couldn't believe Odette was actually here, willing and open. It was all her dreams come true. She unclipped Odette's lacy bra and let the straps fall. Gently, she lowered it over the cast. As the material fell away, Beryl cleared her throat at the sight of Odette's dark nipples, so different from her own. They were as she remembered, taut, inviting, and perfect. "You are beautiful," she whispered and pressed her hand between Odette's breasts, feeling goosebumps and her cantering heart below her fingertips.

"Thank you."

As Beryl mapped her hands over Odette's contours, she pushed her torso forward into Beryl's hands.

Beryl gently pulled her nipples like she did to herself in bed at night, and Odette squirmed.

"Don't you like it?" Beryl asked, wondering if she was doing something wrong.

"I love it. Let me show you." With her good hand, she pulled away one of Beryl's hands and guided it into her knickers.

Beryl moaned when her fingers contacted hot and wet swollen flesh. She stroked and circled and was thrilled with the response. Her own body mirrored Odette's in harmony.

"Undress me, please," Odette said, trying to wriggle out of her skirt and knickers.

Beryl removed her fingers and slipped down their remaining clothes until they were naked, exposed and open. There was no going back. There was no pretending this wasn't what they wanted. Her fingers trembled.

"Come back onto the bed."

Odette pulled her with her good hand onto the squeaky bedsprings and laid back. Her hair was tousled, and the other hair at the top of her thighs glistened with desire. She held up her broken arm so that Beryl could settle on top of her. They rested breast-to-breast, belly-to-belly, with Beryl's thigh between Odette's, coated with the evidence of her desire.

Slowly, Beryl rocked forward and back, spreading the sweet smell of sex all over her legs and responding to Odette's rhythm.

"Go inside."

Wanting to please and also needing to extend this as long as possible, Beryl slipped her hand between their bodies and traced her finger through Odette's swollen folds. Gently, she pushed inside, and Odette responded with a moan so long and sensuous, Beryl's arousal spiked.

How wonderful to be inside Odette, connected in this most intimate way. It was almost too much. She slipped another finger in to join the first. She had dreamed of this moment, this union, but the reality was so much more arousing, with the scents and little moans of delight Odette made almost sending her off. And Odette was so well-lubricated, her fingers glided in easily, and she quickly settled into a rhythm, slow and slightly tentative.

"Harder. Faster. That's it."

When Beryl circled her nub with her thumb in between thrusts, Odette spoke through gritted teeth, "I'm almost—yes, yes."

Then she emitted a cry so loud and primal, it almost brought Beryl over the edge too. Odette shuddered and collapsed below her. Her muscles tightened around Beryl's fingers, stilling her hand.

Beryl removed her fingers and brought them to her nose to sniff the intoxicating smell of sex. Odette smiled, caught her hand, and sucked one finger at a time, which caused her body to throb all over again. Beryl had never seen anything so sexy in her life, and the image seared itself on her brain, no doubt to make an appearance every time she imagined Odette in bed.

Looking like the cat that got the cream, satisfied and coquettish, Odette whispered, "Thank you."

"Wow, oh no, thank you. How wonderful to see you, feel you, smell you, to be with you. It's everything I wished for and more." Words tumbled out of her and cascaded in a flood of elation. To see Odette flushed and laying back with such a look of ecstasy was worth all the waiting, all the anxiety, and the stress of having to be hidden. And unless she kept her mouth tightly shut, she might say something that couldn't be returned.

Odette stretched. "Mm. Give me a minute and then we'll change sides."

"How will you manage with your arm?"

Odette's eyes sparkled. "Roll onto your back."

Beryl complied and stared as Odette shuffled around, holding her injured arm to the side. She nipped and kissed her way down Beryl's body, causing a fluttering sensation that radiated from the point of contact to her outermost nerve endings.

Odette looked up, her pupils wide with desire, and it was so arousing to have this beautiful woman between her legs, Beryl thought she might explode.

"Are you okay with this?"

"Oh, yes, please."

Odette kissed the sensitive skin beneath Beryl's belly button, and she burned in anticipation. Odette shuffled down further and huffed hot breath between Beryl's legs, causing her to clench and spread her thighs wide to welcome her in. This was so much more erotic than she had ever imagined and when Odette licked her there, she moaned in pleasure.

Gradually and torturously slowly, Odette played her tongue between Beryl's folds. Beryl rose from the bed, desperately seeking further contact, more intensity—just more.

Beryl bucked and tensed as Odette set up a fast rhythm with her mouth, supercharging her cells and refuelling her desire, pushing her higher, like climbing in a Spitfire, up, up, into the clouds to roll out in a glorious, tumbling thrill ride.

"Come for me, Beryl," Odette whispered, the words vibrating against her flesh.

Odette's voice, her actions, and the years of pent-up desire brought Beryl to a quick, leg-shaking, toe-curling, mind-expanding release. Odette slumped over Beryl's torso, probably exhausted from her exertion.

Beryl giggled. She couldn't help it, even if it wasn't sophisticated. The joy bubbled up within her and had to escape. "That was wonderful. You are wonderful. Wow." Language escaped her, and she shuffled down the bed to meet Odette halfway. When they kissed, she tasted the strange, salty tang of herself on Odette's tongue.

Odette smiled and caught Beryl's gaze. "It's wonderful you're so open and passionate. I had a feeling you would be." She brushed a damp strand of hair from Beryl's glowing face and kissed her temple. "I'd love you to stay here all night so we could fall sleep in each other's arms, but Maisie and Joyce will probably be back soon."

Beryl groaned and kissed Odette again. "Okay. I hope we'll

do this again." She couldn't have just had her whole life split apart and upended, and then go back as if nothing happened. *Everything* had changed.

"We will. Soon, I promise. Now I need to use the bathroom. Will you help me with my nightie?"

"Of course."

Although her brain still wasn't functioning properly, Beryl managed to put on her trousers and shirt and help Odette with her nightie. She gathered up the rest of her clothes to leave and they emerged onto the landing.

Seeing Odette, with mussed hair and the glow of sex, Beryl couldn't resist snatching a quick kiss goodnight, which turned into a longer kiss. It was a kiss of promise, a kiss to remember, a kiss to seal their future.

Chapter Twenty-Three

"WHAT THE HELL ARE you doing?" Joyce's clipped tones made them spring apart in a second. "I came up here to ask if you wanted anything and to tell you my news, and I find this. It's disgusting. I won't have this going on under my roof. I've always suspected about Beryl, but you, Odette? I can't find words."

All the air was expelled from Odette's lungs. She placed a hand on her chest, willing her heart not to beat so fast. How many of her friends had faced this? But rather than an irate English woman, they had been ripped out of bed by men with guns and bundled off to those awful, awful camps they showed on the news.

Beside her, she felt Beryl stiffen, winding up in her fury. Odette took a sharp breath and was about to speak when Beryl jumped in, shaking with rage.

"Your roof. How typical of the upper classes to be nice until it suits them then what, throw us out? What a hypocrite."

Odette placed her hand on Beryl's arm to stop her, but Beryl tossed it off, hardly pausing to take breath as she glared at Joyce. "How many mistresses does your father have? I counted two at your wedding, and I don't follow all that crap in the papers, so there are probably more. And you know how it is to love someone who your parents disapprove of. Your mother was tight-lipped throughout your wedding, yet you still went ahead. So Tommy's a group captain now and therefore more acceptable, but he was just a pilot when you first met him. And how could you turn on Odette who saved your life? Have you forgotten the day we met when you flew in on a snowstorm? Are you saying you would have landed the plane without her? She talked you down. This isn't how you repay a friend."

Joyce took a step back in the face of such anger, but Beryl was coiling tightly before striking.

"Fine, level your contempt at me, and you're right, it's me who is so clearly the sapphist here. I've been in love with Odette since I first met her, so yes, take out your ire and judgement on me, but not on Odette. If you're going to inform the ATA, just report me. But don't do that to Odette. She's lost everything once already, and she's nothing else apart from the ATA."

Beryl's voice faltered. Pride at Beryl and panic warred in Odette's mind, and her admiration for Beryl increased. Her anger was very impressive, more so because she was normally so placid and serene. And she'd just admitted that she loved Odette. Despite the situation, a tingle shot through Odette's body, warming her all over. Beryl loved her. Not the most romantic of declarations, but it was clearly heartfelt. Both she and Joyce just stared at Beryl.

Maisie clattered up the stairs, and her face appeared at the landing with a frown furrowing her eyebrows. "What's all this argy-bargy? They'll hear you on the other side of the channel."

Joyce was still sparking anger, her face red and scowling. "I came up here to find them kissing, and I don't mean like friends."

Maisie's eyes went as wide as tea plates, but before she could speak, Odette said, "Perhaps we should all go downstairs and discuss this rationally like adults. Beryl, could you take the tray down when you've dropped off your stuff?"

"She's not going in your bedroom. I'll get the tray." Joyce pushed past them to get to the door, and she flapped at the air as if she could eradicate the taint of illicit sex.

Maisie, who'd made no comment at all simply asked, "Do you want a robe, Odette? You'll get cold in just your nightie."

Odette shivered, and her teeth began to chatter, although it was the shock as much as the cold. She nodded in thanks, still unable to arrange her thoughts into a sentence. Beryl had been powerful and articulate, but Beryl shouldn't have to protect Odette. For some reason, Odette couldn't get her brain to engage.

As she followed Maisie downstairs, her mind flip-flopped between fear and honesty. If this was the end of her ATA career, so be it. More important was to stand by Beryl, who attempted to protect them both. She shouldn't face Joyce's wrath alone.

Maisie filled the kettle and set it on the range as Odette and Beryl sat on one side of the kitchen table with Joyce on the other, her mouth a grim line.

"I don't want you in my house anymore."

"Tea?" Maisie asked, clearly trying to smooth the troubled waters, not that it made any difference to Joyce, who sat stony-faced.

"Why, because you don't approve?" Beryl asked, her face going red. "When did we need to seek approval for what we do as consenting adults?"

"It's immoral. A sin. What will people think?" Joyce asked.

Maisie turned from her place by the stove. "Who cares what people think? All these stupid rules help no one. If they want to fuck like rabbits, let them. God, I wish I could've had more time with Rob, and I wouldn't have told him we had to wait until we were married." She stretched up to bring down the crockery which rattled as she placed it on the table. "I wish that I'd said yes, and I was carrying his baby, then I'd have a piece of him. Instead, I'm going through life as a zombie." She caught and held Joyce's gaze. "Don't be hypocritical, Joyce; that's not you. You had sex with Tommy and had a pregnancy scare before you were even married. If they're happy and in love, let them be. There's enough misery and hatred without you adding to it."

They all stared at her as she swilled out the tea pot, rotating it briskly three times. She banged the pot on the table, gripped it in both hands and glared at Joyce. "If you breathe a word about it to the authorities, I promise I'll never speak to you again. It would be particularly cruel, given your news." She turned away from them to add the tea leaves and poured in the hot water.

All three of them gawped at Maisie, who was usually so affable and calm. *What a revelation.* Odette turned her head to see how Joyce would react. Her mouth was a hard, lemon-sucking line.

She jerked up from the table and crossed to the refrigerator to retrieve the milk. As she closed the door, she rested her head against the cool surface and seemed to be struggling to control her breathing.

"Thank you, Maisie. That means a lot to me, to us," Odette said after a few moments of awkward silence. She glanced at Beryl, who nodded assent.

"Aye. You're welcome. I guess that's why Beryl followed you down to Hamble. It wasn't just the Spitfires, was it?"

Beryl grinned and shook her head.

"Well, I think I've seen everything now," Maisie said and poured the tea, which was way too weak because she hadn't let it brew. "Are you going to bring that milk over, Joyce, and come and sit with your friends?"

Joyce didn't move, so Odette rose and extricated the bottle from Joyce's tight grip. She poured out the milk directly from the bottle, expecting an admonishment from Joyce because she hadn't used a jug, but no rebuke came.

Maisie pushed a cup and saucer towards the empty space at the table. "Come and sit down."

Joyce perched herself at the edge of the seat. "It's such a shock. I don't know how you can be so calm." She stared at Maisie and deliberately avoided catching Odette's gaze.

Maisie shrugged. "It's none of my business. You three have been the only thing that's kept me going since Rob died. When this war is over, everything will have changed. If Nye Bevan is right, the previous order will crumble, and the old rules may not apply. But I do know we'll all need the comfort, connection, and support of our friends, of those we love. If they're happy, I'm happy for them. Don't deny them that."

Joyce raised and lowered her shoulders and placed her palms down on the table. She cast her gaze from Maisie to Odette and back again as if she was struggling to decide whose side she was on. Finally, she nodded. "Okay."

Odette raised her cup to Joyce to acknowledge the shift.

"I didn't know you had a pregnancy scare," Beryl said, clearly not prepared to let it lie.

Joyce breathed out a deep sigh, then gave a sheepish grin. "That's not something you need to worry about though, is it?"

Beryl grinned back. "Not last time I looked."

"So are we all going to kiss and make up then, only no tongues please," Maisie said. Everyone laughed, and the tension eased. "Are you going to tell them your news, Joyce?"

Joyce took a sip of tea which gave herself time to readjust. "Tommy is going to be in charge of an airfield in England, and I'm leaving the ATA to join him in married quarters, so we can have a life together."

Odette rose to give Joyce a hug. "That's great news."

"Thank you. I'm sorry I had a go at you. Please feel free to stay in the cottage."

"Thanks. Do you know what the married quarters are going to be like?" Beryl asked.

Joyce gave a wry smile. "I've a horrible feeling it may be a converted Nissen hut, but we'll make do."

Maisie raised her teacup. "To new beginnings."

They clinked their cups as if they were champagne flutes and took a drink of the insipid tea. Beryl screwed up her nose. "Bloody hell, Maisie. You're coming off tea duty."

Maisie smiled. "Then my plan worked. Did you hear the rumour that the ATA are actually allowing women to fly across to Europe soon?"

Joyce and Beryl made matching sets of round eyes and

mouths, and they probably mirrored Odette's own.

Maisie laughed. "I see that caught your attention. Yes, it would appear they still need aircraft deliveries, and the men can't do it all."

Odette placed her cup back in the saucer with more force than was sensible for Joyce's fine porcelain china. "It's typical, only accepting us when they have no choice. Look at all the commercial airlines that are lining up to sign up the ex-RAF men when they are demobbed. The women won't get a look in."

"I have an idea about that," Beryl said. "But tell us what we need to do so we can make delivery flights to Europe."

"Well, you have to be based at White Waltham. Hamble will probably close in a few months anyway except as a diversion airfield, so maybe we should all apply to be transferred."

Odette snorted. Not her most elegant noise, but she didn't want to admit she was feeling left behind and jealous that they were all moving ahead. And she didn't want to lose Beryl having just sealed their future together. "How will they accept me with a busted arm?"

Maisie smiled. "I'm sure you can help with the logistics, and maybe even sign off anybody who needs it."

"But they won't be doing training now." Odette sounded petulant, but Beryl was bouncing up and down at the prospect.

"Surely they'll need your language skills too?"

She doubted that. "Let's see." Odette raised her teacup again. "Maybe we should toast to happy endings. Thank you all for being such wonderful company over the last few years. Let's celebrate in London when it's all over."

"Ooh, yes," Joyce said.

Odette stretched out to take Beryl's hand, but catching Joyce's stare, patted her arm instead. "You should see if you can transfer. This is the opportunity of a lifetime. All I request is you bring back some cheese for me."

Beryl placed her hand over Odette's. "I'd bring you back the world if I could."

As they shared a knowing smile, for the first time in a very long time Odette caught Beryl's enthusiasm and hope. Rather than bringing back the world, after the war they could take a plane and fly to different parts of the world, together.

Chapter Twenty-Four

8 May, 1945. VE day

HER SINGING VOICE WASN'T the best, but what Beryl lacked in talent, she made up for in gusto as she sang *The White Cliffs of Dover* as she flew the ancient Anson back across the channel.

If she never flew again, she would be happy. Flying towards England now, with the sunlight glinting off the iconic white cliffs, was a memory to keep her warm in her old age. For six years, just fifteen minutes of flight time had stood between subjugation and freedom, and it all seemed so precarious and fortunate. Yet, here they were, now Hitler was dead, knowing victory in Europe was any day now, and she was one of the lucky few to fly her dreams.

From beside her, the pure contralto of Odette joined in. Of course she would have a wonderful singing voice. Beryl took her hand off the half wheel control column and gently threaded her fingers with Odette's, so she didn't harm her healing arm. "I've never heard you sing before."

"I've never *felt* like singing before. I'm not interested in singing jingoistic songs about the British Empire. But flying along with you, I want to sing. This is perfect, even if we didn't fly to France."

The short trip to Brussels, delivering supplies and bringing back a rather tired Anson to be repaired, was the highlight of Beryl's flying career, because she and Odette flew together. Odette had flown out and Beryl was flying the return leg. "I plan to do this more in the future."

"Fly Ansons?"

"If that's what I can get my hands on. But I meant flying with you." Beryl swallowed, her mouth suddenly dry. "After the war, I mean. I'm trying to get enough savings to scrape together for a couple of planes so we can provide trips to France and Belgium and joy rides. I'll have to get my dad to put his name on the lease agreement, but he's already said that he's happy to do that."

"You're setting up your own business?"

"Yes." Beryl extricated her hand to adjust the throttle, trim the plane, and double-check the heading. Although it was a glorious day, a heat haze was settling along the coast, but she was spot on with her dead reckoning. She loved the thrill of flying to plan, especially because navigation had always been what she struggled with the most. "I'm going to schedule regular flights to France and offer joy rides for people on the south coast. Part of the condition of getting my dad to guarantee the loan was that I have to have an engineering arm for planes and cars too. I reckon the cars will make the money that will subsidise the planes." Now was the time to ask, and her neck felt surprisingly clammy. "If you're not going back to France, I'd love you to join me as one of the pilots. And more...on a personal side too." How indirect could she be? It was unusual for her to flounder over speaking. She inhaled sharply. "I would love you to stay in England and to be with me, and this seems like a good way to make a living and keep you here. You say you want to visit France, or are you having second thoughts and plan to move back there?" Beryl swung around to check Odette's response, but she was staring out of the side window.

Slowly, she turned her head and met Beryl's gaze. "You saw the state of the country back there. There's nothing to go back for. My family disowned me, my friends are gone, and the north of France is like a Swiss cheese. Paris may be intact, but it isn't the same. You aren't there." Odette cleared her throat.

Beryl held her breath waiting for the "but." Of course she could stay in Britain without being with Beryl. Had she completely misread the signs?

Odette smiled, and her eyes gleamed. "I love that you don't let the constant no hold you back. You adapt and find another way to move forward, as though life is an engineering puzzle to solve. I love that you want to include me in your thinking, and you work towards it. You never let bigotry hold you back. You're so much braver than I am, and resilient. I love you, Beryl."

Beryl's hand flew to her mouth and the skin all over her body tingled. This day couldn't be any more perfect.

Odette nodded towards the windscreen. "But you need to check your heading as we're about to go back over the coast again."

Beryl jumped and scanned the horizon. Odette was right; in her daze, she'd drifted to port. She adjusted course to head for the next waypoint and noted the new bearing. The thrill of those three words sent a shiver down her spine, and her pulse quickened. Her heart seemed to expand like a balloon as though Odette's love was physically filling her, making her big enough to take on anything the world had to throw at her. She allowed the words to seep in.

She'd known she loved Odette for so long, it defined every breath she took and coloured every thought. But now she had to speak it aloud, her tongue was thick and sluggish. "I love you too. I always have. From the moment I saw the figure in the field mending their Tiger Moth was a woman, I knew I wanted to be with you."

Odette raised an eyebrow. "I thought you wanted to be me?"

"No. I wanted to fly like you. To have the freedom you had. To have the freedom we have now. It will be hard work with a business, but I'd love that we'd be doing it together."

"I know." Odette nodded to the windscreen. "I want to kiss you now, but you're drifting again."

Beryl's delighted laughter burst from her, and she readjusted her heading towards the waypoint once more. This was too much to take in. Her dreams were coming true. What could be more perfect? "My head's not in it. I'm floating in clouds. I can't believe that you love me."

"Believe it. Now you need to concentrate on flying us home, otherwise we'll be lost in La Manche forever."

Beryl stared at the ground and realised she'd drifted to port again. She was so grateful to have this perfect moment, loving and flying, sitting beside the woman she had loved for so long, knowing it was reciprocated and sharing her passion of flying. Laughter burst from her in unrestrained joy. It didn't matter that the Anson had an oil temperature that ran hot and was to be repaired or retired when she delivered it to a maintenance unit. They'd only seen the airfield in Brussels, but she didn't care. It was wonderful to see all the signs in different languages and to be addressed in heavily accented English. The Belgians also had a roaring trade in chocolate, and at Maisie's recommendation, Beryl had purchased cocoa, which the locals struggled to get there. A little trade helped to make the extra journey time worthwhile.

The unmistakeable ripe smell of a soft cheese wafted through from Beryl's bag, and she anticipated the look on Odette's face when she presented it to her. As the flight had progressed, the heat in the cockpit must have warmed the cheese, and despite it being tightly wrapped had released its secret one breath at a time.

Odette suddenly sniffed. "What is that smell?"

Beryl grinned. "You mean the smell of oil and fuel?"

"No, I don't mean that. Beryl Jenkinson, what are you up to? You've got the look of a Cheshire cat."

"Look in my overnight bag. There's a present for you."

Odette drew the bag toward her and put it onto her lap. Beryl rechecked her instruments and heading then watched as Odette pulled out the round package wrapped in wax paper and string. She brought it to her nose and inhaled deeply, her eyes closed as she savoured the scent.

"Oh my God, it's a real cheese."

"Camembert from Normandy. I asked Piotr to get it for me and leave it at the airfield when he was passing through. The Belgian controller gave me a very strange look when he handed it over, as it smells a little ripe." It had cost her six packs of cocoa, the contraband of choice, but it was worth every ounce to see the joy on Odette's face.

"You got me real cheese," Odette said, like she couldn't believe it. Tears rolled down her cheeks.

Hopefully they were tears of joy, but Beryl was too far away in her seat to brush them away.

"Thank you, thank you, thank you. What a wonderful gift. We'll have to share it with the others. They'll love to try it again. I haven't had it in years, since long before the war."

"I've never had it before," Beryl said, once again feeling the difference in her experiences from the rest of her erstwhile cottage mates. Would the class differences return with peace, along with the misogyny? Maybe, but she would face it all with Odette by her side.

Before long, they were making their final approach to land, and Odette wound down the crank handle to lower the undercarriage. There was a bit of a cross wind, but Beryl made a daisy cutter landing so smooth, the plane hardly jolted.

"Nice landing, sweetheart," Odette said.

She'd never tire of hearing that. "Thanks." Beryl taxied off the live runway and applied the brakes at the far end of the taxiway. She uncoupled her harness and jumped onto Odette's lap, straddling her, then smothered her with kisses.

"What are you doing?" Odette asked.

Odette placed her hands on Beryl's thighs and even through her trousers, the touch was enough to send her body tingling. "There's no one around up here," she said. "I need to connect with you, to kiss and revel in you. I've been distracted all flight and if I had my wish, I would take you now and show you how much I love you, physically and emotionally."

Odette circled her fingers, trailing fire at her touch.

"Mm, that sounds perfect."

The radio crackling caused them both to jump.

"November three-a five-a. Do you have a problem?"

Odette rolled her eyes. "Damn, I forgot about the radio."

"It was so much quieter before we started flying to Europe and got radios," Beryl said and reluctantly scrambled back to her seat to press the call button. "Just checking the undercarriage."

Odette laughed, and Beryl hoped she had released the call button quick enough so the controller couldn't hear. "So, Mademoiselle de Lavigne, are you ready to face the world? Shall we taxi back?"

"Affirm. But I would like to finish checking your undercarriage later."

"You can oil my undercarriage anytime."

Odette groaned and Beryl laughed. She settled herself back in the seat and taxied back to the control room to check in.

When they reported to the operations room, Josephine, who had also joined them from Hamble, came up and hugged them both. "Have you heard? War in Europe is over. Winston Churchill just made a radio broadcast saying a ceasefire has been in place since yesterday and all hostilities have ended. Those who are free are going to meet in London to join the celebrations. If you've done, you can go off now."

They jumped up and down in a strange three-way embrace and laughed and wiped away a few stray tears, then stepped back.

"Wow! I'll never forget today," Beryl said and smiled at Odette, the beautiful woman who actually *loved* her. She who was smiling at Beryl with such depth and intensity. Odette would understand she was referring to more than just the end of war in Europe. Beryl almost reached out to her but stopped just in time. They had company, and she needed to behave. For the moment, they still had a job, and she had to save as much as possible to put into the business. *Her* business.

Beryl and Odette left Josephine and made their way down the long dark corridor to their changing area. The room was empty.

Odette swung open her locker and leaned against the metal door. When she raised her head, her eyes were glassy and she visibly swallowed. "I never thought I'd live through the war—I almost didn't—and I definitely never believed I could be as happy as I am now with you."

Beryl paused and caught her gaze, and their smiles broke through the tempest of the past, drying the tears. This was one of those moments Beryl knew she would treasure forever: standing on the threshold of a new life, with the love of her life, poised and precarious, but worth every risk. "Are you sure about this, about the business? We'll have to work hard, and I can't promise a large salary. I'm not wealthy like the others."

"I don't care. You are you. Glorious, practical, passionate you, and I love you."

Beryl choked with the emotion. No one had ever told her that before. The landscape of her understanding shifted as her perspective changed. She felt it in her bones, and her heart expanded in cascading joy spreading throughout her whole body. *Odette loves me. She really loves me.* "I love you too."

Odette stroked Beryl's cheek and smiled. It was a hint of more to come, a promise.

"We need to make arrangements with the others."

Odette broke the spell, bringing Beryl back into the present. Today was a multi-celebration: the war in Europe was finally over, and Odette had told her she loved her. Every nerve in her body tingled in excitement. Now they had the rest of their lives together to create something special, something lasting.

Chapter Twenty-Five

BERYL HAD RARELY BEEN to London but had never seen it so packed. Crowds jostled and sang, waving flags and swaying glasses in time to the music. The surging and pressing of the throng of people caused her heart to swell and a lump formed in her throat. People, mostly in uniform, clung to each other and cheered. Odette grasped Beryl's hand and pulled her along to their meeting place, upstairs in a pub where Maisie said they had a room reserved.

Joyce was there with Tommy and some of his flying buddies. "Come and sit here. I've news," Joyce said to Odette after they kissed.

She patted the chair, and Odette put her hand out for Beryl to sit too. Joyce smiled, and Beryl was glad the old differences had been forgotten. They'd hardly exchanged a word since Beryl and Odette had moved to White Waltham, and Joyce had left to join Tommy in a decommissioned Nissen hut. She couldn't imagine Joyce being a housewife rather than a debutante. Would the class differences re-emerge now the war was over? Surely they couldn't go back to how they were before? She had to believe that people coming together from all walks of life, as had been shown in the war, would continue into peace. "Anyone for a drink?" she asked everyone. Although the men usually bought the drinks, Beryl wanted to prove to herself that things would be different now.

"Get what you want from the bar. Tommy is taking care of the tab. I'll just have a tonic, thanks," Joyce said.

Beryl and Odette both stared at her. Joyce always had alcohol if there was a drink going.

Odette's eyes widened. "Is that your news? How far gone are you?"

Joyce nodded, a shy smile on her face. "About twelve weeks, so I'm hoping the sickness will stop soon."

Odette kissed her again, and they both gave her congratulations. Beryl made her way to the bar, and the men parted to let her through. As she waited for her drinks to be poured, Piotr and Maisie entered. They waved and joined her at the bar. Beryl and Maisie kissed hello. Maisie's eyes shone for the first time since Rob died. "What will you have? Tommy is paying."

Piotr made to shake Beryl's hand, but she enveloped him in a hug. She wouldn't allow him to go back to his formal self, not after he had rescued Odette and been so understanding about Odette and her.

"That could cost a pretty penny with this lot." He motioned towards Odette and Joyce. "I'll give Beryl a hand if you want to join the others."

After Maisie had crossed the room to shrieks and welcomes, Piotr tugged on Beryl's arm. "Beryl, if I asked Maisie, would she go on a date with me?"

Beryl grinned. Perhaps that explained the gleam in Maisie's eye. "I didn't even know you knew Maisie that well. She seems to have moved on from losing Rob. But maybe that's because she's been spending time with you."

"We've only met a few times, but she's been flying with me in the Anson delivering oranges to Europe. And we've been talking a lot."

"What have you got to lose by asking? Nothing. Go for it. I'd love to see two of my best friends together."

"You would? You don't mind?"

Beryl hugged him. "Not at all. I want to see you happy."

"Thank you, Beryl. You look very happy too," he said and winked.

She grinned. Nothing would stop her joy from brimming over tonight. "I am."

They collected the glasses and carefully made their way back to the others.

"Your gin-less tonic." Beryl presented Joyce her drink. "Congratulations again."

Joyce leaned in so the others wouldn't hear. "Thank you, Beryl. We haven't always seen eye to eye, but you're a good soul. Odette has just been talking about you; it's clear she's besotted with you. Please look after her."

Beryl's heart skipped a beat, and she couldn't resist catching Odette's eye. "I will. I promise."

Piotr placed the other drinks in front of Maisie and sat beside her, facing Odette and Beryl.

Joyce raised her glass. "To us. To victory. It's so nice to have everyone together again."

"Not everyone," Maisie whispered. "I'd like to raise a toast to those who fell, for their losses, for the unlived years, unfulfilled promise, and dreams. To the fallen."

"To the fallen," they said, and sadness rushed in, displacing Beryl's joy. Everybody had someone close who wasn't returning.

"And I'd also like to propose a toast for all of us who've been affected by the war and have lost eyes and broken limbs in the fight for freedom. For sacrifices." Maisie raised her glass to Piotr and Odette. Today was a day for toasts and speeches, the pinnacle of everything they worked for. It was a day for reflections and taking tally of all they had given and all they had lost and their hopes for new beginnings.

Beryl wanted to hold on to this moment, to capture it and hold it tight in her memories. Her long days of flying were numbered. Even when she had her own business, if all went to plan, she would not have such carefree flying as she'd had today with Odette. Although maybe they could occasionally slip out of work and fly together to France and bring back more cheese and wine.

Tommy had arranged with the pub they could bring in their own food, and she was delighted and astounded when Odette had brought in her treasured cheese to share. Beryl took another slice of cheese and placed it on a cracker. At first, the smell had put her off and she'd been reluctant to try a slice. But the eager anticipation in Odette's eyes would have persuaded her to try anything. Once she tasted it though, the rich claggy taste cloyed around her tongue. It was like no cheese she had ever tasted, and it offset her bitter shandy to a T.

"I'm glad the taste is growing on you. It's a taste I want us to experience a lot when we fly to France."

Odette's whisper and her hot breath left a trail of desire down Beryl's body.

Tommy came over to their table. "Anyone fancy dancing? Are you up for a quick twirl, my dear?" he asked Joyce. "If you need partners, I'm sure I can ask some of the chaps."

Odette shook her head. "We'd love to Tommy, but Beryl and I promised we'd meet up with Mike in another part of town. If we want to get through the crowds, we'll probably need to head off now."

A thrill skimmed down her spine. That was news to Beryl, but she wasn't going to protest. If Odette really meant she was going to take her back to their B&B and make love to her, or even to spend more time alone with her, she wasn't going to complain.

She grinned at her friends. "Piotr, maybe you and Maisie could dance together. You might need to guide him a little though, Maisie."

Maisie flushed. "That's no problem. I enjoy being the boss."

"I noticed. You'll have to watch out for her, Piotr. She'll take over and you won't know what hit you."

"Cheeky! I guess I'll see you at work then. Have a good night."

Maisie's smile indicated she'd been waiting for a chance to dance with Piotr but hadn't wished to snub the two spinsters. Given that Maisie seemed to know everything, she probably had a better idea of where Odette was taking her than Beryl did. Odette had been very secretive.

After they said their goodbyes, Odette led Beryl through the crowds, holding on to her so she didn't get lost. They were jostled from behind, and it was quite a relief when Odette took her down a dank alleyway.

"It's a bit creepy down here. Aren't you going to tell me where we're going?"

Odette turned and smiled. Her whole demeanour was lighter and freer than Beryl had ever seen her. She skipped down the cobbles, tugging Beryl along and finally stopped outside an unmarked door. Now she was curious. Odette hadn't dropped her hand when they escaped from the crowds, and Beryl had no intention of complaining.

Odette knocked on the door and an eye-level slit opened, revealing a stern pair of eyes. Odette muttered a password like she was a spy. The slit closed, and the sound of bolts being drawn came through the wood. Beryl looked around as they entered. A woman staggered towards them dressed in stockings and a garter with tiny tassels covering her nipples. "Welcome, stud," she said in a broad London accent.

Beryl snapped her mouth shut and swallowed. Her pulse rushed in her ears, whether from fear or anticipation she couldn't say. Where were they?

The woman looked Odette up and down. "You two together then?"

Odette nodded and laced her fingers tighter through Beryl's. "Yes."

The woman tilted her head. "Pity. You make a nice couple though."

"Thanks."

"Is it okay to hold hands?" Beryl whispered. Her eyes were becoming accustomed to the gloom of the windowless bar, and she looked around, absorbing what was different. There were a number of women in suits as well as women in dresses. There were people in uniform dancing. Two men together. Two women kissing. She was a kid in a sweet store, and she had to swallow to wait for her mind to catch up with what surrounded her. "Is this what I think it is?"

A thrill shot through her. That there was a place that existed just for this, for others to come together with no lies, no pretence, no judgements was a revelation. What a joy to have somewhere, just for them, where they could relax and be themselves and have a good time. But best of all was the affirmation that she and Odette weren't the only ones.

Odette smiled and pulled her through to the bar area. "If you're thinking it's a place for people like us, then, yes. Come on. Let's go and find someone."

"Who?"

"The person who told me about this place."

As they threaded their way through the couples and groups, someone stroked Beryl's buttocks. She flicked them off, and they just laughed. She stayed closer to Odette, who was forging her way forward, homing in on the clinking of bottles and glasses and higher hubbub of noise. Surely talking about Mike had just been a ruse on Odette's part to escape from their friends? He wouldn't be here, would he? The last she'd heard, he had been flying in Europe again.

She saw Mike at the bar in his RAF uniform.

"Mike? What are you doing here?"

He leaned over to give Beryl a peck on the cheek. "I could ask you the same. Hello, Odette, you found it okay?"

"Very clear instructions, and no problems at the door, thank you."

So it was true that Mike was like them too. She almost laughed. How ironic that she'd been so worried he would be upset if she had turned him down. Mike moved aside, and another man stepped into view in an airman's uniform.

"This is Terry. Terry, these are friends of mine, Odette and Beryl. They live together and work from White Waltham."

The way he introduced them implied they were married, a couple, and she laughed. What it would be, to be accepted for who they were. The dancing, the singing, the smooching. It was all so normal and thrilling all at once. "When did you find out about this?" she asked.

"Last week when you were away." Odette winked. "I contacted Mike to see how he was, and he said there was a place we might be interested in. I wanted it to be a surprise."

"Wow. It is. I can't believe it."

"I know. It reminds me of Paris before the war. It gives me hope for a better future where we can be who we are. Where there is real liberty, equality, and fraternity."

Odette kissed Beryl in full view of everyone, and she loved it.

"Je t'aime," Odette whispered.

Beryl had never heard anything so romantic in all her life.

If this was their future of liberty, equality, and so much more than fraternity, she would rush headlong into it with a joyful heart.

Epilogue

Three years later

ODETTE LEANED ACROSS THE pristine tablecloth as Mike whispered, "Which cutlery do I use now? I thought I understood all the etiquette from years of eating in the Officers' Mess." She picked up the outside knife and fork. "They're trying to confuse us with all the wedding courses."

Beryl, who sat on the other side of Mike at their large round table, was still gawping at the surroundings. A genuine Scottish castle was impressive and reminded Odette of her youth in a crumbling chateau. The dark and gloomy hall Maisie always complained about had been brightened up with white tablecloths. The polished silver cutlery and centrepieces reflected the torch candles, fracturing into pinpricks of light.

Terry, Odette's official date for this evening, checked to see what she was doing and followed suit. "Is this right?"

She shrugged. "What do I know? I'm French."

Bea, a nice young woman with the bright blue eyes, smiled. "I'm sure Maisie and Piotr won't mind. This is a wonderful league of nations amongst the attendees, and everyone has their own distinct cultural etiquette."

There was something about the way she observed the interaction between the four of them that put Odette on alert. Had she worked out they were lavender couples? Bea tilted her head to the side. She didn't seem uncomfortable at all, quite the opposite. And Bea's date for the wedding, Eddie, and Eddie's friend Joseph seemed to be very absorbed with one another.

Way too absorbed. *Ah.* Maisie had put all the lavender couples on one table. Odette smiled at Bea, who returned the gesture.

"How do you all know each other?" Bea asked, her eyes shining as she looked around the table.

They were quite an unusual bunch, Odette supposed, and she smiled. "We're all pilots. Terry and Mike flew with the RAF, Beryl and I with the ATA during the war."

Bea seemed to take everything in. She had worked out who they were. "Ah, yes, the war. That great disruptor of normal life. And what are you doing now? You don't strike me as the domestic type."

What did she mean by that? Odette narrowed her eyes a little, but she seemed to be genuinely interested, rather than judgemental. "Beryl has an aeronautical and automotive engineering and flying business. I fly for her, taking lessons and trial flights. While she's here, she's got a meeting arranged with Maisie's father who's giving her a loan to buy another plane." She didn't know why she was rambling on, but she trusted Bea for some reason; she had the air of someone who was friendly but secretive. Someone like them.

"He must be forward thinking if he's giving a loan to a woman," Bea said.

"I'm sure it wouldn't have been offered if she wasn't big friends with Maisie, but he can see it's a successful business, and the new plane will let her tap into the growing wish for people to travel to the south of France."

"You must be very proud of her," Bea said.

Before Odette could stop herself, she nodded. In her enthusiasm, she had inadvertently confirmed what they were to each other. Odette blinked and inhaled sharply. She was usually more careful, but she felt sure of this woman. They were okay; there were no consequences even if they were exposed. The people who mattered already knew.

Bea smiled and patted her hand, presumably to reassure her

that her secret was safe. Bea raised her glass, and they shared an acknowledgement of who they were.

A fork rattled against a glass with a ting, cutting through the chatter like a disturbed flock of swallows. Relieved she hadn't revealed any more, Odette focused on the speeches. Piotr had been practising his with Beryl's help. As he rose, an expression of sadness flashed over his face. She knew it was hard for him that his family were unable to leave Poland as it was now under the Soviet regime. Then he caught Maisie's eye and his whole face brightened with a smile, radiating love.

"Thank you all for coming to our wedding. We're sorry my mother and sisters can't leave Poland at the moment, but they've written to say they look forward to the day when they can meet Maisie's—I mean Mairead's—family and welcome her to ours."

As he went through his speech, he didn't glance at his notes, which was very impressive. A hundred flaming candles and torches seemed to cast more shadows than light, so perhaps it was fortunate that he'd learned the words. Piotr had once said he missed the brightness afforded by two working eyes and hated the half-darkness. But his life was filled with light now.

Odette had already heard the speech a few times, so she watched Beryl surreptitiously, who was mouthing the words along with Piotr. She bit her lip to hold back the emotions that suddenly flooded her. If only she and Beryl could do this. They could never have their friends stand up and acknowledge them, and there would never be an outward recognition of who they were to each other. They would always be "just friends," with no lasting sign of commitment or security. There was no external acknowledgement for them, just a raised glass and clandestine nods. Her throat narrowed, and her lungs felt too tight, so she clutched her hand to her chest. It was okay to cry at weddings. Even a few stiff upper lips had wobbled earlier.

Beryl caught Odette's gaze and winked. It was so typical of Beryl to be unimpressed by the pomp and circumstance and know what was important, what mattered. She loved Beryl with an intensity that enabled her to bear the trap of silence and censure. And she would bear it, though there was no formal arrangement, no marriage contract they could sign that would say to the world what they were and who they were to each other.

Beryl looked stunning in her bright red dress and new Katherine Hepburn-like hairstyle with rolls at the back and pinned back fringe. Odette was eagerly anticipating retreating to the security of their hotel room, where she could take out the hair pins and slowly unzip Beryl's dress until she stood in her underwear, proud and glorious. Even though they'd had to amalgamate their coupons to get the dress, it was worth it. Beryl had wanted to wear her old ATA uniform, saying it looked more professional, but Odette knew Maisie's father would be more charmed by a glamorous woman.

She hoped they would take some photos at the signing. For a woman to be given a loan was a big deal, and Bea was right, Odette was proud of her. It was wonderful to see Beryl now, and although she had little to do with Beryl's success, she was honoured to have witnessed the transformation from naïve young woman to successful and confident businesswoman. But at her core, she was an enthusiastic pilot who had flown off with Odette's heart. Beryl was frowning at her slightly. Ah, she'd been staring. She grinned sheepishly, put down her napkin, and tuned back to the proceedings.

After the speeches, as people made their way to the long hall for dancing, Mr Stewart approached their table.

"Beryl, do you want to sign that agreement now? Do come along."

"Thank you, sir. Odette, will you join us?"

He nodded and strode to the door. Maybe Beryl needed a witness.

Beryl placed a hand on her arm. "No, wait. I need to tell you something."

She loved it when Beryl whispered to her, although normally she preferred the sweet nothings as a forerunner to being physical.

"I've changed the name of the company from Jenkinson and Daughter to Jenkinson and de Lavigne. Dad agreed to it before you ask."

Odette stopped, and her hand flew to her mouth. She couldn't have heard that right.

Beryl tugged at her arm, pulling her along so they didn't fall behind Mr Stewart.

"What? But why?"

"Because I can't stand up and declare my love to you publicly, as we've just witnessed, and I can't sign write it in the sky, like I'd prefer. But I want to give you something that will bind us together as closely as any marriage contract. Besides, you've earned it." An expression of panic flashed across Beryl's face. "Unless you don't want it?"

Her heart fluttered, and Odette laid her hand over Beryl's. "Of course I do. Merci. You don't know how much that means to me. I love you, and I'm completely honoured to be your business partner as well as your life partner. Thank you, but we'd better go."

They hurried to follow Mr Stewart before he disappeared behind an oak door. He paused and turned and seemed surprised they weren't right behind him.

Beryl smiled with her easy charm. "I'm not used to high heels," she said and hurried forward with a clacking sound on the stone floor.

Odette had the delightful view of her seamed stockings and red heels. Beryl looked positively edible. She would ask her to keep those on later, for a short while, anyway.

"Aye, sorry, lassie. I'm used to a man's stride. All the paperwork is in here. I've asked Corrie to witness our signatures."

He stood behind his desk, where papers were laid out in

triplicate on the green leather top. It all seemed so formal, and the butterflies in Odette's stomach took flight. This was a commitment for life. This was essentially a statement of their love, and Beryl's business acumen had made it possible so that Odette could travel regularly to France. She had carved out an opportunity where there was none, and now they would fly together.

"Corrie, these are the directors of the company. I'll sign first then ask Beryl and Odette to sign."

"Of course, sir."

Mr Stewart sat to scribe his name. He pulled out an expensive-looking pen and rolled it in his hands like a cigar before uncapping it. His signature was tight and neat.

He stood and indicated that Beryl should take his seat. "Sign where indicated by the pencil crosses."

"I will." Beryl scrawled her name in her small precise handwriting.

When she was done and Corrie had blotted the ink, Odette swapped places and settled herself in the captain's chair. Fleetingly, she wondered what her family would think of her now, whether they would be pleased to hear that, despite their predictions, she had made something of herself, and she had found happiness.

When she saw the name of the company typewritten above Beryl's signature, her heart filled with joy.

"Do you also agree to ensure timely payment of the loan repayments?" Mr Stewart asked.

"I do."

With words that echoed Piotr and Maisie's, they sealed their fate together.

Later that night, Odette exited the suite she officially shared with Terry and swapped with Mike in the corridor.

"Goodnight," he said and grinned. "Don't do anything I wouldn't do!"

"I will." She entered the adjoining room and breathed out in relief.

Candles flickered around the room casting a soft vibrant light. Beryl lit the last of the candles and blew out the match, still facing away from Odette.

"Come here."

Beryl's instruction came with an authority that made Odette shiver inside. How different from the shy young woman who had never seen another woman naked before. Now Beryl was comfortable in her body and thrived in her power.

Odette crossed the room and slid her arms around Beryl's waist and kissed the nape of her neck. "Did I tell you how wonderful you look today?"

Beryl half turned and smiled. "Oh, you know you did...in very low whispers, knowing what you were doing to me, and by your eyes undressing me from across the room. How I wanted you to take me then, in the church, at the reception, on the dancefloor. You're a wicked woman."

Odette stroked the material of Beryl's dress over her belly. "Did you see how they were watching you on the dance floor, wishing they could be with you? All the time I was thinking they may look all they want but you are coming home to my bed."

"That would be you they were looking at. You've given off this movie star glamour ever since I met you."

Odette waved her hand. "That's just an image, you know that."

Beryl turned them both around to face the heavy old wardrobe. "Before we get to that, I have something else to show you," she said and opened the closet. She rummaged around behind her clothes and then handed a long parcel over to Odette wrapped in brown paper and tied with a string with a bow easy to undo.

"Open it, open it." Beryl bounced up and down and Odette laughed at her infectious happiness.

The parcel was heavy, and Odette carefully unwrapped the paper so she could use it again. Inside was a wooden plaque shaped like an aeroplane propeller and just as highly polished and smooth. She traced her hand over the blade and marvelled at the craftsmanship.

"Turn it over," Beryl said, her eyes bright.

Odette did so and gasped. On the left blade was carved *Jenkinson* and on the right blade *& de Lavigne*. That ampersand was so important, linking them together, like holding hands in public, which they could never do. In the centre on the hub, a brass rimmed aviator's clock was inlaid, with the numbers 1 to 12 on the outside and 13 to 24 on the inside. Inside the clock face, "Time flies when you're flying" was scripted in black ink.

Odette could hardly speak around the lump in her throat. She had never seen such a potent example of love. "It's beautiful. Thank you. I love it."

"It's for the office," Beryl said. "Most people will look for the clock. But I will look for the name to remind me of you, when you're off flying, and I'm stuck in the office."

"It's perfect. Hiding in plain sight. I love it. What once was a dream is now a glorious reality. Thank you. I've never been so happy in my life." She placed the propeller sign on the desk then turned around and stole first one kiss then many, each one more passionate than the last.

"I think we have some unfinished business," Beryl said and pushed Odette back onto the bed.

With a rustling of skirts and undergarments, they devoured each other and reconnected at their most fundamental level. This was what Odette prized above all else, this unfettered, infectious happiness, demonstrating their love in the physical acts, where their hearts skipped in synchronisation, until Beryl moaned in climax.

In this vulnerable moment of connection, watching Beryl lose control, she loved her more than ever. They were more than two bodies clinging to each other with wobbly legs. They were expressing their love in a way that could only be done behind closed doors in the anonymity of an expensive hotel, but all the more precious because it was so scarce, like the most cherished gemstones.

Eventually, after a few minutes to regain herself, Beryl stretched, laughed, and leaned against Odette's shoulder. "Oh dear, do you think the boys heard?"

"Who cares? We're here exploring our newfound freedom, why shouldn't we enjoy ourselves? I'm sure we're not the first people who've ever made love in a hotel room."

"Mm. Maybe I can leave the business to the managers and come with you on your French trips, then we can stay in hotels all the time."

The prospect thrilled her. They would snatch hours of pleasure where they could and in the quiet of the night, they could be who they really were, maybe with trips to France and to the club in London. And now they had a reason to be together as far as the world was concerned.

"We will."

Beryl was exposed and beautiful in her nudity, sculpted by years of hard work and rations. A surge of love rose and overwhelmed Odette. "You're beautiful from your soul outwards." She had to take in a deep breath to catch her swelling heart that seemed to expand from her chest and into her throat, causing her voice to catch. She couldn't love anyone any more.

Beryl was a revelation; confident, powerful, and secure in herself. Odette didn't need to hide behind walls anymore, she could be raw, vulnerable and she would be seen, because she was where she was meant to be. She was finally home.

"Thank you so much. When I saw what you'd done, how you must have planned it for weeks for me to join you. It's perfect. My heart's bursting with joy and pride and sheer delight. In case I haven't told you, I love you, and want to be with you until my final landing."

Beryl pulled her closer and whispered in her ear. "I love you more than the lift of wings as we break the bonds with the earth. I love you more than the kiss of the ground on a perfectly executed landing. I love you more than the freedom of being unfettered in the fluff of the clouds. I always will."

And Beryl took her with love, till she soared above the hills and valleys and floated in the brightness of radiant sunshine.

Odette reached for Beryl as she came out of her euphoric haze and entwined their fingers. How amazing that Beryl was once a shy girl enthusiastic for her first flight. Now she was a powerful businesswoman, her soul mate, and her lover. She'd given Odette love, and hope, and everything she thought she'd lost. A future, together.

THE END

I really hope you enjoyed reading Virgin Flight. If you did, I'd be very grateful for an honest review. Reviews and recommendations are crucial for any author, particularly one early in her career. Just a line or two can make a huge difference.

Thank you,

E. V. Bancroft

Other Great Butterworth Books

Fragments of the Heart by Ally McGuire
Love can be the greatest expedition of all.
Available on Amazon (ASIN)

Here You Are by Jo Fletcher
.Can they unlock their hearts to find the true happiness they both deserve?
Available on Amazon (ASIN B0CBN935ZB)

Stunted Heart by Helena Harte
A stunt rider who lives in the fast lane. An ER doctor who can't take chances. A passion that could turn their worlds upside down.
Available on Amazon (ASIN B0C78GSWBV)

Dark Haven by Brey Willows
Even vampires get tired of playing with their food...
Available on Amazon (ASIN B0C5P1HJXC)

Green for Love by E.V. Bancroft
All's fair in love and eco-war.
Available from Amazon (ASIN B0C28F7PX5)

Call of Love by Lee Haven
Separated by fear. Reunited by fate. Will they get a second chance at life and love?
Available from Amazon (ASIN B0BYC83HZD)

Where the Heart Leads by Ally McGuire
A writer. A celebrity. And a secret that could break their hearts.
Available on Amazon (ASIN B0BWFX5W9L)

Stolen Ambition by Robyn Nyx
Daughters of two worlds collide in a dangerous game of ambition and love.
Available on Amazon (ASIN B0BS1PRSCN)

Cabin Fever by Addison M Conley
She goes for the money, but will she stay for something deeper?
Available on Amazon (ASIN B0BQWY45GH)

What's Your Story?

Global Wordsmiths, CIC, provides an all-encompassing service for all writers, ranging from basic proofreading and cover design to development editing, typesetting, and eBook services. A major part of our work is charity and community focused, delivering writing projects to under-served and under-represented groups across Nottinghamshire, giving voice to the voiceless and visibility to the unseen.

To learn more about what we offer, visit: www.globalwords.co.uk

A selection of books by Global Words Press:
Desire, Love, Identity: with the National Justice Museum
Aventuras en México: Farmilo Primary School
Times Past: with The Workhouse, National Trust
Young at Heart with AGE UK
In Different Shoes: Stories of Trans Lives

Self-published authors working with Global Wordsmiths:
Steve Bailey
Ravenna Castle
Jackie D
CJ DeBarra
Dee Griffiths
Iona Kane
Maggie McIntyre
Emma Nichols
Dani Lovelady Ryan
Erin Zak

Milton Keynes UK
Ingram Content Group UK Ltd.
UKHW021832011223
433620UK00013B/537